INTERFERENCE

"Linda. I've come to appeal to you for Hester's sake. You can see that Gregory Merton is very much attracted to your sister, can't you? I am sure that if he had a chance to see what a charming girl she is he would adore her."

"Do you think that I'm interfering with his chance to see her?"

"You'll see him this weekend at his sister's." Her mother sat forward in her chair. "I'm asking you to give up the visit, Linda."

"I'll phone my regrets as soon as you leave."

"You've made me very happy, Linda."

"Perhaps it will make you happier to know that I couldn't love Gregory Merton if he were the only man in the world."

Bantam Books by Emilie Loring
Ask your bookseller for the books you have missed

EMILIE LORING

THERE IS ALWAYS LOVE

BANTAM BOOKS
TORONTO · NEW YORK · LONDON

The names of all characters in this novel, all episodes, are fictitious. Use of a name which is the same as that of any living person is accidental.

This low-priced Bantam Book
has been completely reset in a type face
designed for easy reading, and was printed
from new plates. It contains the complete
text of the original hard-cover edition.
NOT ONE WORD HAS BEEN OMITTED.

THERE IS ALWAYS LOVE

A Bantam Book / published by arrangement with
Little, Brown and Company

PRINTING HISTORY

Little, Brown edition published June 1940
2nd printing____October 1940
Grosset & Dunlap edition·published September 1947

Bantam edition / December 1965
2nd printing_____February 1966
3rd printing_____December 1966
4th printing_____December 1966
5th printing_____August 1967
6th printing_____June 1968
7th printing_____October 1968
8th printing_____April 1969
9th printing_____May 1970
10th printing

Published simultaneously in the United States and Canada

Bantam Books are published by Bantam Books, Inc. Its trade-
mark, consisting of the words "Bantam Books" and the por-
trayal of a bantam, is registered in the United States Patent
Office and in other countries. Marca Registrada. Bantam
Books, Inc., 666 Fifth Avenue, New York, New York 10019.

PRINTED IN THE UNITED STATES OF AMERICA

I

FOR THE space of a split second Linda Bourne thought that the man in the open, low-slung black roadster speeding out of the orange-red sunset had waved and called "Hi!" to her. As he came on she realized that he was a stranger. Instinctively she turned to see whom he was hailing with such exuberance.

No one behind her. On each side of the broad, tree-bordered New England street, white houses with green blinds had the appearance of having sat placidly in the midst of their shadowed lawns for generations. No sign of life on the porches. No curious eyes at the windows—none visible. Had he waved to *her?*

"Don't tell me I'm wrong. That this isn't the date you set for me to dine with you."

Linda wheeled. The opulent, clean-lined black roadster had drawn to the curb. The engine breathed softly as only a top-drawer engine would breathe. The smile of the hatless, dark-haired man leaning toward her waned, his eyes widened with surprise. Was he putting on an act? If so, he was doing it well. She shook her head:

"Sorry, but that's the story. Wrong number." There was a hint of amused derision in her voice.

"You don't have to tell me." He was out of the car looking down at her. "I know now that you're not the girl I thought you were. Just to keep the record straight, it isn't my habit to speed about the country hailing strange females. Your name isn't Bourne by any chance?"

Linda smiled suddenly, adorably, with a flash of perfect teeth and a deep dimple in each flushed cheek.

"Not by chance, by marriage. One Evelyn Carter did become the wife of one John Bourne and I'm an offspring, one of them."

"Then I didn't make such a break after all." He drew a long breath of exaggerated relief. Now that they were clear of surprise she could see that his eyes were a warm gray, at the moment brilliant with laughter.

"Last week in Plattsburg where I've been in training, I met one Hester Bourne." His imitation of her inflection was perfect. "She invited me to dine at her home tonight on my way back to New York. You have a sister, Hester, haven't you? Stop me if I'm wrong. You look enough like her to be a twin. She, also, wore white with a big cartwheel hat. Same tawny hair with a hint of auburn; same brown eyes that just now look enormous. Same heart-shaped face. Your mouths are different. Yours tips up at the corners and you have a dimpled chin, she hasn't."

"You've forgotten something. Hester is in possession of four wisdom teeth and I lost one last week, impacted, in case you care."

She wondered that she could speak flippantly when her throat was so tight. She knew why her mother had urged her to accept Ruthetta Brewster's invitation for the evening. She had wanted her out of the way when Hester's guest, this tall, lean, bronzed, terribly good-looking gray-suited man arrived. It had happened before. She had been bitterly resentful when two men had cooled toward her elder daughter and had tried to rush the younger, who had promptly snubbed them. But that last fact hadn't helped.

"Hope that it isn't the prospect of having me for a dinner guest that has struck you dumb, Miss Bourne?"

His voice was light but too sharp, vertical lines had cut between his eyebrows. His intent regard was oddly disturbing. It was as if while listening to her words he was reading her mind and knew of the hurt suspicion simmering there.

"Disappointment, not the prospect, has stolen my tongue." Her voice matched his in lightness. "I'm not going home, worse luck. I'm on my way to keep a supper date, Mr.——"

"Gregory Merton's the name. My friends call me 'Greg.' Going to be my friend?"

She smiled as she placed her hand in his extended.

"Of course, any friend of Hester's is mine. I'm Linda. My friends call me—"

"'Lindy,' I'll bet my hat. 'Lovely Lindy,' if you ask me. Hop in and I'll take you to your date. Noble of me to offer because I'm pretty sore that you weren't enough interested to stay home when you knew I was coming."

"But, I didn't . . ." She broke off the admission and substituted, "I made this date long before I ever heard of you." Which was gospel truth. No need to tell him that she had felt something festive in the air when she reached home from the office, that her mind had been so full of the not-to-well-suppressed ogling of her boss that she had dashed up to her room without stopping to speak to anyone, that later as, refreshed by a shower, she was dressing, her mother had tapped at her door to tell her that Ruthetta Brewster was on the phone, wanted her to come for supper and go on to the Clubhouse Committee Meeting with her.

"You'd better go, dear. Ruthetta is so alone since her parents died suddenly. She needs you. Living with that hatchet-faced Liberty Hull must be trying. Of course she's a marvelous housekeeper, but I'd rather wade in dust and have a few more smiles."

She had intended to sidestep the committee meeting, had told Skid Grant not to call for her, had planned to devote the evening to intensive consideration of what to do about her job, which was fast becoming unendurable, but if Ruthetta wanted her she would go. And here she was stopped on her way by one Gregory Merton who was regarding her with narrowed eyes.

"Apparently you're not a believer in the spoken word, Lovely Lindy," he teased. "Do you always go into silence when you meet a new man or shall I attribute it to my devastating charm? What's the matter? Afraid to get into my car? Don't you believe that your sister invited me to dinner? Come on home and let me prove it." The hand with which he indicated the tan-leather seat of the sleek roadster was strong, perfectly shaped. A green signet ring was on the little finger.

"Of course I'm not afraid. Of course I believe that you're dining with Hester, but I want to walk. I've been sitting at a desk all day. I'm a working girl. Good-by."

She looked back once as if attracted by a magnet. He was still standing beside the car. She waved and hurried on. Exit Mr. Gregory Merton from her life.

His face and smile were disturbingly clear on the screen of memory as she and Ruthetta sat on the porch steps after supper. The western sky was a faint crimson. One adventurous star blinked in the cool twilight blue above. There was a premonition of autumn in the August air.

"The days are shortening too fast," she regretted. "I like the country but when the afternoons get dark I love the bright lights of the city."

Ruthetta caught a leaf as it flitted past like a green butterfly.

"So do I and I'm going. Nothing to keep me here, now. I've been living in the past, in an atmosphere of collector's items acquired by my forebears before they were antiques. It's deadening. I'm about to tear up my roots. I've always wanted to paint—don't laugh when I say portraits —never had a chance to take a brush in my hand. I'm starting from scratch, but the point is I'm starting. I've made all the arrangements. Come with me, Lindy? You aren't happy or satisfied here. That isn't a criticism, that's an observation—your job is a bed of nettles. There is only one common-sense move when you don't like your life. Do something about it. Get out. Go somewhere. Follow a rainbow. Who knows, you may find the legendary pot of gold at the end of it. It's not only the office that's getting you down, it's your mother. She has hurt you again, hasn't she? I recognize the symptoms."

Linda nodded and looked at the girl beside her as if seeing her for the first time. She was twenty-five, only two years older than herself. They had been friends for years but never before had Ruthetta admitted that she wanted more than she had in a life which had been devoted to parents who were middle-aged when she was born. She had lately been through tragedy but her hazel eyes were steady and unclouded, her lips parted in a gracious curve; her satin-smooth dark hair was waved and gathered in a soft knot at the neck. She was not pretty, but her face was interesting: there was color under her skin which made it lovely. She was an understanding person and an I'm-here-when-you-need-me friend.

"You've guessed it, Ruthetta." Linda tried to keep her voice clear of resentment. "Is it my fault that Mother hurts me so often? She is a wonderful woman in many ways. Am I touchy and supersensitive?"

She told of meeting the man in the black roadster, of her ignorance of the fact that a guest had been invited for dinner, of her realization that her presence at home was not wanted. Something in her friend's face prompted her to ask:

"Did Mother suggest that you invite me here tonight? You needn't answer. You've gone the color of a red, red rose."

"Suppose she did? Mighty thoughtful of her. She knows that I adore being with you. You're so gay, so incredibly sincere, so absolutely without malice and so lovely to look at. She knows that I hesitate to ask you to come here now that I'm living quietly." She indicated her black frock. "Don't think for a minute that she isn't proud of you, doesn't love you, Lindy. It's only—"

"I get you. It's the 'Not that I love Caesar less but Rome more' tradition. For Rome substitute Hester."

"Don't be bitter. I understand your mother. She doesn't love Hester more, it's just that she feels a deep sense of protectiveness. She realizes that her elder daughter hasn't the younger's take-it-on-the-chin spirit; in short, that she's a trifle dumb, that Life is bound to step on her; and she's trying to stand between her and Life. It's a fool thing to do. She'd better let her get knocked down and struggle to her feet again, especially when it comes to boy friends."

"I agree with all you say but this last crack makes me so mad I could cry. It's so unjust. I've never, never tried to attract a man, never have encouraged one who has shown the faintest symptom of liking Hester."

"You're telling me. Haven't I seen you shunt them off with a flippancy that made me want to beat you? No matter what your mother thinks, Hester isn't entitled to the attention of every male who blows into this town. She'd be a whole lot better off if she had a job."

"Mother wouldn't let her take one. She insisted that Dad left a sufficient income for us to live like ladies. Hasn't that a before-the-World-War flavor? However, when I proved to her that there wasn't enough if I depended on that same income for my expenses, she consented to the secretarial course for me. I believe I drew the world's worst boss. He brings out the savage in me. Sometime I'm going to forget I was brought up to be a perfect lady and slap his fat face hard or bite him." She snapped her teeth. "So what?"

"Change. Break away. New friends. New surroundings. New problems, harder ones perhaps, but new. Your father left you a legacy, I heard."

"You heard right. A legacy and his stamp collection which is quite valuable. Hester resents that last. She stages an aggrieved, he-left-you-more-than-he-left-me act, when even an ordinary postage stamp is mentioned. To my mind one of the most tragic aftermaths of a death is the fact that *things* are so apt to cause trouble in families."

"Was Hester interested in your father's hobby?"

"Bored her to distraction. I loved it. After Dad was confined to the house I spent hours working with him, mounting and sorting stamps. He had a lot of cronies with whom he traded and he and I would tingle with excitement when he acquired an item we had needed. I haven't looked at them since he—he went. I—I couldn't."

"I understand, Lindy. You feel that way now, but someday you'll begin arranging and collecting again and it will bring him very near. You have money enough to stake yourself till you find work. Come to New York with me."

"New York!"

"That's what I said, dearie. Your voice wouldn't have been more shocked had I suggested Timbuctoo. Take a chance. It might not be such a chance. The sensational blond guest of the Grants' who camped on your trail last June told you he would give you a position, didn't he?"

Linda braced her elbow on her knee and rested her chin in her pink palm. Her eyes were on the one blinking star.

"You mean Keith Sanders? Sure, he offered me a job in his real-estate office."

"Mr. World-Wise in the flesh plus a sardonic smile."

"And the yellow hair of a Viking, the biggest, bluest eyes I've ever seen, colossal charm, and a caressing voice for which I fell hard. I had had all the childhood and adolescent diseases but I never had an attack of love at first sight before. I burn with humiliation when I remember the night I sat beside him at dinner at the Grants'. I felt like a million when I entered the dining room in my spiffy gold-dotted white net; when I left I felt like thirty cents."

"You with an inferiority complex! I don't believe it."

"It's true. I had fairly prattled of tennis, Club affairs, our dramatics. When I rose I could see 'Small-Town Girl' in his sophisticated eyes, such cold eyes, as plainly as if the words had been set in neon lights."

"Pity you couldn't have given a demonstration of your capability on the spot. Your present boss, fat Sim Cove, boasts that he has the smartest secretary who ever took dictation. He has. I haven't forgotten the hours I read aloud to you that you might gain speed in shorthand. The Sanders person may have thought you small-town but I noticed that he trailed you like a G-man in pursuit of a suspect while he was here. He had your steady, Skidmore, Heir to the House of Grant, glaring at him until I sniffed battle, murder and sudden death."

"Skiddy isn't my steady, Ruthetta, and you know it. He's a sort of cousin. We've grown up together. As for Keith Sanders' devotion, that was what is known to the literati as character-study. He had helped finance a show and had picked up the writing bug in the process. He declared that as far as he could see playwriting was a cinch, he intended to make a stab at it when he had time. I heard later that he was being trailed by a night-club singer who wanted him to back her in a musical comedy."

"If he was after copy he should have stayed one week longer to have been at the Grants' when the priceless diamond bracelets, rings and other jewels were stolen. He might have caught the merry burglar while a-burgling. Small-town girl plus an experience like that would given him material for a smash hit. So long as he offered, why not ask Mr. Worldly-Wise for a job?"

"I'm not quite so naive. Were I to send in my name I wouldn't crash even the outer gate of his business citadel; besides, I'm in real estate here, I want to try something else. I'll keep him for a last resort. You've given me an idea, though. Father used to say that there is more power in an idea than in anything else in the world. You're a grand person, Ruthetta. My heart has stopped smarting about the dinner at home. I hope Mother and Hester are enjoying their precious Greg."

"So, his name is Greg. What's he like?"

"Not too young, early thirties, perhaps. Military setup. He has just come from training at Plattsburg. Hester was there for a week, you remember. Uncanny perception, I'd say. New Yorker. Up-to-the-minute clothes. Snappy car. Gray, almost black eyes, clear and compelling. Determined mouth till he smiles, then it's rather touchingly boyish. I'd hate to clash wills with him. He'll be perfect for Hester. Something in his voice makes you feel that he belongs in the till-death-us-do-part school."

"The direct answer to a mother's prayer. It's your cue for a dignified exit. How about it? Will you go to New York with me? I've leased an apartment, modern to the last saucepan, I judge from the description. That's what I want, a sophisticated background. I shall leave 'Ruthetta' with the other antiques. From now on, I'm Ruth. I'll take Liberty Hull to keep house for me; I can't leave her, she's been with us so long she's family. She's all excited about it and for a wonder hasn't lisped a word about my plan in the village. I hear Skid's whistle. He has tracked you down, Lindy. Quick, before he gets here. Will you come?"

"If I may pay my way."

"Of course you may, silly."

"Then I'm following your advice and getting out. I'll take a chance. I'm just a little gambler at heart. You've struck a spark."

"So glad I'll be there to watch the fire. Something tells me that there will be one big blaze." A horn and a clatter sounded simultaneously at the edge of the lawn. "One would think that the son of plutocrats would have a car that didn't rattle and groan like the rigging of a ship in a gale. For goodness' sake, tell Skid we're coming, Lindy, before he cuts up the grass any more."

II

LINDA glanced at her wrist watch, compared the time with that of the clock on the wall. The hands of each had moved only five minutes though she felt as if an hour had passed since she had looked at them before.

It was such a silent place, this office set back on a terrace thirty stories above the city street. She could almost hear the hard beat of her heart. One wall was a sheet of mirror, the others were paneled in a light, satin-smooth wood. Closed doors of the same shut out whatever business transactions were going on behind them. The pile of the carpet was as deep and springy as the pine-needle-covered ground in the woods at home. There were a few inviting tan-leather chairs with low tables beside them on which lay large portfolios. Did they hold the photographs of the property offered for rent or sale? There were no pictures of houses and estates. She had expected to see the walls covered with them like the walls in Sim Cove's office.

In an alcove a girl was busy at a typewriter which was as soundless as the room. She wore a tailored navy-wool frock with crisp, narrow turnover piqué collar and cuffs. From the top of her smooth, dark hair to her glistening nails she had the same polished look at the office. Beyond the window behind her the tower of the Empire State Building slowly emerged from the morning mists and took form like a Maxfield Parrish magic castle.

Linda's eyes left the receptionist to regard herself in the mirrored wall. Not too bad. The hair visible below the brim of her moss-green felt had a satin-sheen, her teeth were beautifully white, her skin smooth and delicately tinted; her lips were vivid and still persisted in tilting up at the corners though she had been looking for a position for two weeks. Her amethyst jacket and her skirt of a plaid which combined green and amethyst were expertly tailored; her mother had given her the money for them as a going-away present. She would much rather she had protested against her leaving home. Instead she had encouraged the experiment. Had she been glad to have her go because of Hester?

She slammed shut the door of memory. She would allow none of the problems of the past to blur this new life. Besides, she had enough to think of in the present. It had taken her two weeks to reluctantly decide to remind Keith Sanders that he had promised her a job. She hadn't wanted to go into real estate again but she wanted less to be idle. She had been waiting an hour to see him. Had he slipped out another door to avoid her? Better to know it at once if he had.

She crossed the room and stopped at the desk which offered the information in gold letters on a small black oblong that Miss Dowse was the incumbent.

"Are you sure Mr. Sanders will see me this morning?"

The girl looked up from her work. "Gee, I'm sorry. You were so quiet I forgot you were here. I'll speak to him again."

She touched a button on the inter-office phone. A sound which was a cross between a grunt and a growl responded.

"Miss Bourne is still waiting, Mr. Sanders."

"Who?" Quite plainly Linda heard the impatient question and visualized his cold blue eyes.

"Miss Bourne."

"Who the dickens is Miss Bourne?"

"Tell him that she sat beside him at dinner at Mrs. Grant's last June. That he told her he would give her a position if she came to New York," Linda whispered instead of dashing from the office as anger prompted.

The girl faithfully relayed the message. It brought a laugh from the other end of the line before a voice exclaimed:

"The little country girl with the naive line! Tell her I'm busy. No opening here at present. Wait a minute. Get her phone number. That's all."

"You needn't tell me, I heard," Linda assured before the girl could speak. "I couldn't help hearing."

"I'm sorry. He's always like that in the morning. Try in the afternoon. His secretary walked out on him yesterday. She thought she had him eating out of her hand, didn't believe he would let her go. I'll bet she got the surprise of her life when he said 'O.K.' He'll need someone. Be sure and come back though I'll warn you now he's a hard man to work for. He's a slave-driver. That secretary could afford to walk out; I, the receptionist, can't. So think it over."

"Thanks for the tip, but no one could be harder to work for than the boss I left. I will be back this afternoon if I don't find something before. Good-by."

She was half-way across the room when a man entered.

"Tell Sanders that I'm—Miss Bourne! When did you blow into town?" It was the driver of the black roadster,

Gregory Merton, smiling, undoubtedly glad to see her. "What luck to run into you like this!"

Linda gently extricated the hand she had laid in his, eagerly extended. Her heart, which had been smarting from Keith Sanders' indifference, went all melty with pleasure.

"What are you doing here?" he demanded as if only then aware of her surroundings. The sharp lines she remembered cut between his eyebrows, his smile was gone.

"If you mean, by 'here,' New York, I'm living in the Big City; if this office, I'm looking for a position. I met Mr. Sanders last summer and he assured me that when I wanted a job he would have one all tied up in pink ribbons for me."

"Look here, don't decide until I've talked with you. I . . ."

A door behind them opened. Keith Sanders appeared on the threshold. His rather thick red lips made his small, clipped mustache appear even more blond than his hair. He seemed taller, more good-looking than Linda remembered him and that had been good-looking enough. His blue eyes flashed from the face of the man beside her to hers and hardened.

"My receptionist notified me you were here, Merton. You were so long appearing that I came to see what had happened to you. By Jove, Miss Bourne, I'm glad you haven't gone. I was deep in a business problem when Miss Dowse phoned and for a minute your name meant nothing, then all of a sudden I remembered a lovely girl in a fluffy white dress. I'd started after you when Merton was announced. Of course I have a place for you. You're just what I need. You . . ."

"Wait a minute." Gregory Merton's interruption was cool and unhurried, his gray eyes clear and disconcertingly direct beneath his sharp-drawn brows. "I need another secretary. Want the position, Miss Bourne?"

"Keep out of this, Merton. I engaged her first. You can't . . ."

Linda laughed suddenly. The tilt of her mouth above her sturdy dimpled chin was challenging.

"This situation isn't real. It's something out of a radio

skit. Two businessmen clashing over a girl of whose capability they know nothing. It doesn't make sense."

"Your mistake. I do know something about your work," Sanders corrected. "I played golf with your boss, Sim Cove, last summer. When he wasn't disputing the score he was broadcasting the fact that he had the world's best secretary and saleswoman, that you practically ran his real-estate business, so you see I'm not engaging a girl because she's charming."

"And I'm making the offer because I recognize ability when I see it. I'm a 'sensitive,' one of those psychic chaps you hear about, Miss Bourne. I can tell by looking at you that you'll fit into my organization like the missing piece of a picture puzzle. I'll guarantee to be the world's best boss."

Greg Merton's voice was light but his eyes were grave as they met hers, almost as if he were warning her to go slow. She liked him, liked him more than at their first meeting, and he had set her heart glowing then. That first meeting. On the screen of her mind flashed a picture with sound effects. She saw him leaning forward in the roadster, heard him say:

"Don't tell me I'm wrong, that this isn't the date you set for me to dine with you."

He was Hester's friend. Her mother and sister hadn't wanted her to meet him. He had really been the occasion of her leaving home, though the cause was deeper, much deeper. That settled it. She would keep as far away from him as possible and judging from the animosity between the two men which was thick enough to cut, Keith Sanders' office would serve. She looked from one to the other and smiled.

"I've taken time to consider the offers. Thanks for wanting me, Mr. Merton, but . . . but I'll stay here."

"Fine! Fine!" Keith Sanders exulted. "Miss Dowse, show Miss Bourne into the office she will occupy. I'll be right along to talk terms. Now, Merton, we'll settle the matter about which I phoned you."

"But not so easily as you have settled this." The ice in Greg Merton's voice gave Linda a premonitory chill before the closing door shut off the sound of Keith Sanders' reply.

That night after dinner she and Ruth sat in front of what the advertisement of the apartment had described as a

wood-burning fireplace, in which danced and capered midget flames. It was a large room. The casing around the fireplace was of blond mahogany, the wall above it was one vast mirror, which reflected her lime-green frock and Ruth's violet crepe. Tables and piano were of the same sat-in-smooth wood. Large chairs and a capacious couch were upholstered in cotton tweed the shade of the beige hangings which were striped horizontally with a deeper beige, brown and Chinese lacquer red. Ceramic lamp bases were of the same red, with pale shades. A brown *sof-tred* rug was on the floor. A bowl of Chinese lacquer on the table.

"Weren't you in luck to get this place?" Linda exclaimed. "It does seem strange, though, not to see you against an antique background. Stranger to see your hair cut and in short curls all over your head. Sometimes I wonder. if you be really you. I love it, though, the change, I mean. If you were after sophistication, you found it, plus, in this apartment. The furniture is the last word in modern design."

"Heavens knows I needed the change. I like this room but I'm stumped when it comes to flowers. Nothing seems to fit. I expected that the walls would close in on me in protest when I put that silver vase with three yellow roses on the table and the copper bowl with that mass of near-white chrysanthemums on the piano, but I had to have them."

"A room without flowers is a room without a soul. After the racket of the city this apartment is like a walled-in enclosure of color and quietness. Speaking of quiet, you've hardly spoken since I told you of my lucky break. I'm still a bit dazed, myself. It's unbelievable. Of course there was something behind it. Two modern businessmen wouldn't fight over securing a certain secretary—the woods are full of them. After I accepted Keith Sanders' offer, I felt as if I were a leaf tossed into a current, that having started I must go on or be dragged under. Queer feeling. I wonder what it meant. Was it a premonition of danger?"

"Danger! Don't be ridiculous, Lindy. If you ask me, I think the Sanders man was pretty lucky to get a girl with a conscience, who didn't boost her price. I gather that in his eagerness to block Merton you might have asked for anything and got it."

"I was practically office manager for Sim Cove, buyer and seller and publicity specialist. He boasted that he never let business interfere with his golf. I inquired when I first came to New York what the pay was for that sort of work and asked for it. Sanders was a bit staggered but came across, although he remarked:

" 'For a country girl you do know your way around, don't you?'

" 'But, you see, I haven't always lived in the country,' I explained sweetly. 'My father was a Federal Court judge in Boston. We lived there winters for many years.' "

They had been such happy years. Her father and she had been boon companions. Had he sensed his wife's absorption in her elder daughter and tried to make up for it to the younger? She shut her eyes tight to keep back a rush of tears as she visualized his noble head crowned with short, silvery curls; his humorous dark eyes. She could hear his deep voice encourage:

"You can do anything you want to do, Lindy. I hope you'll want to be a grand wife and mother, but whatever it is never forget that your Dad believes you can be tops."

If only she could remember, forever and ever, the light in his eyes and the tenderness of his voice as he had said it.

"What is Gregory Merton's business?" Ruth's question brought her back to the present.

"We didn't get that far. He spoke of his 'organization.' After he left I was so busy learning the ropes that I didn't think of him again. Have I told you that I have an office to myself with the skyscrapers and towers of Manhattan vanishing into the mists or emerging gold-tipped from the sun just outside the window?"

"Only twice, dearie. Look up Gregory Merton in the telephone book. I'm curious to know why there should be a feud between him and your boss. Is it *cherchez la femme,* or business? Whichever it is it spells drama to me."

Linda ran her finger down a page.

"Merton. Albert. Donald. Here it is, Gregory. Real estate. Lives at his Club, apparently. It isn't a woman. It's rivalry in business. And I thought for one crazy minute that each man really wanted me because I was I. Lucky I found out, else I might have had an acute attack of swelled

head. Anyway, we know now that the feud isn't about a woman."

"Do we? I'm not so sure. I begin to smell smoke. I warned you that there would be fire if you came. Even if the quarrel is about business many an able-bodied blaze has been started over that, my child."

Linda crossed to the window and stepped out on the terrace. There was light enough to see the swaying trees in the Park below. Beyond the Park tall towers pierced by tier upon tier of lighted windows drew an irregular line against a sweep of star-sprinkled sky. Orange, green, blue and yellow lights flashed and faded. Rows of street lamps glowed like opaline quartz. The hum of motors rose from the Avenue. An airplane hummed overhead. Somewhere a man's voice was singing "With All My Heart."

She listened till the last caressing note was lost in the hum below. Her eyes swept over the lighted skyline.

"What an amazing world!" she said aloud. "And I'm part of it."

Her breath caught from sheer excitement as she entered the room and closed the terrace window behind her.

"I never tire of our view at night, Ruth. It's blazingly, unbelievably beautiful. It twinkles and sparkles and glows like a fabulous city. It is hard to realize that across the ocean cities are being blacked-out through fear of an attack from the air."

"And that even here, under the enchantment, lie secret depths of uncertainty as to what may come to dim its glow. Come in, Libby."

The tall, angular woman in the gun-metal mohair dress came within the light of the fire. Her long, narrow bony face with its high-bridged nose, its fold of loosened skin under the sharp chin, was redeemed from ugliness by brilliant black eyes set in a fan-work of lines at the corners. Her mouth with its mobility, its tilt of humor was as surprising in her otherwise austere face as would be a rose found tucked above the granite ear of the Old Man of the Mountain. Her pepper-and-salt hair was strained back and bunched in a tight twist at the nape of her neck. She held out a letter.

"Thought you'd like to read this, Ruthetta. It's from Lucy Lane at home. What with one thing an' another there's lots goin' on there. She writes that Hester Bourne raised such a rumpus' cause Lindy was in the city for the winter and she was left in the country that her Ma has leased the house an' them two are goin' somewhere for the winter. Skid Grant has told his Ma and Pa that he ain't goin' to Florida with them this year, he's goin' to live in New York." She sniffed and looked accusingly at Linda. "An' the whole town's talking 'bout the reason why."

III

LINDA rose from her office desk and stretched her arms above her head. She had been typing steadily since she had returned from an early luncheon. Keith Sanders was a fascinating person, agreeable, friendly; but he exacted his business pound of flesh. His salesmen were on the jump every minute. If one lingered in the office after his report was made he had to tell the reason why. He kept her after hours to take dictation. Both Saturday afternoons since she had been in his employ he had sent her to inspect houses which he had been commissioned to sell or rent, had even casually suggested that she might turn a Sunday to advantage to him, a suggestion which she had forthrightly declined to consider. He had left her to keep office today while he took Miss Dowse with him to take notes on an estate in the country.

Not that she was complaining, she told herself. She loved the work, liked the type of customers with whom she talked when Sanders was out, liked the stimulating give and take of business. The experience was doing a lot for her. She felt a growing confidence and courage. It was as if her blood flowed more warmly and redly through her veins and gave a rosy cast to life. She met people more easily and by their response knew that she gave out something of the glow within her and—she glanced at herself in the mirror—she was acquiring that intangible patina which, for want of a better word, is called style.

She crossed the cool quiet room to the great window

and looked down upon roof gardens gay with the scarlet, orange, lemon, bronze and purple of zinnias. She watched men at work on the steel skeleton of a skyscraper. Held her breath till the red-hot rivet tossed into space was caught in a bucket by a steel-helmeted workman; relaxed as it was set in a shower of golden sparks. Whichever way one turned in this miraculous city one saw something stimulating, exciting, inspiring. Suppose she hadn't taken Ruth's advice, to "do something" about the life she didn't like? She would have missed all this.

The low roar of traffic came up to her like the sound of the ebb and flood of a mighty tide, with an obbligato of the tap, tap of rivets. Mid-September in New York with bulletins of air raids, bombed ships, cities reduced to shambles broadcast constantly from one radio station or another; with theaters opening, with enchanting places to dance to music caressingly sweet, or blatantly saxophonic, and not a man to ask her to step out with him. Not even Skiddy Grant had appeared. Lucy Lane must have been misinformed about his decision to come to New York. She would have seen him long before this were he in the city.

Why be sorry for herself that there was no one to invite her out? What had she expected? Of the two New Yorkers whom she had met before she came, one was her boss. Cross him off. Hadn't office flirtations always seemed to her the lowest form of business life? They had and of course he wouldn't ask her. The other, Greg Merton, had been turned down with such chilly disdain when he offered her a position that it was no wonder he had never again appeared within her orbit. She didn't want him to. He was Hester's friend and as such taboo for her.

Was there someone in the city who was even now moving toward her? Someone to whom she would say one day, "I knew you were coming. I waited for you"?

Perhaps he would come from one of those buildings which loomed tall and great against the skyline; divided into floors and those floors into offices, each one a hive of industry where men planned and schemed, trusted and failed, worked out transactions essential to their existence, fought fierce burning competition while passionately believing that fortune if not fame awaited them just around the corner.

"Mr. Sanders not back yet?"

Linda turned from the window. A girl entered the room with the assured, languorous grace of a professional model, swinging a little at the hips, smiling—white teeth gleaming between vivid lips; hard green eyes appraising under delicately darkened lids—shedding the faint sweetness of expensive perfume as she moved. She appeared to be quite aware that the hair which showed below her ultra-smart black hat had the sheen of minuted gold, that her purple orchids were costly, that her slim black frock accentuated the barbaric heaviness of her gold necklace and that the secretary regarding her was taking the measure of her ensemble and finding it flawless.

"Mr. Sanders is not in. May I take a message for him?" Linda inquired in her best office manner at the same time wondering if this were the night-club singer who, she had heard last summer, wanted Keith Sanders to finance her in a Broadway show?

The girl sank into a deep chair, crossed her knees, produced a vanity and began, unnecessarily, to restore her make-up.

"I'll wait."

"He has an important engagement when he returns and . . ."

"He will see me. I am Miss Crane, Alix Crane. You're new here or you would know. It may save you a heartache later to understand that he is never sentimentally interested in hired help. It's a scream the way the girls in his office have fallen for him."

Linda was acutely conscious of the hint of taunting patronage in a voice which was out of character with the exquisite appearance of its owner, that in quality, cadence and diction was commonplace.

"In that case, doubtless he will see you. You'd better wait in the reception room. I have work to finish and my typewriter is not so silent as it is advertised to be."

"Invitation to leave, what? I'll go, but not to the reception room. I'll wait in Keith's office. I always see him there. I will find plenty to amuse me. Mr. Sanders is careless about his correspondence."

She threw a mocking glance over her shoulder before she closed the door behind her. Of course, the spectacular

Miss Crane shouldn't have gone into Mr. Sanders' private office, but equally, of course, could she have been stopped without staging a scene? "She could not," Linda answered her own question. When the girl had come in she had indexed her as beautiful but dumb. Was she as dumb as she appeared or so shrewd as to be dangerous? Whatever she was, it was not a secretary's business.

"Sst! Where's the boss?"

Linda looked up with a start. She had been so immersed in a column of figures, which refused to add to the correct total, that she had not heard the door open. She was a fearless person, but there was something about the slender, medium-height man, with the cadaverous deadpan face that sent her heart to her throat. It wasn't that he was shabby; he was exceedingly well-dressed.

"If you mean Mr. Sanders he won't be back for half an hour. He went out of town. He may not return to the office tonight. You'd better leave your name and call again."

"Out of town, is he?" Something crafty came into the man's eyes, it was as if a hunted animal were looking for a way of escape. "I can't wait. Important date. I won't leave my name. I'll be back tomorrow."

As the door of the corridor closed behind him Linda returned to her figures. If Mr. Sanders had not come in by the time she finished this piece of work, she would lock up and go home. Miss Crane flung open the door.

"Was that Keith talking? Did you let him go without telling him I was waiting?"

"It was not Mr. Sanders."

"You needn't get mad about it. If it wasn't Keith, who was it?" There was a hint of suspicion in the question.

"I haven't the slightest idea." Linda looked at her wrist watch. "It will be useless for you to wait. Mr. Sanders said that if he were not back by this time he wouldn't be in until morning." She closed the typewriter into her desk. "As soon as I file these papers I shall call it a day and lock up the office."

"Terribly keen to get me out of the place, aren't you? I'm going. Tell Mr. Sanders in the morning that I was here. Tell him also that I can't spend my life waiting for him. There are other men eager to back me."

She crossed the outer office, swinging a little at the

hips, trailing expensive scent; and banged the door to the corridor behind her.

Temperamental party—plus, Linda reflected. That was that. Now if she could have a half hour uninterrupted by jack-in-the-box appearances she could clear her desk and start from scratch tomorrow. She hated being faced with yesterday's unfinished work when she came into the office in the morning. She would rather remain, no matter how late, and finish.

She was slipping into the amethyst-wool jacket when Keith Sanders entered. He frowned at her.

"Going? So early? Any callers?" He entered his office. She followed to answer his question.

"One didn't leave his name, the other—"

"It's up to a secretary to get names." He had a way of tugging at his blond mustache when annoyed.

"I realize that, Mr. Sanders. The man was in a hurry and didn't answer when I asked him. The young lady, Miss Crane, waited for a while—"

"Miss Crane! Alix! I've told her that there is nothing doing. Miss Dowse would have known that I wouldn't have seen her had I been here."

"But you took Miss Dowse with you. She plays Cerberus as a rule you may remember."

He laughed, became the smooth, charming person she had first met.

"I don't like your simile. Cerberus was the dog who guarded the entrance to the infernal regions, unless I have forgotten my mythology. Is it so bad, here?"

"There are days when the atmosphere is slightly sulphurous, but on the whole it's not too bad."

The mischievous daring in her response brought him a step nearer. His bold blue eyes smiled possessively into hers.

"I say, you've got a gay little devil inside that lovely prim shell, haven't you, Miss New England?" He stuffed the paper into his pocket and glanced at the clock on his desk.

"Wait till I phone, then we'll go somewhere for a drink and no nonsense about having another date. You've earned a party."

"But perhaps I have a date and perhaps it isn't non-

sense." Linda pulled on a glove. "The young man who called seemed anxious to see you. He couldn't wait, said he would be back tomorrow."

"A young *man!* What was he like?"

"Cadaverous with a crafty smile." Linda wished she hadn't been so quick with her answer as his eyes bored into hers like steel points. The caller might be a relative. Positions had been lost for less reason than her curt description and she didn't want to lose hers, she liked it. It was easy to understand that a person as successful as Keith Sanders would have needy hangers-on, though the man in question had been smartly clothed.

"All right. That's all. You may go." He frowned dismissal, dropped into a chair at his desk and drew his private telephone toward him.

Already he had forgotten that he had invited her out, Linda realized as she stepped into the corridor. So much the better. She wouldn't have gone with him and if he had persisted, and if she had steadfastly said "No," she might have lost her job. Besides, he wouldn't have believed her if she had said she didn't drink. She didn't and didn't intend to.

As she went through the bronze revolving doors of the great building she wondered again why the cadaverous man with the furtive eyes had the power to disturb Keith Sanders. He had been disturbed, she hadn't imagined it.

Why think of that unpleasant person when the setting sun was gilding the lofty tops of buildings? When lights were snapping on behind millions of windows? When this amazing city was beginning to dress in incandescence for the evening? It was the time of day she loved best.

"Even a badly-stepped-on worm will stage a comeback and here I am," announced Gregory Merton beside her.

IV

"WAS I as crude as that?"

There was the same beauty of timbre in Linda Bourne's voice, the same mischievous softness that had lingered in his memory since their first meeting in her home town. Greg Merton had the same feeling now that he had had then, that he had happened on a rare person, fresh and unspoiled, naturally gay of spirit, making no effort to attract, with a genius for comradeship, and extraordinarily lovely to look at.

"You didn't give me an even break that day in Sanders' office," he reproached. "You owe me something for turning me down so hard. Have tea with me, will you?"

He wondered what was passing in her mind as she regarded him. Her lips were curved in a faint smile which didn't touch her eyes.

"I'm really a most respectable person," he urged. "I can produce any number of references—clergyman, banker, a sister—"

"Of course you're respectable. I may have come from a small town but we have human nature there. I know it from A to Z."

"I wonder if you do?" He thought of Keith Sanders and of her prompt acceptance of his offer of a position. At her quick look he asked: "Where would you like to go? To the Ritz or to the country? I have my car just round the corner."

"I haven't forgotten that sleek, sporty roadster. Thanks a lot; the country, please. This frosty air makes me think of blazing logs in a big fireplace and leaves turning and the smell of ripening apples." He saw the muscles of her white throat contract.

"I believe you're homesick for the country. I know just the place to ease the hanker. Come on."

She was the loveliest-looking girl he had ever seen, and he had seen them by the glamorous score, Merton told himself, as he sat opposite her at a small table in the long, heavy-beamed, pine-walled, many-windowed room at the Inn. At one end huge logs spouted scarlet and yellow flames in the brick fireplace. There were hollyhock chintz hangings, choice highboys and secretary-desks, and many small tables, polished till you could see your face in them. An ebony cat dozed on the hearth rug, its white-tipped paws folded sedately beneath its black velvet bosom, its eyes like topaz-jewels, opening wide at every sound.

Outside the window an old-fashioned box hedge enclosed a garden with a sundial in the center. Its borders were a gay patchwork of yellow, russet and rose chrysanthemums, invincible purple petunias, valiant orange-king calendulas, towering white and orchid asters and feathery pink cosmos. Beyond that lay lush green fields patterned with color where the afterglow stained them crimson.

His eyes followed hers about the room, into the garden and back. He smiled at her across the table.

"Was I right? Is this the place?"

"You were wholly, completely, entirely right. It's perfect."

"Not homesick any more?"

"How did you know? I wasn't really. It was only that just before I left the office I had looked out at the lights and realized that I didn't know a man in this huge town who would ask me out. And—and then you appeared and here I am. It's the Cinderella motif. For pumpkin-coach see your snappy roadster."

"Doesn't Sanders take you out?" he asked quickly and then as quickly wished he hadn't. He felt her withdrawal. It was as if a mist had drifted across her gaiety.

"Forget I asked that. It's none of my business. Let's order. I can recommend the popovers. They always pop. They never let you down. Like jam?"

She said she loved it, black-currant if they had it. Her gaiety had returned. After that, the conversation ran lightly, ran above a deep current of protest in his mind. He had assured her that it was none of his business if her boss took her out, but he knew already at this third meeting that it had become intensely, passionately, his business with whom she associated. Take a girl whos character seems fixed and expose her to the attention of a predatory animal like Sanders and what might be the result?

"Just in case you've forgotten, I'm still here," she reminded. "What were you thinking about?"

"You." Then lest he repel her by his fervent answer, "I was wondering what you do out of office hours, how you like your job, if you find real estate interesting. That's my business too."

"I know it. I looked you up in the telephone book to find out what sort of a position I had so snootily turned down. I do plenty after office hours. I have joined a Red Cross class, I'm training to be an ambulance driver in case . . . Why think of that now, this is a party. You were right, these popovers fairly melt in one's mouth. I could die eating this black-currant jam."

"Don't. Overeating would be such an inglorious way of passing out. Comparable only to being run over by a horse and buggy in this automobile age. You haven't told me how you like your work."

"Immensely, especially when I am sent to look over houses. I adore meeting people. It hurts though, when I know they are giving up a home they love because they can't afford to run it. It seems to me that in this town it's money, money, money, whichever way one turns. I'm beginning to be afraid it may get me, too."

"It won't, but it's a pretty necessary thing to have. I—I —hope you are being properly paid for what you're giving, apparently you're doing more than the work of a secretary."

She told him the amount of her salary and he nodded approval.

"That's fair. Watch out that Sanders doesn't overwork you. He is a driver as well as an organizer."

"You don't like him, do you?"

"Personally, no. But he's brilliant, quick-witted, resourceful and makes a whale of a lot of money, apparently."

Her laugh was as refreshing as the cool sound of water rippling over the pebbly bed of a shaded brook.

" 'Damn with faint praise, assent with civil leer.' "

"Ever been told that you have a lovely laugh? I wasn't

damning Sanders. I didn't know that anyone in this age quoted Alexander Pope. How come?"

"If you had grown up in my family you would have had quotes from the classics at your tongue's end. From the time I could hear anything I heard my father theatrically declaiming extracts from favorite plays or poems as he shaved. 'We have come to bury Caesar not to praise him.' Remember that one? He had a marvelous voice, rich and mellow with a hint of *vibrato* when he was deeply moved. I've been told that lawyers would gather in court when he was about to charge a jury." Her voice caught before the last word, she furiously blinked long bronze lashes.

"Where were we when I began to quote? Talking about Keith Sanders, weren't we? I like him, but I'll admit that he's restless, always on the go, impatient, aggressive, and terribly suspicious; I wonder why? What a lovely woman!" she exclaimed as a party of four entered the room. "I mean that perfect brunette with eyes like big black-velvet pansies. Did she bow to you?"

Gregory Merton answered by rising as the woman, after a word to the three who had seated themselves, approached their table.

"What luck to find you here, Greg," she greeted. "I have just left Aunt Jane. I'm fairly simmering with news."

"Hold everything. I want you to meet Linda Bourne. Lovely Lindy, this is my sister, Janet Colton; Mrs. Bill, to be explicit."

He knew by Janet's cordial acknowledgment of the introduction that she felt as he had about the girl, that she liked her at first sight; and Linda's eyes had glowed in response.

"Won't you have your tea with us," she invited.

"I'd love to but I've just come from a meeting of a committee and I must join the members for tea. Take it from me, Miss Bourne, committee meetings are the best little-wasters-of-time in the world. Talk. Talk. Talk about anything except discussion that will advance the subject which the members have been summoned to decide."

"Easy, easy, Janet, we didn't call that committee meeting; don't take it out on Miss Bourne and me," her brother protested.

The soft color that mounted to Mrs. Colton's hair increased her beauty.

"I'm sorry to have inflicted you with one of my blow-ups, Miss Bourne."

"No apologies needed. I've been on commitees. If you get me started I could say even more than you said and *more* colorfully."

"You're a girl after my own heart. My brother and I always like the same people. Greg, Aunt Jane told me this afternoon that she has finally decided to sell her white elephant before it eats her up. It's the chance of your lifetime. The commission will be princely. Go to see her, quick, and get in on the ground floor."

"Can't. I'm going out of town on business tomorrow. Won't get back for a week. I doubt if she would let me in on the deal. She's still sore because she heard that I said she thought herself smarter than her business adviser. The little bird who carried that juicy titbit neglected to finish the sentence, 'and darn it, she is most of the time.' "

"She'll forget that, she really adores you, Greg. Write to her if you can't get to see her. Forgive this family digression, Miss Bourne, but I've been tingling with excitement ever since I heard of this possible grand break for my brother." She held out her hand:

"Come and see me, *please*. I know just by looking at you that you'll love my garden and adore young Mr. Colton; young Mr. Colton is Billy Boy our son and heir, in case you care. The girls are looking daggers at me while the popovers cool. Bring your lovely Lindy to tea soon, Greg dear." Without waiting for a response she departed.

"Whew! I always feel as if I had been caught up in the middle of a cyclone and then dropped with a bang when Janet breezes in on me like that." Merton resumed his seat.

"She's a dear and so lovely. Her husband is a lucky man. I hope he appreciates her charm and beauty. Is he nice?"

He thought of Bill Colton as he had seen him the night before with a gay party at the Ritz, of which Keith Sanders appeared to be the host, leaning against the bare shoulder of the girl beside him, a girl whose hair was too yellow, whose eyes were too shadowed. He didn't, he wouldn't believe that Bill would go so far as to be unfaithful to his wife, but he'd been a spoiled kid, he was rich and the natural prey for an unprincipled woman, and he was selfish, too absorbed in himself to realize that he was hurting Janet horribly.

"Depends upon what you call nice," he evaded. "To borrow from Hollywood, he has a 'colossal' country place. He keeps a stable of racers which takes care of his surplus income very nicely. He doesn't beat Janet; he loads her with presents, jewels, especially, and he worships his boy."

He promptly switched the subject. They talked about real estate. About taxes. About the war overseas. About his commission as Captain in the Reserve. About social conditions. Wondered if they were suddenly to become perfect what sort of a world it would be. Came back to business.

"You may not think it by my calm exterior," he observed lightly, "but I'm as much excited over Janet's news as she was. I think I know just where I can dispose of the estate, 'white elephant' to you, of this aunt of mine, great aunt really, which is one of those big unsaleable places no one wants now. I've been talking with an architect who is eager to get hold of a proposition like that. He thinks he can get a backer for a development from his plans. Aunt Jane's a prickly person with personality plus. I call her 'Duchess.' She likes it. I've been in her blackbook. I've appeared not to notice it, have kidded her along as usual, while all the time I have been scared stiff for fear, if she decided to sell, she would give her business to someone else to handle."

"I'm so glad for your good fortune. It's amazing how Life straightens out problems if one sits tight and works one's head off to help, isn't it?"

"You believe in Life, don't you? Believe in the best."

"I do. Isn't it stupid not to? My father used to quote, 'The alert men in all walks of life are men of faith.' Shall we go? Ruth will think that this great, gay city has swallowed me if I don't reach home soon."

"She'll have to get used to it, to your being out with me, I mean. I sure am glad you didn't accept my offer of a position."

With one arm in the amethyst-wool jacket he was holding she looked up at him.

"Do you know, I suspected at the time that you didn't really want me, that you were asking me to annoy Keith Sanders."

"I wanted you, all right. But not for a secretary. Come on." She thought that he added under his breath, "Sweet thing," but she wasn't sure.

V

THE ESTATE on the Hudson which Keith Sanders had that morning detailed Linda to visit and report on was another of the relics of a fabulous age before taxes had begun to overthrow those palaces stupendous on which the modern upkeep is tremendous.

She drove the green convertible supplied by her employer between tall, ornate iron gates and followed a pebbled drive the tortuous curves of which must have been designed before the days of automobiles. She thought of the estate Greg Merton's sister had been so eager for him to handle. Was it as immense as this? And she thought of the late afternoon a week ago when he had driven her home from the Inn and Hester had greeted them at Ruth's door with the news that she and her mother had subleased an apartment near for the winter. She remembered that she had stood speechless for an instant as she realized that since the moment Greg had invited her to tea she had forgotten that he was her sister's special friend. She had said something to Hester about having an important message to telephone, about changing her frock and had bidden him an icy good night. Her cheeks burned now as she thought of her rudeness and visualized his face, which had gone white with surprise and anger. She hadn't seen him since. She didn't know whether Hester had or not; she had been too busy to see her often.

Why think of it? That was that. This trip was business, business which required her entire attention. As she passed green, velvety lawns, orchards reddening with ripening fruit, garages, stables, greenhouses and two stone lodges, she had a curious feeling that she was intruding. Silly, hadn't Keith Sanders told her this morning that he had been urged to take on the sale and that an appointment for this afternoon had been arranged for her with the owner?

She could see the deep, rich coloring of the Palisades beyond the silver blue and cobalt of the river, the house looming under a cloudless sky. The Castle, the place was named appropriately. It must have proved to be the architect's pot of gold at the end of a rainbow, it was so immense, so blatant of unlimited expenditure. The sun shining on the windows gave it the appearance of an enormous palace checkered with gold plates. It was lacy with wrought-iron balconies, a house too great and splendid to have been conceived by human brains and built by human hands; rather it was something which might have been conjured into being by the wave of a magician's wand. On the terrace wall a gorgeous peacock spread his green and scintillant jeweled tail and preened in self-approval. He moved slowly, proudly until he disappeared around a corner.

As she stopped the roadster at the door a gray-haired man with a just-my-luck droop to his mouth, in maroon livery, the coat adorned with many silver buttons, ran down the steps. She inquired for Madam Steele, told him that she had come by appointment.

"I know, Miss. She's expecting you. She's in the garden. Take that path. I'll have your car sent to the garage."

There is nothing truer than the saying that one half the world doesn't know how the other half lives, Linda told herself as she followed the gravel walk. "I've known any number of lovely, luxurious homes but nothing so unbelievably colossal as this. Glad I wore my snappy navy ensemble with the moss green turban and bag. It helps keep my chin up. Here you are, gal. Remember you are expected."

In the brick-walled garden a woman sat in an Oriental fan-back chair which made a charming background for her white hair. Two Great Danes lying on the ground rose and took a forward step. There were white chairs with gay orange cushions and a glass table with tea things, massive silver and delicate china. An open book was in her lap. Her purple-blue gown made one think of a huge iris blossoming late and unexpectedly among the welter of pink, bronze, Lavender Lady and fluffy sulphur-yellow chrysanthemums in the flower borders. A crystal shower was being blown high into the air from the pipes of a bronze Pan in the middle of a lily-padded, fern-bordered pool.

Life had etched lines at the corners of the woman's piercing black eyes, eagle eyes, between which loomed a Roman nose of no mean proportions. The bitter line of her mouth was out of character in skin still soft and young. Her long-fingered hands, glittering with rings, were beautiful. As Linda approached she spoke sharply to the dogs.

"Cash! Carry! Come here." At the command of their mistress they crowded against her chair.

"Don't be afraid of them. They won't hurt you. They are not worth their keep as watchdogs, are merely part of the stage setting. You're the young person from the real-estate office, I presume?"

Her austere and uncompromising voice set Linda's heart thumping in her throat. "Remember, pussy-footing won't get you anywhere. Self-belief has power." Her father's words echoed through her mind and restored her poise.

"Yes, Madam Steele. It is part of my work to make memoranda of houses Mr. Sanders is to handle before he gives them his personal attention. He assured me that you would see me."

"Stop talking like a real-estate advertisement and sit down. Pour yourself a cup of tea. There are sandwiches and cake. Perhaps you don't drink anything so commonplace as tea?"

"Oh, yes I do," Linda answered lightly, determined to ignore the woman's acridity. "I was brought up in a family which had to have its afternoon tea though the heavens fell. You'd be surprised how much I miss it now that I'm in business. May I prepare some for you?"

"I've had mine. So you grew up in a tea-drinking family. English?"

Linda set her cup on a small glass table, settled into an orange-cushioned chair and prepared to enjoy herself.

"Yes, Madam Steele, but we left that country in 1672."

"You have a sense of humor, I see. What have you been doing since?"

"Oh, we've been governors, in business, lawyers—my father was a federal judge in Boston. After he—he left us we lived in the country house in which he was born, winters as well as summers. I was put through the stereotyped 'coming-out' paces. Teas, balls, dinners, modeling at fashion shows, social-service work and I even had a motion-picture test. Then I took a secretarial course. The bright lights of the metropolis lured me and here I am."

"You'd be much better off in that country village. Like this man Sanders for whom you're working? Think he's honest?"

"Of course! Would I be working for him if I didn't?"

"Don't be so excitable. How do I know what you would do, never having seen you until you walked into this garden? There are racketeers even in the real-estate business, I presume. It could be used as a cover for a lot of deviltry. Your employer was recommended to me by a man whose advice I wouldn't take about buying a draft horse, after I had waited and waited for a person who ought to have shown interest enough in my affairs to come to me and ask to handle the sale. I don't know why I listened to him about this. I did and you're here as a result. If you've finished your tea run along to the house. Tell Buff, the butler, to show you over it. Come back here before you go."

"I will, Madam Steele. I'm sure that I will prepare perfect notes after that delicious tea."

Linda lingered in the great flagged hall of the house. Stairs curved up each side to a gallery. The banisters were beautifully turned, the curve of the handrails was perfect. At the back against the wall, stately gladioli were banked. The broad base was of purple spikes. Shades of amethyst, orchid, pink, pale yellow mounted to pure white at the peak. The fragrance of long-stemmed crimson roses drifted from the mirrored gold-and-ivory drawing room at the right. In the library at the left bowls of giant yellow and flame zinnias blazed against the mahogany walls.

Disapproval fairly oozed from the butler's ramrodlike back as she followed him up the stairs. As she glanced into room after room she wondered if Madam Steele had had children, if one of them was the person whose advice she wouldn't take about buying a draft horse.

The sound of bells chiming the half hour drifted through an open window.

"How beautiful. Is there a carillon near, Buff?" she asked.

"Yes, Miss. A very fine one. It chimes every quarter and on important days like Christmas and Armistice plays tunes. The Madam presented it to the church in memory of the village young men who died in the World War. She lost a son in it." He sniffed and brushed a hand across his eyes. "Would you like to see the servants' quarters?"

"Are they above this?"

"They used to be, Miss. Now the third-floor rooms are not occupied. One is used for storage. Except for the housekeeper and myself who have apartments in the ell, the staff is in a separate cottage which is connected with the main house by an enclosed corridor. Shall I take you there?" His choice of words and manner of speaking were in character with his precise personality.

"No. I was told to make notes of the house and a diagram of the second floor only. I have those." She slipped a notebook into her handbag. "Madam Steele asked me to see her before I left. I shan't be but a moment. Please have my car brought around."

"Very good, Miss."

As she approached the garden she heard voices. Visitors? Not so good. The owner would doubtless question her in her sardonic way about her impressions of the house. It would be most unbusinesslike to air them before a stranger. Should she wait or go on? As she hesitated Madam Steele's voice cut through the still, fragrant air.

"I don't agree with you. I love jewels. I can afford to buy them and I shall continue to keep them in my home even if the insurance people won't cover them here. What pleasure would they give me interned in a bank vault? No more than if they were stolen. I don't see any point in storing them where I can't see and handle them. I have a permit to keep revolvers in the house, and I'm a straightshooter. Buff puts new servants through the third degree to make sure of their honesty before he engages them. The alarm connected with the locks is guaranteed to rouse the

dead, or words to that effect. Judge Reynolds has made my life a burden with his warnings about burglars and now you."

Lingering, outside the gate was own cousin to eavesdropping, Linda decided, and entered the garden. She could see the top of a dark head above a luxurious lounge chair, a hand on the arm; heard Madam Steele say:

"You're too late. I waited and waited for you to come. I made up my mind you didn't care for my business so engaged another realtor. Here's the young person who represents him."

A man extricated his long body from the chair and stood up. His eyes widened with surprise as they met Linda's, his face crimsoned, went white.

"You!" he said. *"You!"*

"What's the matter, Gregory? Have you met this young person before?"

"I've met Miss Bourne before."

Linda could have hugged him for the substitution of her name for the patronizing "young person." It restored her sense of individuality which, for an instant, Madam Steele's condescension had laid low.

"We are both realtors," she volunteered, not knowing what else to say to crash the silence which was getting ominous.

"Rivals, in fact," Greg Merton elaborated sarcastically. "Miss Bourne, apparently, is a business-chaser for Keith Sanders. I'm for myself. Janet told me the day before I had to start on a business trip that you had decided to sell. I couldn't get here last week. I preferred to talk with you, rather than write. You can give your business to whom you please, Aunt Jane. I can take the count, but you might at least have given me a whack at it before you turned it over to Keith Sanders."

Linda's knees gave way and deposited her in a chair. Janet! Aunt Jane! Was this the estate of which Greg Merton's sister had told him that afternoon at the Inn? Did he think she had advised her boss of the conversation? That she had put him on the track of this sale? Was that what he had meant by "business-chaser"? He couldn't believe she would do such a thing, he *couldn't*. She started to her feet.

"Keep out of this, Miss Bourne; when I've finished

you may have the field to yourself. I'm out of the deal, but first, Duchess, I want to know who advised you to call in Keith Sanders."

"It was Bill."

"Bill Colton! So that's why Sanders has been palling with him. To get your business. How long since you've been relying on *Bill* for advice?"

"Don't speak to me in that tone, Gregory. I told Janet that I had decided to sell and, when you didn't come or write, I concluded that you still believe 'I think myself smarter than my business advisers.' " Madam Steele's voice was hurt, slightly unsteady.

"Please, please, may I be excused?" Linda interrupted. "I must get back to the city."

"Must *hurry* back to make your report, I presume." Greg Merton's voice was savage, his eyes black fire. "You pulled a fast one, lady, when you reported to your boss the family conversation you heard while you were my guest."

"I didn't report it." His angry accusation lashed her into furious response. "How could I know who your 'Aunt Jane' was? She must be proud of her nephew after the exhibition of temper you've given. Good-by, Madam Steele."

Her heart smarted and burned, she seethed with fury as she ran along the graveled path. A man opened the door to her car. She gave a fleeting glance at him as she said, "Thanks," thought he was about to speak to her, shot the convertible ahead before he had a chance. How could Greg Merton think she was a double-crosser? How could he, she kept asking herself?

Twilight dropped over the world like a mantle of soft violet malines. The river rippled darkly. A star came out. Lights sprang on in windows. Amethyst smoke spiraled from chimneys. The air was fragrant with the scent from gardens and ripening fruit. Her heart ceased smarting as she drove on and on.

She lived over the gaiety and comradeship of the afternoon at the Inn, winced as she remembered her frigid goodnight to Greg Merton in Ruth's apartment—he must now believe that she had decided then to turn informer—saw again his white face when he had learned the reason of her presence in that garden; could see herself running along the path, dashing into the car. The man who had brought it round had been about to speak to her. Had he wanted a tip? Did one tip a servant on a great place when one came on business? Had he looked dissappointed? She tried to visualize him. Now that she thought of it, there had been something familiar about him. She had seen him before.

Where? In the office! Her heart did a handspring and dropped back with a thump. It was the cadaverous man with the dead-pan face and crafty eyes.

VI

IT WAS after the usual hour for closing. The buzzer sounded on Linda's desk. Keith Sanders had come in for the first time that day. His long absences from the office were becoming more and more frequent. He explained them, when he explained them at all, as business trips to see estates.

"Hoped I'd find you here," he greeted as she entered his room. The eyes that met hers were strained; there were haggard lines about his mouth. "How did you come out yesterday? Did old lady Steele give you any trouble?"

"On the contrary, she gave me tea. Don't make the mistake of thinking her an old lady. She's one of the ageless type. Keen, executive and up-to-the-minute. You should have seen her modish frock and her hair-do and her rings. Her fingers blazed."

"I've heard of her jewels; who hasn't? Did you make notes of the interior of the house?"

"Yes. Here they are."

With reluctance she presented the notebook. She had spent part of a sleepless night wondering if she had better speak of her meeting with Greg Merton in Madam Steele's garden, tell of his angry accusation that she had informed her employer that the estate was in the market. The question had bobbed up at intervals during a day packed to the brim with interviews with customers who had expected to talk over their business with Sanders. Now that she was face to face with him she decided not to refer to it at present. If Greg Merton believed that her boss had barged in on his territory, let them fight it out; it was not part of a secretary's duty.

"Good work, Miss Bourne. This diagram is just what I need. Curious second floor, isn't it?"

She looked over his shoulder and followed the plan with a pencil.

"Yes. The large hall is oval with rooms opening from it. At the end opposite the stairs is Madam Steele's suite. A sitting room on the front with a view of the river is connected with a bedroom at the back of the house by a solarium. Its windows extend from ceiling to floor on one side. Long glass panels, behind which are marvelous Chinese screens, shut it off from the hall. Gorgeous red-lacquer cabinets almost cover each of the two walls between windows and glass panels. I noticed them particularly because at home we have a small one which is the darling of our hearts. An ancestor brought it from the Orient."

"Know what they are used for?"

"No. I didn't consider that my—your business."

"Righto. I asked because I wondered if they were built-in and would be included in the sale. We'll inquire about that later. Did you look into the other rooms on that floor?"

"Yes. The doors were closed when we went up. They were identical. Each was finished in ivory paint with gold moldings and a small, ornate knocker. I wondered how a guest would be sure of his own room. It seemed more like a hotel than a private residence. Most of the furnishings were old-timey, heavy and elegant. Perhaps half a dozen were chintzy and modern." She told of the arrangements for the "staff."

He dropped the notebook to his desk, clasped his hands behind his blond head and tilted back in his chair to regard her through speculative eyes.

"So she gave you tea, Miss Bourne? I have it on good authority that usually Madam Steele is a Tartar. Must have fallen hard for you. That gives me an idea. I'll turn the buying of the estate over to you. You can swing it with me behind you to advise. I'll keep out of the spotlight and when I sell I'll cut you in on the commission. That's fair, what?"

Linda had a searing vision of Gregory Merton's burning eyes as he had accused her of being a "little business-chaser."

"But, I don't want to handle it. Buying and selling isn't part of my job."

"It is if I say it is," Sanders declared arrogantly; then as her eyes flashed he smiled with the charm which had fascinated her the first time she had met him.

"I'm doing it for your good, Miss New England," he cajoled. "You don't want to be a secretary all your life, do you? Learn to buy and sell and you'll get somewhere, so don't talk any more nonsense about not handling the old lady—my mistake, the ageless lady. I have a prospective customer for the estate already. If the deal goes through I'll break my own record for speedy sales."

"A man would have to be a super-billionaire to take on a place that size these days. 'The Castle' is right. I didn't see the whole of it but enough to know that the grounds must require a small army of laborers and that ark of a house a retinue of servants."

"My prospect is buying for investment. Plans to make over the house into apartments, have a community garage and build modest-income cottages all over the place. It's within easy commuting distance of the city. It's a contractor's pipedream, but with a mile of river frontage, I think he has something. You put through the deal with Madam Steele. I'll engineer the sale. If the buyer's scheme proves a dud it will be just too bad—for him. I'll be sitting pretty with the double commission and good lord, can I use it! What's the rush?" he demanded as Linda took a step toward the door.

"If you don't need me any longer I'll leave you building air castles, no pun intended, and go home. I'm hungry. I had time only for a sandwich which Miss Dowse brought in to me." Her dimples came out of captivity. "I hope you'll be able to shed the light of your presence on this office tomorrow if only to save me from being torn to shreds by disappointed customers who expected to see you today."

"Look here, I'm confoundedly sorry you've had to starve." He glanced at the clock. "Come along and have dinner with me. I've been too busy to eat myself. We'll go to a spot down town where the food is Grade A and one doesn't have to dress."

Why not? She had vowed she never would appear in public with a man for whom she worked but that had been in a small town and fat Sim Cove had been no temptation. This was New York and there wasn't a hint of an office flirtation in Keith Sanders' invitation. As if he had followed her train of thought he urged ingratiatingly.

"Really, it's part of your job to dine with me. You can tell me what happened today, the customers whom I must see tomorrow and we can start in the morning with a clean slate."

He was right. It would help tremendously if she made her report this evening. After all, it wasn't as if she were going out with a man she never had met before he had employed her. She had played tennis, walked, driven, danced with Keith Sanders during his visit with the Grants. The memory of that dinner when she had sat beside him—Skid glum with annoyance at being ignored on her other side—and prattled of small-town affairs had grown sharp little tentacles by which it clung tenaciously. Try as she would she couldn't shake it out of her mind. She owed it to herself to show him that she wasn't so naive as he had thought. She had gone out of her way to demonstrate her broad viewpoint to Greg Merton when they had driven home from the Inn. She had refused to be lured into personalities.

"It's a date," she agreed. "It won't take a minute to get my hat and coat."

As she applied her lipstick lightly before the mirror in her office she was glad she was wearing the black-wool frock with a touch of gold at neck and wrists and the matching reefer. Her black turban did a lot for her hair.

She remembered that once before he had asked her to go out with him and had promptly and, apparently for all time, forgotten the invitation when she had told him of his cadaverous-faced caller with the crafty smile. That same man had brought her car from Madam Steele's garage yesterday. Curious that he should have been there. Was there any connection between him and the man who was taking her to dinner?

"Any cash in the safe?" Sanders inquired from the doorway between his office and hers. "Had to dine and wine a customer. I'm cleaned out."

"Your agent Pokoski brought in the rents from the apartment house."

"Give me fifty bucks from that. Charge it to the expense account. That will square what I used of my own today."

The question she had asked herself about the mysterious caller recurred to her as she faced Keither Sanders across a table for two in the balcony of the restaurant. From a gallery at the other end of the large room drifted the wooing music of violins and flutes. She had told him of her conferences with his customers. One had been pathetic as a woman had besought her to hurry up the sale of her home. She needed the money, she had explained, needed it terribly to tide her son over a business crisis. If he could only hold on, the European war was bound to start a boom. Linda's throat had tightened as she told of it, her voice had been husky, but Sanders laughed.

"Don't take these hard-luck stories to heart. Better for her and the boy if we don't sell it. Better for him to fight it out for himself. I was sent to a good school, had two years in college, before the bottom dropped out of the family fortune. After that no one helped me. I've fought and schemed and battled my way to success without hanging on to anybody. He can do it. It takes all sorts of men to make this world—Lindy. Mind if I call you that away from the office?"

She didn't, she told him, and it was then that she thought of asking him about the cadaverous-faced man; his reference to all sorts of men had brought him to the surface of her memory. While she was framing a tactful question he went on:

"Do you know that you're a most companionable person? It isn't a recent discovery. I realized it when I met you at the Grants' last June."

"But not enough to remember me when I applied at your office for a position."

"You're one up on me there, but you have forgiven me, haven't you?" he wheedled with an appealing small-boy air.

Before she could answer a girl in smart black and pearls with a sensational corsage of purple orchids stopped at the table with a start of theatrical surprise. Alix Crane. A tall, black-haired man, suavely groomed and tailored, loomed behind her.

"Keith! How *marvelous* to see you! Dining the new little watchdog secretary! It's a trend. Meet my friend, Señor Lorillo. Pedro, Keith Sanders is the man who promised to back my show—and didn't." Miss Crane's voice was charged with venom.

If eyes could freeze, Keith Sanders' icy blue ones would have frozen her then and there. His curt nod in acknowledgment of the introduction set little flames dancing in the eyes of Señor Lorillo who bowed with exaggerated formality. Only an overpowering emotion could turn a man so white, Linda reflected, as she glanced at her employer; was it jealousy? Had the callous indifference he had expressed toward Miss Crane that afternoon in the office been pretense?

"How are you, Alix? Still sore at me for not being willing to finance a sure loser, I see." Sanders' voice had spikes in it.

"Your mistake, darling. I'm not sore, I have a better backer." Miss Crane smiled seductively at the man behind her. "Señor Lorillo is from Brazil." She touched her corsage and laughed suggestively. "Where the orchids come from. He's here to size up the effect of his country's exhibit at the Fair. What luck at the races today, Keith? Did you miss your little mascot?"

So he had been at the races and had not been dining and wining a customer? Was that what had cleaned him out so often lately, Linda wondered. As if drawn by a magnet her eyes met the brilliant eyes of the Brazilian. His wirelessed a we'll-meet-again message.

"Come, *carisima,* we are *de trop* here, yes?" His smooth, rich voice had a mere trace of accent.

"I guess you're right, Pedro. *Au revoir,* Keith."

Sanders nodded. The color had returned to his face but his eyes were cold and hard, his mouth was set in an ugly line as he sat down.

"Where did Alix pick up that tailor's dummy?"

"Dummy! His clothes were perfect." For some

inexplicable reason Linda rushed to the defense of the smooth señor. "He's my idea of a typed cinema lover. I thought him fascinating, with the come-hither in his eyes developed to the nth degree."

"Don't fall for that come-hither if you care for your job."

"Was that growl a threat or a warning?"

"Figure it out. I *was* entertaining a customer—at the races, believe it or not."

"I believe you, why wouldn't I? Races must be fun. Sensational horses, smart people, smart clothes and exciting crowds. What is this delicious thing I'm eating? I wonder how it's made. Seems to be coffee ice cream in meringue with brandy-flavored hot chocolate sauce." His low laugh stained her face with color.

"Still 'the little country girl with the naïve line,'" she quoted. "Country girl or not, I adore cooking. I believe it's as much of an art as interior decorating." She glanced away from his satirical eyes. "My word, there's a boy from home."

"Who is it? You look as if you'd discovered a diamond mine."

"You know him. Skidmore Grant." What could there be about unromantic Skid to make Keith Sanders scowl?

"Of course I know him. Wasn't I visiting his people when I met you? Is he your Big Moment that you've gone all sparkly?"

"Life has funny twists, hasn't it?" she evaded. "A week ago I was standing at the office window looking at the lighted streets, feeling sorry for myself that in all this great city I didn't know a man who would invite me out and now —presto, there are three."

"Three men and a girl. I presume the boy from home is one, yours truly makes two. Who's the third?"

She opened her lips to say Gregory Merton. Thought better of it. He never would ask her out again. She must account for three.

"Perhaps it's the charming Miss Crane's fascinating friend from Brazil, 'where the orchids come from,'" she suggested gaily and wondered what demon of contrariness had prompted her to make that senseless reply.

"Where have you met him before?" The low, fierce question startled her.

"Before! I've never met him before. Can't you recognize the light touch when you hear it?"

VII

IN THE square entresol of Ruth's apartment Linda lingered to listen to the caressing baritone. Who was singing? Something about moonlight and love. She never had heard the voice before. It did things to her heart. Made it ache. Why? Hadn't she everything she wanted at present? She had a fine position; tonight a man had invited her to dinner, the theater; they had had a sandwich at Reuben's after. And here she was being sorry for herself. Silly, she'd better go in and break up this attack of blues.

As she entered the living room Greg Merton's eyes met hers. It was he who was singing to his own accompaniment. Hester leaned against the blond-mahogany piano. Her tawny hair and lovely face, her white shoulders framed in diaphanous azure and silver net, were reflected in the satin-smooth surface. She applauded effusively as the song ended.

Her sister's smart evening frock made Linda unpleasantly aware that she was tired, that her mouth and eyes were showing the result of a sleepless night, that her nose would be better for a dab of powder, that her lips needed color, that the black frock and coat she had thought so smart at the office looked pretty uninteresting at eleven-thirty P.M. Gregory Merton was in white tie and tails. Had he and Hester been out together? Ruth Brewster glanced up from the mass of rose-color yarn in her smoky gray-and-silver lap.

"Well, see who's here? Our career woman, as I'm alive! You stole in like a ghost, Lindy. Guilty conscience? What kept you so late?"

"Business."

"Business! The wage-and-hour law should be required reading for that boss of yours. Had your dinner?"

"I have, Ruth, thanks."

She pulled off her reefer and hat and smoothed her
hair, trying to think of something casual to say to Greg
Merton who was standing in front of the fire now, lighting
a cigarette; trying to imagine what was passing in his mind
as he regarded her with that faint, cynical smile, trying to
forget his face and voice as he had accused:

"You pulled a fast one, lady, when you reported to
your boss the family conversation you heard while you
were my guest."

"Business!" Hester daintily shrugged dismay and linked
her arm in Merton's. "I'm glad you don't have to work so
late, Greg. We would have missed that gorgeous revue.
You really must see it, Lindy."

"I will. Who's calling at this ungodly hour?" she wondered aloud as she opened the outer door of the apartment.
"It's Skiddy," she announced breathlessly to the room behind her.

"Looks like old-home week," Grant exclaimed as he
entered. He was a man in his late twenties, of medium
height, with ruddy skin and sandy hair. His pug nose was
freckled. His short-sighted eyes, framed in bone-rimmed
spectacles, were brown, large and extraordinarily expressive. His wide smile was infectious, he fairly sparkled with
vitality. His tweeds were smartly tailored.

"You're a cute trick, Lindy."

"It's all done with mirrors, Skid."

He laughed and patted her shoulder; greeted Ruth,
who had sprung to her feet and dropped her knitting at his
entrance, with a resounding kiss. He struck an attitude of
stunned admiration as he looked at Hester.

"By the great horn spoon, the dame is beautiful!" He
caught her hand. "Got a kiss for me, Sugar?"

Hester's face flushed an annoyed pink. She shrank
back and tightened her grip on Merton's arm.

"Don't be ridiculous, Skid. Greg, this is my *Cousin,*
Skidmore Grant."

"Cousin several times removed," Grant corrected indignantly. "Everybody is a cousin to everybody else in our
town."

"My name is Merton." Gregory freed his arm from

Hester's and offered his hand. "Glad to meet you, Grant."

"That goes double." He glanced around the room and grinned. "Pretty swell layout you have here, Ruthetta, what? Modern and then some. Seems queer not to see you against a background of period pieces. You're different, too. My gosh, you've cut your hair! I'll have to get acquainted all over again."

"Begin by calling me Ruth, Ruthetta is out, Skid. Sit down, everybody, sit down, *please*." Ruth picked up her knitting. "You've been a long time finding this 'swell layout,' Skid. We heard some time ago that you were in New York."

Grant slumped into a deep chair and with elbows on its arms fitted the fingers of his two hands together.

"Always come at this time of the year to have a look-see at the theaters before my doting parents drag me South. I've stuck. This time I stay. Mrs. Grant's little boy is going to work."

"Work!" Ruth, Linda and Hester exclaimed in amazed unison.

"That's what I said. What's so surprising in that? I knew you wouldn't believe me so decided not to look you up till I had landed something. Finally sold my gigantic intellect for forty bucks a week. Not too bad for a guy who's never worked before."

"I'd say it was sensational," Greg Merton approved. "What's the business?"

"Investments. It's about time I grew up and learned to handle the property I'll inherit someday. I'm sick of traveling round for golf tournaments, living up to my stubby nose by being conciliatory and amiable. From now on I'm a smart fella, whose 'No' is no, and no kidding."

"And a working man. Somehow I can't picture you in overalls with a dinner pail, Skiddy," Linda teased. "But you are right. You should know how to take care of the property which will come to you. Speaking of property, has your mother ever traced her stolen jewelry?"

"Not even a sparkle of it. Hung around waiting for you to come out of that restaurant tonight, Lindy, but you and Sanders put on a disappearing act. Where'd you go? It made me so homesick to see you that soon as I could shake off the guy who was entertaining me I looked up your address and beat it over here."

Linda was uncomfortably aware of the three pairs of eyes that flashed to her face.

"Dining with her boss and she called it business!" Hester's exclamation was drenched with jealousy. "Do you hear that, Greg?"

"Why not? Many big deals have been discussed and put across over a dinner. I presume it was an important deal, Miss Bourne?"

"Very important." Linda hotly resented the tinge of sarcasm in Gregory Merton's question. Was he implying that the sale of the Steele estate was the "deal"? "Why didn't you come to the table and speak to me, Skid? Ashamed of your country cousin?"

"You, country! You knocked the spots out of every female in that room for looks, Lindy." His voice was rough with affection. "I didn't want to meet Sanders. I've never forgiven him for cutting-in and making a play for you, last summer. You wouldn't expect me to give him the glad hand, would you? He was a guest at the house and I had to treat him decently, but in little old New York, that's another thing again. He's a four-flusher."

"I'm working for him. And what's more I like and admire him very, *very* much."

"Well, I'll be—"

"Linda, ring for Libby. She's preparing a snack for us." Ruth Brewster's calm voice interrupted Grant's explosive protest. "I don't know why, but here we feel that we must eat at midnight. I never in my life did it at home."

"One of Libby's snacks makes the perfect ending to a perfect day." Linda touched a button in the wall.

"Has this been a perfect day for you, Miss Bourne?" Gregory Merton spoke directly to her for the first time since she had entered the room.

Her sturdy chin went up a trifle.

"Super-perfect. I borrowed that 'super' from Hollywood. There hasn't been an unoccupied moment since I entered the office at nine-thirty A.M. The batteries of one corner of the real-estate market appear to have been recharged. Ours, in case you care. The World and his Wife are either buying, building or selling houses. It's the war in

Europe, I presume. I understand that during the last one prices rocketed. Apparently people do not intend to be caught again. 'Buy now' has become a slogan. I hope the boom has hit the Merton office, also," she added with exaggerated concern.

"Is dickering in houses and land your business, Merton?" Skidmore Grant inquired.

"Dickering has been the word for it during the last few years, though, as Miss Bourne says, there is a decided upswing. The bulk of my business is the management of buildings and apartment houses for our clients."

"Then I'll bet you're the man I'm looking for. I've just inherited a city block from an uncle. I don't like the agent and—"

"Skiddy—"

"No, you don't get it for your boss Sanders, Lindy. I won't give it to you."

"Nobody asked you to, 'smart fella.' I was about to say that I hoped it wasn't your granduncle Paul who had died."

"Nope. It was another you never met." Liberty Hull entered carrying a laden tray. "Lib, if you open your mouth like that something's bound to fly down your throat and then—here give me that tray before you drop it."

"Well, of all things, if it ain't Skid Grant!" The woman's face, usually austere, broke into a wide smile. "Jest pull out that table, Mr. Merton, and open them leaves."

"Do you call this a snack, Ruth? I'd call it a gorge," Gregory Merton observed as Grant set down the laden tray.

"Land's sake, Mr. Merton, I've got to have somethin' to do to keep me busy. What with one thing an' another, it don't take no time 'tall to slick up this apartment an' Ruth an' Lindy are so 'fraid they'll get fat I don't have much real cookin'. That's fine. I always say, it takes men to do things right. Now you an' Ruth go an' set down, Lindy—never have to tell Hester not to help—Skid an' Mr. Merton an' me'll do the passin'.'"

Ruth smiled at Linda who nodded understandingly in response. Libby Hull liked men. Not in any sentimental way, just thought them as a whole grand persons. She was never happier than when feeding them. If it is true that a man's heart is in his stomach, she must have won scores of

male hearts. She was a wonderful cook. She didn't care
much for women except for Ruth and Linda whom she
loved devotedly—didn't trust the rank and file.

"My stars, Skid," she exclaimed, "must have felt in
my bones that you were coming, when I trekked out to
market just after lunch to get mushrooms for these sandwiches. You were always wheedling me to make 'em when
you an' Linda dropped in to Ruth's for tea an' the Lord
knows that was often. And that makes me think—why
haven't you been to see us before? Folks at home said they
knew when Lindy left town you'd be a-following."

"Oh, come now, Libby, don't be so modest. You know
it's you and your mushroom sandwiches I'd follow to the
ends of the earth," Grant wheedled, though her words had
set a deeper shade of color in his already sufficiently ruddy
face.

Linda, looking up suddenly, met Gregory Merton's
eyes. Was there a question in them or had she imagined it?

"Looks as if Cinderella had another Prince to take
her out, Miss Bourne," he observed. "Grant, added to the
one you have, makes two, doesn't it?"

What had he meant by the one she had? Himself or
Keith Sanders?

"The more the merrier," she responded lightly. "Libby, the sandwiches are wonderful. I must bring my boss
home someday for tea. He would love them."

VIII

"SO YOU think I was rough with Linda Bourne, Janet?"
Gregory Merton inquired, looking down at his sister as she
curled up in a chair in front of the fire in the huge living
room in her home. "Think I was unjust when I accused her
of being an informer, of telling Keith Sanders that Madam
Jane Steele was about to sell her estate?"

"I do. I think you were crazy. Did I mention Aunt
Jane's surname that afternoon? If I did, I don't remember
it and if I didn't how could Miss Bourne know of whom we

were speaking? You're off on the wrong foot, Greg. You're a dear until you get your back up about something and then you're unbearable. Heaven help your wife."

"Heaven won't have to get busy at present." A laugh cleared his eyes of moodiness. "And I'll never have one if a girl comes to you for a recommendation."

"You have your points. I'd be willing to stake my soul that if you once loved and married a woman you would be true as steel."

Her wistful dark eyes, the unsteadiness of her voice, hurt him unbearably. How much did she know of her husband's philandering? As if she sensed his troubled regard she said quickly:

"We're off the track; let's get back to your lovely Lindy."

"She isn't mine. She's Sanders'."

"Don't growl over a mere figure of speech, Greg. I thought she was charming, natural, with a special quality of sincerity. What did she do? She must have done something before you met her in Aunt Jane's garden to shake your confidence in her or you wouldn't have been suspicious of her all in a minute. You say you saw her there a week after she had tea with you. Was she unfriendly at the Inn?"

"No. We had a grand drive back to the city. She's a lot of fun. We had discussed the European war while at tea so we pushed that horror into the background. Talked of books, the plays that were coming and discovered that surrealism in its rawest state induced in us both a slight stirring of nausea. We were in the midst of an animated argument as to politics when we stopped in front of the apartment house. She had worked on a getting-out-votes committee in her home town and had views, but emphatically."

"Did she say anything about her family, her life before she came to New York?"

"Not a word. I tried once or twice to steer the conversation in that direction but she as steadily switched it back. It was almost as if she were determined to talk only of impersonal affairs."

"I can't believe that she passed our conversation on to Keith Sanders. I thought her one of the most attractive girls

I had met in years and I fell hard for her speaking voice, it is so beautiful, so alive. Sure you've told me everything?"

"Not quite." He kicked a log in the fire behind him, watched the shower of sparks fly up the chimney before he turned again to his sister.

"Not by a long shot. The moment we entered the entresol of the apartment where she lives, she turned frigid —perhaps .you can explain that—murmured something about telephoning and darted down the hall. Apparently she couldn't wait to get word to Sanders that the Steele estate was in the market. Left me standing there with her sister staring after her as if I'd been struck dumb."

"A sister! You haven't told me of her before." Janet Colton came out of her curl and sat erect. "The plot thickens. When did you meet her?"

"At Plattsburg. I was on my way to dine at her home when I saw Linda on the village street, mistook her for Hester and hailed her."

"Was she at dinner that night?"

"No. She had a previous date."

"Is the sister pretty?"

"They look a lot alike but Hester hasn't Linda's zing. Ruth says that Mrs. Bourne has spoiled her elder daughter. She doesn't work, isn't interested in much that I can discover but clothes and good times. She indulges in a high-frequency pout that is amusing at present, but which, I suspect, won't age well."

"I get it. Clinging-vine type?"

"That's the general idea."

"Who's Ruth? Another sister?"

"No. Ruth Brewster is their friend. Lost both parents in an automobile accident; left comfortably fixed financially, I judge. She decided to pull herself out of a rut, came to New York, subleased an apartment on Fifth Avenue opposite the Park—it's the last word in modern décor—and brought Linda along with her. She has taken up portrait painting. She's a grand person."

"Sounds like an interesting setup. Take me to call sometime, then I'll invite them here for a week end. Something tells me that the lovely Hester would intrigue Bill. He likes them beautiful but dumb. He has been away two days. I wonder where a man like Bill stays when he isn't at home." She blinked long lashes. Gregory Merton ached to get his hands on his brother-in-law and beat sense into him.

"Stays at his Club, of course. Don't get ideas, Janet. Bill loves you and the boy; nothing can touch that love, it's unshakable. It's a sort of devil in him that takes possession at times and makes him run around with other women to reassure himself that he still has what it takes. Don't think I'm approving of it; I'm trying to explain the make-up of some men, that's all."

"You never would be like that, Greg."

"How do we know? Fat chance I've had to go play-boy. It takes money and leisure. I had darned little of the first for a while and now that I have more of that I have none of the second. When Father died the summer after I left college I beat it home from abroad to find the business in a mess, that I must cut out all thought of studying law, roll up my sleeves and duff into real estate to save what I could for you and Mother."

"Mother needed your sacrifice for so short a time."

"It wasn't a sacrifice, don't get me wrong. I like business. I have taken evening courses in law, the kind I need in real estate. Now, because you insisted on making over your share of the family property to me when your husband settled a small fortune on you, I'm on Easy Street. As for Bill, I'd stake my life he's on the level with you. Try to sit tight till this crazy brainstorm of his blows over."

"I have tried, Greg. I loathe scenes. The first time he was away for days I froze him when he came home. I was frigid as the North Pole. I know better now. I'm still loving him after five years of exposure to his sizable rages and passionate repentances, but we're mentally and emotionally out of tune. I wouldn't divorce him no matter what he did and I don't believe he would cut the boy and me out of his life for the most glamorous woman in the world, but, unless I can feel sure of that until the feeling returns that brought us together, I'm afraid I'll tear our life to shreds."

"Someday a cyclone of emotion will shock him to a realization of what you mean to him; he'll be all yours, af-ter that. Hold on tight, Janey, he's worth it. There's no woman living who can see it through better than you. You'll never be downed. You won't have to depend on youth for attractiveness, either, no one will think of years in connection with you. You have a spirit and zest which are ageless."

"Thank you, Greg." Her eyes spilled tears. Her mouth curved in a tremulous smile. "I feel better. A whole lot better. It's been pretty tough on you, to have me sob out my troubles on your shoulder."

"That's what a male shoulder is for, I've been given to understand. To return to Bill. He went to the races, didn't he? He usually puts in several days when he goes, doesn't he? If he were winning he wouldn't leave and if he were losing he'd hang on like grim death hoping to make up the losses. He's traveling round with Keith Sanders and his lads. It's a high-power outfit. I wonder where that guy gets his money? Seems to have it to burn. He's self-made. Real estate hasn't been paying any extra dividends lately. At least not to me and I've been fairly lucky."

"Greg, you're such a comfort." His sister smiled through tears. "And here's another!" she exclaimed as a four-year-old boy in periwinkle-blue linen dashed into the room. His eyes were the color of his suit, his hair curled in gold rings on his beautifully-shaped head. Teeth like little pearls gleamed between his laughing lips. He dashed into the arms his mother held wide.

"If it isn't young Mr. Colton, in *person*," she exclaimed. On her knees she snuggled her nose into the child's chubby neck till he squirmed with laughter.

"You tickle," he gurgled, "tickle like the debil."

She sat back on her heels and regarded him incredulously. Her brother broke into unregenerated laughter.

"Don't laugh at him, Greg. William Colton, Jr., where did you hear that word?"

"Debil? Don't you like dat word?" His eyes were sapphire stars of surprise. "Dat debil, he's a friend of Yohnny's. Yohnny's always talking to him, even when I can see him. Guess dat debil hides when I come. How's my goldfishes?"

He ran the length of the room. Hands on his knees he stooped to look through the glass side of the large aquarium. His mother's eyes followed him. They came back to her brother as she curled up in her chair.

"Johnny's the new groom. I have warned Bill that the child shouldn't be around the stables so much and he laughs at me, points out the fact that he was brought up with horses, that it never hurt him. He's determined to make a rider of Billy Boy, but the child is so little to begin."

"You think that because you and I weren't brought up with horses, but we began to learn to handle a boat when we were his age. He's only four but he sits his pony like a veteran. Don't worry about that word 'debil.' He'll drop it and pick up something worse, probably, if that suggestion helps any. Bill is right about—"

"Do my ears deceive me or are you really pinning a medal on your brother-in-law, Greg?" Bill Colton inquired sarcastically from the threshold.

He crossed the room to his wife and pressed his lips to the top of her satin-smooth hair. His gray suit looked as if it had just come from the tailor's, his blue shirt and tie were impeccable but his face carried the stigmata of hours of tense excitement. There were deep creases on his high forehead, heavy lines between his nose and the corners of his thin lips, a slight puffiness under his brilliant hazel eyes. He dropped a velvet case into Janet's lap. Was it a conscience-gift? Greg saw her recoil before she smiled and opened it.

"Thanks a million. I adore presents." The contents of the case blazed and sparkled in the firelight.

"What a gorgeous bracelet with that sensational yellow diamond set in the band of white ones! It's perfect."

"Glad you like it. Hope you'll wear it. I bring home jewelry that was designed for a lovely woman and Janet parks it in her jewel case, Greg."

"I do wear it, Bill; only when I have guests who can't afford jewels, I don't like to put mine on parade."

"You're a sweet thing and you may wear diamonds or not as you please." Colton slumped deeper into the chair. "Boy, I'm glad to be home." Apparently there was to be no explanation offered of his absence. Janet was a sport. She had made no query, uttered no reproach.

With a squeal of joy the boy dashed from the other end of the room and flung himself against his father.

"Where you been, Daddy? The cat had some lovely little kittens an' Flossie, the brown setter, an' her five puppies slept on Yohnny's best riding' coat. He was awful mad.

He says he'll put a jinx on her if she does it again. What's a jinx, Daddy?"

"Oh, it's a sort of spell a magician casts on a person he doesn't like so that bad luck will follow him." Bill Colton laughed and rumpled the golden curls.

"What's bad luck?"

"It's what I've had for the last two days—dam'—" he caught back the word as his wife drew a sharp breath of protest. "There's something for you in the nursery, Billy Boy. Something red with a steering wheel and—"

"It's a mautomobile! It's a mautomobile!" The child's shout drifted back as he charged the stairs.

"Sorry about that damn, I almost let it out, Janey, but I've had a rotten time."

Gregory Merton tossed his cigarette into the fire.

"I'm off, Janet. Any day you're in town at teatime give me a ring and I'll take you to call on Ruth Brewster et al. So long, Bill."

"What's the rush? I'm not poison, am I, that you leave just as I appear? Stay and cheer me up, I'm low in my mind, so help me."

"Sorry, but I have a date."

"Sore at me, I suppose, because I turned Aunt Jane's business over to Sanders. Didn't know you had a prayer at it, she's been so down on you. He was cleaned out at the races, said he needed more business and would I get him a chance with the old lady. I felt darn sorry for the guy—know what it is to lose, myself—so went after her and sold him to her."

"Who told him that she had decided to sell the estate?"

"How do I know? Such things get on the air, don't they? Perhaps that secretary of his heard it and tipped him off. I hear that even in the short time she's been there she about runs the office. Somebody told me her name is Bourne and that she's too darn beautiful to be so smart."

Janet Colton glanced at her brother.

"That sounds as if you had been right and I wrong, Greg," she admitted regretfully.

IX

LINDA looked up from the letter she had finished reading. She was in her office; she hadn't dreamed the thing. That was the Empire State Building, looming outside her window, its tip gilded by the morning sun. She felt of the sheet of heavy notepaper with a dashing gold monogram and a faint scent of sandalwood. It was real. She focussed her attention on the Spencerian script, firm as copper-plate engraving, and read again:—

> Dear Miss Bourne,
>
> You will doubtless be surprised at the contents of this letter. I am asking you to come and live with me as my secretary. The duties will not be heavy. Attending to my household accounts, correspondence, checking-up on my village philanthropies, accompanying me to the city for business, concerts, theater and social affairs, wherever they may be, and acting as daughter of the house when I entertain. You would have plenty of time to yourself, a car at your disposal.
>
> Don't answer at once. Take a week to think it over. Then come and see me. A personal interview is more satisfactory than correspondence. I am sure that the matter of salary can be adjusted to your satisfaction.
>
> If you come or write before the week is up I shall not see you or open the letter. I want you to take time to consider.
>
> This is a confidential proposition. Please treat it as such.
>
> Very truly yours,
> JANE STEELE

Linda slipped the letter into its envelope and dropped it into the drawer of the desk in which she kept her own papers. She didn't need a week in which to consider that proposition. She didn't need an hour. She visualized Madam Steele's stern face with its bitter mouth, its eagle eyes, heard again her acrid voice. The position was not for her no matter how beautiful the house and grounds or how glittering the salary. Besides, what would Greg Merton and his sister think if she were to accept it? That she had moved in to influence Madam Steele in Keith Sanders' favor, of course. That settled that.

To her annoyance the colorful vision of the imperious woman in the lovely garden kept flashing and fading in her mind like an on-and-off electric sign during a hectically busy day. Why should it? Hadn't she decided once and for all that she wouldn't accept the position? Thank goodness Skid was taking her to a new Club tonight; that ought to erase "Aunt Jane" and her furiously angry nephew from her memory. In the smarting awareness of Greg Merton's distrust of her, Skid's sturdy honesty was a comfort. She swept up a pile of letters and entered Keith Sanders' office.

"If you'll look these over and sign, I'll post them on my way out. That cleans my desk. If you don't mind I would like to go home now."

"I do mind but as you've stayed here till seven the last two nights I'm afraid I can't do much about it. Whither away so early?"

"Is four-thirty so terribly early? I'm dining and dancing tonight and I would like a little time before I go. Ladies must beautify."

He laughed, pushed the letters aside and rose.

"These can wait until morning. My car is outside. I'll drive you home."

"Please don't trouble. It won't take me any time to get there in a bus."

"None of that nonsense about going in a bus. I said I would drive you home," he insisted, in his most dictatorial manner. "I want to hear how the Steele-estate purchase is coming on and you can tell me on the way."

She was thankful for the traffic jam as the car crawled and stopped, crawled and stopped. He was too engrossed with driving to have time or thought for conversation. She must tell him that she would not handle The Castle deal and dreaded it. If she could get home before he mentioned it she would be in luck. What would he say if he knew of that "strictly confidential" proposition from Madam Steele?

Ahead blazed the star on the flagpole, the "Eternal Light" which burned day and night in honor of those who had given their lives to make the world safe for democracy. Would there be occasion for another sometime soon? She hoped not, prayed not. High up a moving sign flashed the latest news. It brought a rush of tears to her eyes. In sharp contrast were shopwindows already lighted to display sumptuous furs, glittering evening frocks in all the colors of the rainbow, bronzes, paintings, jewels and silver.

Her hopes were dashed. He had not forgotten. When they reached a less crowded part of the Avenue Sanders asked:

"What's doing in the Steele proposition? Have you been to The Castle again?"

Linda swallowed hard.

"No."

"What d'you mean by 'No'?"

"That I haven't been there."

"Why not? Someone may cut in ahead of us. Merton for instance. The owner is his aunt." He shut his lips hard as if regretting too late the admission.

"I know she is. He was in the garden when I went to look over the house. He made it unmistakably plain that he felt we were encroaching on his territory. I told you when I came back that I didn't want to handle the buying of that estate and I meant it. I haven't the sales technique."

Sanders' whistle was long and low.

"I begin to understand. Been seeing much of Merton lately?"

"I'll have to consult my line-a-day book before I answer."

"Meaning that it's none of my business. Here we are." He manipulated the roadster between two parked cars. "You wouldn't be hospitable and invite your boss in for tea would you? I'm dying of thirst," He added in a hollow whisper.

"Perhaps there isn't any."

"Didn't I have tea at your house last summer and didn't you say that it was as much a family custom as breakfast?"

"I did. But this isn't home."

"But there will be tea?"

"You win. Come in."

As she opened the door of the apartment she heard the tinkle of spoons on china, a low laugh, the murmur of voices. Was Ruth entertaining?

She stopped on the threshold of the living room uncomfortably aware of Keith Sanders' lingering to lay down his hat in the entresol. Mrs. Colton sat in a low chair near the fire; Skid Grant, perched on the arm of the divan, was talking to her. Ruth at the tea table was handing Greg Merton a cup. They all looked up as she entered.

"As, I'm alive, here's Lindy!" Ruth exclaimed. "Has your slave-driver boss absconded or have you lost your job, that you've come from the mart of trade at a civilized hour? Oh!—" she exclaimed as Keith Sanders loomed behind Linda.

"You see what a reputation you've earned, Mr. Sanders," Linda said lightly. "Mrs. Colton, it is wonderful to see you here." She nodded to Greg Merton, smiled at Grant. "Not surprising to find you, Skiddy. When do you work or do you?"

"Not till seven-thirty P.M. when I take you out to dinner." Grant pointed his remark at Sanders, bending over Ruth who was filling a cup.

"Give this to Lindy, Greg. How will you have your tea, Mr. Sanders?"

"As it comes. I like to taste the tea."

Merton set a small table beside the chair Linda had moved nearer Janet Colton and set down the cup and saucer.

"Thanks." She ignored him and turned to his sister. "It must be gorgeous in the country now." She could think of nothing less banal with the memory of Greg as he had raged at her in Madam Steele's garden dominating her mind.

"It is. I have asked Miss Brewster to come to us for next week end," Janet Colton answered cordially, "and I want you also, very, very much. It is not too cold for the swimming pool and—"

"We hoped we would find you at home. We're famishing for tea," interrupted a voice from the doorway.

Her mother and sister. Linda realized at once what

this meant. An invitation for Hester to join the week end would be wangled out of Mrs. Colton. Why not? She herself hadn't the least intention of going. She appraised her mother from a stranger's viewpoint. Her modish "burnt-sugar" hat was the essence of style, her smart matching wool suit accentuated the slim perfection of her figure. Her chestnut hair showed no touch of gray. Her brown eyes were brilliant. Her creamy skin was unlined.

Linda tried to remember when she and her mother had begun to grow apart. She had been such a devoted mother. Was it the day Skid Grant had invited her to the Club dance, when before he had always taken Hester?

"I'm so happy to meet you, Mrs. Colton." Mrs. Bourne's voice held just the right tinge of warmth. "Gregory talks of you constantly. Keith, it is delightful to see you again. I've often wondered what we did to you the last time you dined with us that you ran away without bidding us good-by."

Linda bit back a smile. For the first time since she had met him she saw Keith Sanders nonplussed. She sensed him reaching mentally for an answer which wouldn't materialize, as he tugged at his blond mustache. With a wicked grin Skid Grant came to his rescue.

"You mustn't check up on these city fellas, Aunt Evelyn. They haven't time to remember the manners they learned at their mother's knee. Now take Mrs. Grant's little boy, he's grown up in the way he should go."

"Don't be ridiculous, Skiddy," Hester interrupted curtly. "I hope my little sister is giving satisfaction, Mr. Sanders?" She smiled invitingly. He drew a chair beside her.

"She is, but I could use another Bourne—for decoration. You're not by any chance looking for work, are you?"

"Is he ribbing me, Greg?" Hester appealed to Merton who was standing with one arm on the mantel.

"Sure. He has the world's smartest secretary now and he knows it. Why should he want another?"

"Apparently you didn't hear me, Merton. I said 'for decoration,'" Sanders reminded smoothly. "I hope you'll allow me to make up for my lack of manners last summer by taking you and your daughter to dinner and the theater, Mrs. Bourne."

"Thank you, Keith—you don't mind if I call you Keith, do you—you young men seem like boys to me. I won't go, I'm spending my evenings improving my contract, but Hester—"

"I didn't mean Hester, I meant your other daughter," he corrected curtly.

Linda could have cheerfully strangled him as her mother's face stiffened and the color flew to Hester's hair. How abominable of him. It wasn't the first time he had shown claws, sharp, tearing, cruel claws. She had seen it happen in the office. Janet Colton's voice broke the uncomfortable silence.

"I'll send the car for you next Friday, Miss Brewster. Mr. Sanders, I want that perfect secretary of yours for the week end. So don't send her to the country on an assignment." She hesitated before she added: "Miss Hester, you will join us, won't you? If convenient the chauffeur will pick you all up here."

"Thank you. I'll love to come."

Janet Colton laughed in response to Skid Grant's suggestive cough.

"Don't tell me I can't count on *you*, Mr. Grant?"

"Skid to you, Mrs. Colton. The invitation is so sudden. Thanks, I'll be there with bells on. Sanders, this is where you get completely and utterly left."

"I'm afraid there is a reason for my being left, Grant. You see, while I'm a pal of her husband's, I've cut Mrs. Colton's brother out of a big piece of business. Naturally she's sore about it."

For an instant Greg Merton's anger beat against the silence.

"Don't talk like a darn fool, Sanders," he protested, "and don't lug business in here."

Something woke in Linda, something savage, resentful. Greg Merton had accused her of having told her boss that Mrs. Steele was about to sell her estate. This was the moment to have that straightened out.

"Keith," she said reverting to the familiar name she had called him last summer, "I want you to tell Greg Merton that you did *not* hear through me that the Steele estate was to be put on the market, that I had never mentioned it to you."

Sanders looked from her face to Merton who had taken a step forward. His eyes were at their coldest. His smile was at its most sardonic. He stroked his clipped mustache.

"I'd do a lot for you, Miss Bourne, but I can't lie about a matter of business. Where else would I hear of it if you hadn't told me?"

Linda's gasp of amazement was lost in Greg Merton's cool laugh.

"That makes it just perfect. Come on, Janet. Let's go."

X

THE MUSIC had fiddles and piccolos as well as drums. It whimpered and whistled. To its rhythm Spanish Infanta skirts drifted and swished against Victorian velvets in the crowded space between the Tables. A touch of Watteau. A touch of pre-War hobble. Glimmer of paillettes. The Orient in jewels. The pulled-back look. Skirts yards wide in the Degas ballet manner. The covered-up effect. The near-nude. Sleek heads snuggled against black broadcloth shoulders. Eyes smiling alluringly up into eyes that flamed in response or smiled back with amused detachment. A shimmering kaleidoscope of color. A sea of perfume. A blaze of jewels, real or simulated.

"Here we are Lindy, geared to a session in the world's newest, most jammed night club. How do you like the joint?"

"Garish but dramatic."

"You've said it. Now that we have dined do we move on, dance or set?"

"If you don't mind, Skiddy, let's just 'set' and watch the dancers for a while. This is certainly the season to dress as one likes. There is about every type of costume on that floor but slacks."

"That's a pretty slick outfit you're wearing, half white and half green. What's the slithery stuff?"

"Silk jersey. I like the way it drapes."

"Suits you down to the ground. It's photogenic to the nth degree. What'll you have to drink? Your usual riotous orange juice?"

"With soda to make it sparkle. I love the tickle as it goes down. It's really quite stimulating, believe it or not."

"Oh yeah? I'll take champagne. The brew must be exciting. Your eyes are all twinkle, twinkle in anticipation."

"That isn't what makes me laugh, it's the thought of coming to a de luxe night spot and drinking orange juice. Aren't the women's clothes scrumptious? I could care for that little silver number that just waltzed past."

She watched the dancers as he gave the order. It was a relief to be here, to see something that would push Keith Sanders' face, his voice from her mind as he had declared:

"I'd do a lot for you, Miss Bourne, but I can't lie about a matter of business. Where else would I hear of it if you hadn't told me?"

As he had spoken the solid ground of faith in him, in his honesty, had cracked and crumbled under her feet. He had said he couldn't lie. He was lying and he knew it. She closed her eyes tight as if to shut out the vision of Greg Merton's masklike face as he listened. Instead she shut it in. What difference did it make? Sanders' lie was but a confirmation of Greg's belief that she had repeated his conversation with Janet Colton to her boss, wasn't it?

"Come back, Lindy." Grant tapped her hand lightly with a stubby finger. "Living over that scene at Ruth's this afternoon, aren't you? What was it all about?"

She regarded him thoughtfully. His evening clothes accentuated the roundness of his ruddy face with the blunt, freckled nose, the brown of his large, expressive eyes behind the bone-rimmed spectacles. His smile was heartwarming. In short, he was a rock of refuge in an ocean of uncertainty. She would get his viewpoint.

"I'd like to tell you, Skid, if you'll regard it as confidential?"

"Sure. Come across. I'm worth my weight in secrets. Nobody loves me but they all confide in me. I'll be silent as a tubeless radio. Shoot."

To the accompaniment of muted violins she told him of the conversation between Greg Merton and his sister at the Inn about their Aunt Jane and her estate; of being sent

by Sanders to The Castle, which he had been commissioned to sell; of meeting Greg in the garden there, of his
stunned surprise, of his furious accusation that she had
rushed back to town from the Inn to inform her boss that
the estate was in the market.

"It hurt, hurt terribly, to have him think I would do a
thing like that, so, while the two men were together at
Ruth's this afternoon, I had a crazy hunch to bring it into
the open, to have Keith assure Greg Merton that he had
not learned of the proposed sale through me. You heard
his answer."

"Then you didn't tell him?"

"Skid! Do you believe Keith Sanders and not me?"

"Take it easy, Lindy. Of course I don't. What are you
going to do about it? Chuck your job? Have you heard Opportunity calling? I'll bet you haven't. That's a busy line
these days. If you check out and hunt for the perfect boss,
you'll have some hunt. Business isn't conducted on purely
altruistic lines, now."

"I can't work for a man whom I believe to be dishon-
est, can I?"

"I suppose you can but you don't have to. If you
didn't tell Sanders—hold everything, I'll change that 'if' to
as—how do you account for his so quickly finding out that
the Steele estate was in the market?"

"I can't acount for it. Madam Steele told her nephew
that Bill Colton had recommended Sanders and that she
had taken his advice. Greg Merton immediately jumped to
the conclusion that I had rushed the news his sister had
told him at the Inn to my boss, who had then asked Mr.
Colton to say a good word for him."

"Bill Colton! Husband of that stunning woman we
met this afternoon?"

"Do you know them?"

"By reputation only until I met her today. They are
real people and I don't mean maybe. I wonder why Colton
is herding with Sanders and the high-flying bunch he trav-
els with."

"You don't like Keith, do you?"

"I do not. He's an exhibitionist. But that doesn't mean
that I'm advising you to throw up your job with him until
you are sure of another, if you want another. You wouldn't

prefer to marry me, would you?" His voice was light but the earnestness in it hurt her.

"No, Skid, but I—"

"None of that I-love-you-like-a-cousin stuff, and don't blink your lashes. I can take it. There are plenty more fish in the sea with tawny hair and big brown eyes and—"

"Like Hester's," Linda suggested eagerly.

"That's an idea," he grinned. "But she's gone off the deep end about Merton, hasn't she? I rather got that impression."

"You're right. But perhaps he'll throw her over because he can't stand her 'business-chaser' sister. In spite of your advice, Skid, I've made up my mind to leave Sanders' office."

"You didn't think I believed you would act on it, did you? Ruthetta is the only female I know who will ask a man's advice and take it. If you step out of your present job what will you look for? Employers aren't sending out scouts to bring in secretaries. Got anything in your mind?"

Even as she shook her head, before her eyes flashed a sheet of creamy letter paper with bold Spencerian script. Madam Steele had offered her a position. Opportunity calling? Was it a rainbow to follow which might have a pot of gold at the end of it, or was it a blind alley from which she would have to back out?

"Lindy! Lindy!" Grant's low, strained voice roused her from her preoccupation.

"What is it, Skid? You're white." She followed his eyes. He was staring at the back of a woman at a nearby table. Linda couldn't see her face, could see only the gold-sequined sheath which outlined her figure as if she had been melted and poured into it. She was laughing and gesticulating with an arm glittering and flashing with diamonds. Someone he knew?

"Have you seen a ghost, Skid?"

"Let's dance."

As they stepped onto the crowded floor he put his lips close to her ear:

"Get this, Lindy. I'm about to go screwball for a purpose."

She bent back her head to look at him. What did he

mean? His face was still white. He sounded mysterious. It wasn't what he had been drinking. He hadn't finished one glass of champagne. However, he was Skid Grant whom she had known for years. She could trust him.

"Can I help?"

"You sure can. When we get back to our table I'll pretend I'm blotto. Pull me away and get me out of the room. It'll be darned unpleasant for you, but you'll do a great favor to me. Are you game?"

Linda swallowed hard. She hated to be conspicuous and to drag a man who was tight out of a night club was going some. But it was Skid. He had a good reason or he wouldn't ask her to do it. She nodded. Her voice wouldn't come.

"Don't call me Skid. Call me—Tom. Tom—Sterling's the name. Here we go."

His face was still colorless as they returned to their table. Linda was cold with apprehension. What was he planning? He swayed on his feet, picked up his glass and drained it. Grinned at her vacantly.

"Let's go, Sugar. This is a rotten Club an' . . ."

The guests at a table turned to look at him, laughed and whispered. Skid heard them and swung in their direction. He glared at the woman in sequins and the man beside her who had sprung to his feet. Linda's heart stopped beating. Alix Crane and the suave Señor Lorillo! Now what?

"Laughing at me were you?" Grant demanded cockily. "I'll teach you . . ." Linda saw the blaze of jewels as Miss Crane put up her arm to ward off his hand before it descended on her shoulder. The men in the party were on their feet; she must get Skid out before they knocked him down. Why, why was he making a spectacle of himself and her? She seized his arm.

"S—Tom! Tom! Come," she begged. She looked pleadingly at Lorillo; the tears in her eyes were genuine. "Please don't call the manager. I'll get him away, really I will. Tom—Tom, dear—please come."

"She—she was laughing at me." He made an attempt at dignity and scowled. "No—no one can get a—away with laughing at me—Sugar." He smiled at Linda vacantly. "W—what we standing here for? Garçon! Garçon! L'addition!"

As the excited waiter presented a slip, he flung it to the table with a bill. "Come on, let's get out of this joint where a guy—"

"Pedro! Don't follow them! It's Sanders' secretary watchdog with her boy friend who's on a binge! What d'you know—"

Linda jerked Skid out of hearing of Alix Crane's piercing whisper. A hundred red-hot eyes burned into her neck, left bare by the heart-shape opening of her frock. Snickers and murmurs followed her as she passed between the tables to gay music which had swung into a rumba. The rhythmic motion of the orchestra leader's baton seemed to mock her.

Waves of embarrassment flamed through her as she steered Grant past the zebra-striped banquettes in the azure-and-silver foyer toward the coatroom. She knew now what it must feel like to be burned at the stake. A man followed and stood near while she helped Skid with his coat and thrust his hat into his hand.

"He never has been like this before, really he hasn't," she explained to the person with the pouter-pigeon figure, pendant cheeks and cold eyes whom she took to be the proprietor.

It seemed to her years before she had slipped into her long white coat with the enormous gold frogs and they were through the revolving doors, swaying down the steps, walking toward the avenue.

"Perhaps you'll explain now what all this melodrama is about, Skid Grant," she demanded indignantly. He straightened his opera hat which had been tipped at a ribald angle.

"That woman in the sequin frock was wearing one of Mother's stolen bracelets."

"Skid! Are you sure? That was Alix Crane, the night-club singer!"

"Well, I'll be darned! Who was the guy—"

A hand seized his shoulder. Whirled him round. Linda had a hectic vision of a patrol wagon with its clanging gong.

"What in thunder is all this about, Grant?" a furious voice demanded. Greg Merton! Topcoatless. His finely modeled head uncovered. "What d'you mean dragging Lindy through that disgusting scene?"

So he still thought of her as "Lindy"! Nice of him when he believed her to be a double-crosser.

"Keep your shirt on, Merton." Skid's voice was low but steady. "Lindy and I were putting on an act. Take her home, will you? I've got to hang around here. Hi! Taxi."

With one foot on the step of the cab Linda looked over her shoulder.

"I don't need anyone to take me home, thank you."

"Just the same I'm coming."

She sprang in and slammed the door before Merton could follow.

"Go on! Quick, driver," she ordered. And the driver, who knew his business, went on.

XI

THE TWO men watched the red light of the cab dim in the distance. Merton linked his arm in Grant's.

"What's it all about, Skid? You'll have to have a pretty smooth reason for putting on that act with Linda Bourne. I sat a few tables beyond. Tried to reach you to help, but people got in my way."

Grant told him.

"Your mother's bracelet! There must be dozens of diamond bracelets in that room. How could you be sure?"

"She was told years ago that eight was her lucky number. She had the figure 8 in small diamonds set somewhere in every piece of jewelry she owns, which is always made to order for her. This time there was an 8 on each side of a large emerald."

"Do you mean you could see the numbers in the bracelet of a woman at another table? You must have the eyesight of a condor."

"Not at first. It was the arrangement of the stones that caught my attention. Mother always comes to me to clasp her bracelets. She's awful sweet. Then I kiss her and she says, 'Thank you, dear,' and smiles at me the way mothers do and we're both all warmed up inside. It's a sort of family ceremony."

Sand in Greg Merton's eyes. His mother had had no diamond bracelets for him to fasten but he knew that smile.

"After that, I had to get near enough to see if that 8 was there," Grant explained. "Luck was with me. I saw it, but what do I do now? Linda says that the dame is Alix Crane the night-club singer!"

"Alix Crane! The girl gossip had Sanders backing in a musical comedy? Are you sure?"

"For the love of Pete! *Sanders!*"

"How did Linda know her?"

"Probably has seen her in the office. Gosh, I remember. I heard the Crane woman whisper, 'Pedro! Don't follow them! It's Sanders' watchdog secretary.' I lost the rest."

"Who's Pedro?"

"The boy friend with her, I presume. Wait a minute! Wait a *minute!* Grant stopped under a light. "That's an idea! Who *is* Pedro? Got to find out. How? I ought to follow that couple, but if I go in after my imitation of a high-roller on high, I'll be chucked out, pronto."

"I'll go for you. I was with a party, but as an extra stag only. I won't be missed. I'll ask questions. This is a new place but I know the proprietor." He anticipated Grant's warning. "Don't worry. I know that all you've told me is off the record. I won't breathe a word of it. Thanks for letting me in on the excitement. Boy, I feel like a cross between J. Edgar Hoover and Philo Vance. Drop into my office in the morning. I may have something to report."

"I'll be there. My name is Tom. Tom Sterling, in case anyone cares."

The proprietor was in the foyer when Greg entered. He had been there when he had dashed past in pursuit of Linda and Grant.

"Did you find your friends, Monsieur?" The Frenchman's outlines swelled like those of a balloon figure being inflated. He puffed pendant cheeks.

"Put 'em in a cab, François. When fresh air straightened him up was darned ashamed of himself. He was cleaned out at the races today and was trying to forget his troubles, not that that is an excuse for such a hick performance."

"I agree with you, Monsieur Merton. Eet would be better eef your friend nevaire try to forget here again. You tell heem. You know heem well?"

"No. My interest was in the young lady. Old family. Not used to Café Society. Tough spot for her. She thinks she dropped a vanity case when she jumped up from the table. I'll look for it. I remember where they sat."

"Very good. *Bonne chance,* Monsieur Merton."

He had been pretty garrulous about the affair, Greg realized, as he went on to the supper room. François, whom he had known for years, must wonder what had made the agent for the premises suddenly so communicative but he knew that said agent could accommodate the proprietor if he lagged in his rent payments or could close him out. He would not talk.

As he entered the supper room, he told the maître d'hôtel his errand. That dignitary was all concern as he ushered him to the table Grant and Linda had occupied. The girl in the gold-sequin frock stared up at him, shrugged and whispered to the man beside her. He glanced at them casually, but not so casually that he wouldn't recognize them again, before he began to hunt for the missing vanity case. Alix Crane and Pedro! Who was Pedro?

"Not here," he said to the maître d'hôtel. "In the excitement the young lady must have forgotten that she put the vanity into her bag. Thanks."

He slipped a bill into the man's hand and returned to the foyer. The proprietor hurried up to him.

"Did you find the vanity case of the charming mademoiselle, Monsieur Merton?"

"No. If it should be found send it to my office, will you, François?"

"*Certainment.* But you are not leaving so early, Monsieur?"

"Not until I know the name of the party who engaged the table at which the girl in the gold-sequin dress is sitting."

The cheeks of François puffed and deflated.

"But, Monsieur, there are so many charming ladies in gold—"

"Listen, François. I need the name of the man who was host at that table. Perhaps my tipsy friend wants to send to the lady, via him, an apology in the shape of flowers. Whatever my reason for wanting the information it will not affect you in any way. You don't think I'm fool enough to get a tenant who is paying the enormous rent of a place like this into trouble, do you?" A wireless of understanding flashed between them.

"You may not be a G-man, may you, Monsieur Merton?" The proprietor's strained expression eased in response to Greg's laugh.

"No. No, François. I am exactly what you know me to be, a hard-working realtor trying to help a friend ease a guilty conscience. Poor Tom—"

"What did you say his name was, Monsieur?"

"Never mind his name. He won't come here again, but if he should I'd advise you to be cordial. Scads of money. I'll wait in your office till I get that name."

As he paced the floor of the walnut-paneled room with its scarlet-leather chairs, he thought of his incredulous surprise as he had heard Grant's voice and had seen Linda, cheeks aflame, trying to drag him away from the table. And he thought of his impetuous rush after them and of her contemptuous dismissal of him as he had attempted to follow her into the cab. Quite as if *she* were the injured party. Hadn't Sanders reluctantly admitted that he had had the first news of Jane Steele's decision to sell from her?

He looked up as a red-faced man with baggy jowls, sparse brown hair and gray-green ferret eyes, in sleek dinner clothes, entered and closed the door behind him.

"Jim Shaw! What are you doing here?"

The man gave an excellent imitation of the proprietor's shrug and bared his prominent teeth in a grin.

"The same to you, Monsoor Merton?"

"I told François what I wanted."

Shaw abandoned his Gallic imitations.

"I have it, the name of the host whose guest your tipsy friend tried to discipline for laughing at him. The man is Señor Lorillo. A rich Brazilian. He arrived in New York recently."

"Thanks, Jim. I can't explain now why I want that

name. I may need your help about it later. Keep all this under your hat. I'll be seeing you."

The next morning Greg Merton grinned as he looked at Skidmore Grant, seated on the corner of the broad, flat desk in his office.

"Why the dark glasses? Why the stubble on your upper lip which, experience tells me, indicates a budding mustache?"

"Disguise, boy, disguise!" Grant hissed. "Can't take a chance of being recognized as the heel who got fresh with a lady, and a night-club singer at that, can I?" He removed the dark spectacles, replaced them with his own and squinted at the slip of paper he held. "Señor Pedro Lorillo. Did you get a good look at him when you went back?"

"I did. Thought him a regular fella till his eyes met mine. It was like an electric shock. Sort of Doctor-Jekyll-and-Mr.-Hyde stuff. He gave me the shivers."

"What's his line?"

"He's working at being a rich Brazilian. You know the brand, they have 'em in the movies—stupendous coffee fazendas, sensational cattle ranches, or what have you."

"Think he's a phony, I take it. The others at the table had the New Yorker look all right. Suppose we try to locate him at a hotel? Mind if I use your phone?"

"Just a minute, Skid. Wasn't that jewelry insured? Hasn't the insurance company set scouts tracing it?"

"It has. But I have views. I'd like to try trailing the thief or thieves myself. I'm really in the big city to find Mother's diamonds, if you want to know." He grinned. "I'm psychic. Something tells me they are here."

"Are you sure it was her bracelet? One diamond bracelet looks a lot like another to me. My sister has several but I couldn't pick one of them out of a bunch to save my life."

"As sure as I can be about anything but death and taxes. The one I spotted last night was one of three stolen. The thief got a load of other expensive gewgaws, but I wouldn't be able to identify those in a crowd. If I can trace this one bracelet I may get the others and unearth a gang of international jewel thieves. Lindy knows what I saw last night but you're the only soul on earth who knows the whole story of what I'm after. I've got to have someone to talk to or bust."

"Why me? Why not Sanders? He's a friend of your family."

"Sanders! A friend of the family! He's a friend of the girl who's wearing Mother's bracelet, isn't he? That's an idea! I'll smoke him out. He might give us a tip about the Brazilian. Nope, on second thought, can't do it. He might suspect what I'm up to and it would get around that I'm sleuthing and spoil everything. Besides, I've never liked him since he tried to cut me out with Lindy. Mother admires him. We met him on a North Sea cruise. He has a smooth line with women, especially older ones, and gosh, how they fall for it. You struck me as being a straight-shooter the first time I saw you. I've liked you more since I turned the office building over to you to handle. If you can bear up under the strain I'll sob out my troubles on your shoulder."

Greg wondered if he would be so friendly if he knew that Lindy's charm, her smile *and* her treachery dominated his thoughts.

"Thanks, Skid. I hope you'll never change your opinion. I'll help all I can. After I left you last night I ran into Jim Shaw, who was at the Club on plainclothes duty. He's a detective who has worked for me tracing tenants who have the wanderlust, tenants who pick up goods and chattels and depart leaving the rent unpaid. You'd be surprised how often that happens in the best-regulated families and most expensive apartments. He's good. What say, if we set him sniffing along the trail?"

"You didn't tell him why I put on the act?"

"Hold everything. I didn't tell him that it was an act. He's keen. He can snoop out the thief if anyone can. Shall I phone him to come here?"

"Not yet. We know where the bracelet is. Our combined intelligences ought to find out how it got there. Let's go it alone."

"You're the doctor. It's your hunt. I'll have my secretary ring up the hotels and when or if she locates our man switch me onto the wire. Better let me talk for you."

"Fair enough. Get busy."

It was twenty minutes before a voice came through the inter-office phone.

"I've located Señor Pedro Lorillo at the Ritz, Mr. Merton."

"All right. I'll take over."

"The desk clerk speaking," announced a voice at the other end of the wire.

"Connect me with Señor Pedro Lorillo."

"The Señor is out, sir."

"Then I'll talk with Señora Lorillo."

"She is not registered here."

Greg Merton spoke to Grant but not so softly that his voice would not be audible to the desk clerk.

"Dolores isn't at the hotel, Tom. That's queer. Pedro wrote she was coming with him." He spoke into the transmitter. "That's all. Sorry to have kept you waiting."

"Just a minute. Señor Lorillo left word that if anyone inquired for him to say he'd gone to the Brazilian exhibit at the Fair to meet a friend who recently had arrived in the United States."

"That's a break. Thanks. I'll get in touch with him there." He cradled the phone. "You heard, Skid?"

"Yeah. I heard. Bright boy, Greg, to pretend we knew the Señor's wife. That got you the information. Just where do we G-men go from here?"

"To the Fair, of course. Brazil, here we come!"

XII

TRAILING SENOR PEDRO LORILLO had not been the cinch he and Grant had anticipated, Greg Merton reflected as he leaned against the iron rail of the balcony of the Brazilian Restaurant above a flowery little court and under a sky like an inverted indigo sieve with gold just beginning to shine through its myriad holes. Below hummed and flowed unceasingly a stream of humanity, on foot, in roll chairs, in buses. The delectable aroma of coffee scented the crisp air. Gay, swinging music rippled and crashed and tinkled. Changing lights turned white pillars to rosy marble, walls to amethyst, amber and translucent green jade, the Perisphere to cloudy sapphire. He had haunted the place since he had heard this morning that the Brazilian would be here. Skid and he had decided that the best way to follow up the emerald and diamond bracelet was to establish friendly relations, if possible, with the escort of the woman who had worn it.

He glanced at his wrist watch. Grant was due in fifteen minutes. If the Señor didn't appear soon their plan for him to get fratty with the Brazilian and pave the way for Skid's abject apology for last evening would go smash.

A girl leaned over the balcony to look at the garden, a slender girl in black. He recognized the costly simplicity of her ensemble, Janet's clothes were like that. She wore a corsage of orchids, a litte more yellow than the hair which showed below her feather turban. His heart stopped and pounded on. Alix Crane! Was she here to meet Lorillo? He must talk with her. Establishing rapprochement with a strange female wasn't in his line. What was his best move?

He didn't need one. Green eyes glinted in his direction between artistically darkened lashes. A gold bag dropped. He recognized the technique. Girl wanted to talk to boy. Girl would talk to boy, pronto. He retrieved the bag.

"Darn slippery things, aren't they?" he sympathized and smiled. Her eyes traveled from the top of his head to his feet, rested on the green-ringed hand which held his soft hat and came back to his eyes.

"They are when one is too weak from hunger to hold them," she agreed.

This was quicker work than Greg had anticipated but he rose to the bait like a veteran and swallowed the line to the tip of the rod.

"Never could bear to read about the starving," he attested with just the right amount of eagerness. "Won't you have dinner with me? I'm a stranger in a strange country." That was right, he was in Brazil, wasn't he?

"I'm really waiting for—"

"Lovely woman should wait for no man." Greg wondered how he could think up such clichés. "Let's begin with an apéritif. They serve them on this balcony. After that, how about a charcoal-broiled beefsteak. They're sensational."

"The apéritif first. Perhaps I shall not find you entertaining enough to go on to dinner, Mr.—?" She shrugged her shoulders, looked up into his face as he drew out a chair for her.

"Merton's the name." He laughed and seated himself across the table. "You knew that, didn't you? Just as I know that you are Alix Crane, the singer, whom I've always admired. Never thought I'd have the luck to meet you."

"It isn't so hard."

"So I see. Boy, think of the time I've wasted." He gave an order to the waiter. Elbows on the table she clasped her ungloved hands. It was then that he saw the emerald-and-diamond bracelet glittering against her black sleeve. If that were Mrs. Grant's, Skid's mother had a millionaire-taste in jewelry, all right. It was superb.

"I knew your name when I dropped the bag, Mr. Merton, or I wouldn't have dropped it. I'm not that easy to meet. When you came to the table next ours last night to hunt for a vanity, which I suspect you knew was not there, I asked the maître d'hôtel who you were. He told me that you are the nephew of a filthy-rich woman; filthy is my word, not his."

"The great-nephew, only. And in case it makes a difference to you, quite out of favor with her."

"You look too keen to let that happen. You're in real estate, aren't you?"

"Guilty."

She tapped on the table with finger tips that shone like pink jewels. Her eyes glinted vindictively.

"Do you know Keith Sanders?"

"In a business way, only. Do you?"

"Don't be quaint. You know I do. Is there anyone who reads the papers who doesn't know that he was to back me in a show and wriggled out? You have only to look at those icy blue eyes of his to know that he would stab his dearest friend in the back if it would forward his own fortune."

The venom in her voice didn't improve its tone which Greg had been surprised to find coarse. It was out of character with her exquisite appearance. Her face was flushed now. South American brandy was potent. As if following his thought she nodded toward his untouched glass.

"What's the matter with it? Why don't you drink? Not trying to poison me, are you?"

"Who's being quaint now? Why in heaven's name should I want to poison you? I told you I've been keen to meet you. I don't drink." He achieved a hollow cough. "Doctor's orders."

She regarded him between sweeping black lashes.

"On the wagon? It's a trend. I wouldn't take you for an invalid. You look as fit as they make 'em." She pushed her empty glass toward him and reached for his full one. "Your doctor won't object if someone else drinks yours, will he?"

"On the contrary, he would doubtless prescribe it." He looked around the balcony. The tables were full. No doubt but that the girl had been waiting for Lorillo. Why the dickens didn't he come? Time was stepping on the gas. Skid might appear at any minute and it was up to him to get in a lick or two with the Brazilian in preparation for the apology.

"Looking for someone?"

"A man promised to meet me here, Miss Crane. I rather hope he won't come. It would break up our little party. Where are you singing, now?"

"Miss Crane is at liberty." Her correction was bitter. "But I shan't be long. I have a backer—and here he is!" She held out her hand to the man who stopped at the table. He pressed his lips to it and nodded to Merton who had risen.

"Pardon, *carisima,* I am grateful that I am late. Alas, I am acquiring the bad habit of the businessmen of your country who keep a lady waiting. I do not know the gentleman who has been so good as to entertain you, no?"

"Stop acting like a stuffed shirt, Pedro, and meet Gregory Merton. Señor Pedro Lorillo, from Brazil—" She touched her corsage and giggled. "Where the orchids come from, diamonds too, eh, Pedro?"

Greg couldn't see the Brazilian's eyes—they were looking down at the girl—but there was a hint of eagerness in his voice as he answered:

"That is for you to decide, *carisima*. The diamonds will be yours when you say you will make me the happiest man in the world. The table is waiting inside—shall we—"

"Join us, Señor Lorillo, for a drink," Greg interrupted hurriedly. He must hold them till Skid came. He glanced surreptitiously at his watch. Two minutes more to go.

"Sit down, Pedro. I'm happy where I am," Alix Crane urged. She laid her hand on the Brazilian's sleeve. "Mr. Merton is most amusing. He—Well look who's here!"

The eyes of the two men followed hers. Lorillo quickly dropped to a vacant chair and intently studied the wine card as Keith Sanders and Linda Bourne crossed to the balcony. They leaned over the rail to look down into the court.

"Did you know they were coming here, Mr. Merton? Is this a plant?" Alix Crane's low, harsh query was more an accusation than a question.

"A plant!" Greg echoed in disturbed surprise. Skid mustn't come in now! Linda might call him by name and he was to be known as Sterling, Tom Sterling, to this man and girl at the table. He shook his head and leaned forward.

"You're a suspicious person, aren't you? First, about the cocktail and now about Sanders. Why should I 'plant' *him* here? I hate to admit that I can't get along with anybody, but I'll have to confess that he gets my goat. I see red each time I meet him. Perhaps it's business jealousy. He's the wonder boy in our line in this city."

"You're not the only one who sees red when he appears. I'm just waiting to setfle my score with him." Miss Crane's voice was edged. "Señor Lorillo doesn't like him either, do you, Pedro?"

The Brazilian twisted the stem of his empty glass and smiled. The whites of his eyes stood out with startling distinctness in contrast to his olive skin. Greg's hair prickled at the roots. Something ghoulish about the man.

"I do not know him *carisima*. I know only that he has made you suffer. For that I will challenge him."

"To a duel! For goodness' sake, don't, Pedro." Alix Crane was breathless with anxiety. "It would be grand publicity for me. Front page. Headlines. But it would be the end of you in this country." She smiled with alluring charm. "I would much rather have you alive than Sanders dead. They are going. Good riddance."

Greg Merton held his breath as both Alix Crane and Lorillo watched Linda and Sanders cross the room to the corridor. Time for Skid. If he were to meet them at the door and Linda called him by name the little scheme of making friends with the two at this table would blow sky high.

"I have an apology to make to you, Miss Crane?" he confessed hurriedly. Immediately their eyes turned to him. Now if he could hold them till Lindy and Sanders were out of sight the situation would be saved. "It is from my friend, Tom Sterling."

"The gentleman who objected to being laughed at? So Sterling's the last name. Sanders' current secretary supplied the first." Her eyes narrowed speculatively. "What form will that apology take?"

"You must not accept the apology, I will handle that, *carisima.*"

Alix administered a conciliatory pat on the Brazilian's hand.

"No, you won't. I will. I've had considerable of this sort of thing to do during a life that wasn't all sweetness and light before I met you, Pedro. Is Mr. Sterling rich, Mr. Merton, or is he just another white-collar worker? What is so funny about my question?"

Greg caught the flash in Lorillo's eyes before he looked down at the lighter he was holding to his cigarette. Into what sort of a mess was he getting Skid? It didn't look so good. Good or not, he must put over the plan.

"If you knew Sterling as I do, you, also, would have laughed at the question, Miss Crane. He's not a New Yorker. Woolly West. Oil. Wells of it pouring out liquid gold. Hasn't many friends here—"

"The charming Señora who clung to him last evening would make up for a dozen others. She has what you call here in the States, the glamour, yes?"

"No use, Pedro." Alix' voice was sharp as a knife thrust. "Keith Sanders has her fascinated. The night we saw them dining together I knew her number was up. She devoured him with those enormous brown eyes of hers. Tell me more about your friend Sterling, Mr. Merton."

"I've said he is rich; did I forget to add that he is sensationally generous, to those whom he admires? Like Señor Lorillo, he says it with orchids and diamonds. Why not? A jeweled bracelet counts no more in his expense budget than a corsage of gardenias does in mine. He's sensitive, though, has an inferiority complex I've never seen equaled. There he is now! Just coming on the balcony. Mind if I call him over? If he comes, don't be too hard on him about last evening; he's terribly cut up to think he made such a hick of himself."

"Me, Alix Crane, hard on a man with wells of oil pouring out liquid gold? How do you get that way? Invite him to join us." She lifted her chin, smoothed her slim hips. "Something tells me I shall like your sensitive friend. Be quick. He looks as if he were about to burst into tears."

Skidmore Grant's lachrymose expression brightened as he saw Merton's beckoning hand. At the table he looked from Lorillo's inscrutable face to Alix Crane's smiling one. His brown eyes, humble with apology, rested there.

"Say, this is—is darned good of you, Miss—Miss—"

"Crane," she supplied graciously. "Sit down again, all of you. I understand you have a little speech to make to me?" She was smiling at Grant, with the smile which made her so attractive, as he sank gratefully into a chair beside her.

"I have. I'm on my knees in apology for—" He swallowed hard and betrayed all the symptoms of an inferiority complex.

"Suppose we forget it, shall we, Mr. Sterling, and be friends?" She extended a slender hand which Skid grabbed as if it were a life-preserver flung to a ship-wrecked sailor on a wide, wide sea.

"Friends! You betcha! I'll say it with flowers and—"

"Señorita Crane is most forgiving," Lorillo's suave voice interrupted, "but I was her host. It is with me you should settle accounts, Señor, is it not?"

"Righto, Señor Lorillo." Grant's ruddy face took on a purplish tinge. "I'm sorry, I'm darned sorry it happened. What can I do to make you believe it?"

"You don't have to do anything for him," Alix Crane intervened testily. "You're doing all right. I'm the injured party. I'll name the penalty."

"As you say, *carisima*." Lorillo twisted his glass. For an instant his eyes appeared to be all white.

"You're a sport. Miss Crane, for giving me a chance to square myself. As a guarantee of our peace pact, be my guests at dinner, will you?"

"Sure, we'll be your guests at dinner, with pleasure, Tommy darling."

Grant looked down at the hand she had laid on his. His ruddy color faded a trifle.

"My eye, what diamonds!" he exclaimed. "How do you dare wear that gorgeous bracelet in this crowd?"

Alix Crane shrugged disdain.

"Why not? The stones aren't real. It's a piece of costume jewelry I—I bought off a friend who was tired of it."

XIII

STANDING at her office window Linda watched flags waving from the tops of buildings, looked down upon networks of wires stretched above the canyons which were streets. The sounds of the city rose from below. A backfire like a shattering explosion, bang and clash, the harsh grind of brakes, the banshee whine of a fire siren, the musical fanfare of a motor horn, the toot of a distant tugboat, the hiss and drill of rivets merged into a muted roar.

Her thoughts switched back to the subject which had occupied them almost to the exclusion of everything else for the past week. It was just a week ago this day that Keith Sanders had "reluctantly" admitted to Greg Merton that "Miss Bourne" had tipped him off about the sale of the Steele estate. She had taken dictation from him every day since, had interviewed clients, had visited property which had been put in his hands for sale, had even dined with him at the World of Tomorrow the very night after. She realized that since then she had been disagreeable in the office, had moved in a frozen aura of resentment while all the time round and round in her mind had gone the question:

"What shall I do? I don't trust him. I like him in a way, my heart jumps up and takes a bow when he smiles at me and I love my job. Skid was right; it may be months before I get another."

With Skid's name flashed the scene at the night club. What a situation! Her cheeks burned from the mere memory of it. Had it been necessary for him to make such a spectacle of himself and her? Had he really seen his mother's bracelet on Alix Crane's arm? How could it have come into her possession? Had he followed up the clue? He hadn't even phoned her since that night. What had Greg Merton thought of her curt dismissal? She hadn't seen him either. This was the week end she had been invited to spend with Mrs. Colton. At first she had thought she wouldn't go, then had asked herself, "Why should Greg Merton's unjust suspicion of me cut me out of a delightful visit? It shouldn't and it won't! I'm going. Will he be there?"

"I'm in luck to find you alone, my dear."

Linda wheeled from the window. Her mother was closing the office door. What did she want? What was behind this visit?

"Well, see who's here! Mrs. Bourne, as I'm alive!" She pushed forward a chair. "How in the world did you find your way down into what Liberty Hull calls a dive of iniquity? She's called it that since she took a flyer in worthless stocks. Anything I can do for you or did you come to see where your business daughter labors?"

She realized that she was chattering but she was giving her mother time to formulate her errand. Of course she hadn't come to make a social call, she told herself with one half of her mind, while the other was admiring her visitor's youthful figure, her chic black costume, the sheen of her hair which was almost as tawny as her daughters'. Her mother seemed to have moved so far off she never felt near her, never felt as if she belonged to her any more.

"Linda. I've come to appeal to you for Hester's sake."

"Does Hester know you're here? Did you send you?"

"No. *No.* You—you can see that Gregory Merton i much, very much, attracted to your sister, can't you? It i easy to understand why a typical New Yorker like him would be fascinated by her simple charm."

That simple-charm stuff's a joke. Hester does nothin

that hasn't been figured out like a move in chess, she knows all the answers, Linda thought bitterly. She couldn't remember that Greg had given any indication of high blood pressure when he had seen her sister but she acquiesced with a nod.

"Hester is terribly in love with him," Mrs. Bourne went on, "and I am sure that if he had a chance to see what a charming girl she is he would adore her."

"Chance! He hasn't a chance not to see. She's being forcibly-fed to him. I'm sorry I snapped, Mother," she apologized. "Just why are you telling me this true-story romance? Do you think that I'm interfering with his chance to see her? Wrong number. I haven't laid eyes on him since that afternoon at Ruth's and then I didn't say three words to him."

Too late she remembered the meeting in front of the night club. Why go into that now?

"But you will see him this week end at his sister's." Mrs. Bourne sat forward in her chair. "I—I'm asking you to give up the visit, Linda."

"Give up the week end! Not go! But I admire Mrs. Colton. I accepted the invitation because I like her. She's sending the car for us this afternoon. How can I get out of it at this late date?"

"You can have a sick headache."

"I never had one in my life. Next, you'll be asking me to faint. A faint gave the last irresistible touch of lure to the heroine of the novels you read as a girl, I presume. I shan't have a headache and I shan't faint. So what?"

Mrs. Bourne rose. Her still-lovely brown eyes filled with tears. Tears had always been the final touch to bring her husband to terms, Linda remembered.

"Very well, daughter." Her voice and pose were the personification of injured dignity. "I thought you would be glad to help your sister to happiness. But—"

"What's the matter with Hester's helping herself? How's she going to hold a man after she gets him? Will she engage you to 'shoo' every other girl out of the way? I'm sorry," she apologized again, as color tinted her mother's face. "You win. I'll phone Mrs. Colton that I'm detained in the city on business—not that Greg Merton would pay me any attention if I were there, I'm poison at the box office to him, but anything to make your mind easy."

"Thank you, my dear. Perhaps when you have a daughter you may understand a mother's anxiety for her child's happiness."

"I'm your daughter. I've never known you to lie awake over my future." There was a hint of unsteadiness in the reminder.

Mrs. Bourne drew her sable stole about her shoulders. An expression that was not all pain, not all shame, but the two blended, clouded her eyes.

"From the time you were a small child you were a law unto yourself, backed up by your father. You didn't need me then, you don't need me now—as Hester does."

"Don't I? I'd like to put my head in your lap this minute and cry out my perplexities, have you tell me what I should do about keeping this job," Linda thought.

"Lucky I don't, isn't it?" she said. "Lucky you haven't the destinies of two daughters to settle. Cheer up, as soon as you've gone I'll phone my regrets to Mrs. Colton." She opened the door for her mother.

"You've made me very happy, Linda."

"I'm glad someone is pleased. Perhaps it will make you happier to know that I couldn't love Gregory Merton if he were the only man in the world. Good-by."

"Mrs. Bourne! What luck to have a glimpse of you before you got away," exclaimed a smooth voice in the outer office.

Keith Sanders speaking. Linda shrugged as she closed the door. Had he heard her few valedictory remarks about not being in love with Gregory Merton? Suppose he had? Every word of it was true, wasn't it? If she did love him would she step aside for Hester? She would not. She'd put up a fight to the finish for the man she loved.

Elbow on the desk, chin propped in her hand she relived the last few minutes. Her mother had said that her younger daughter had been a law unto herself backed up by her father. Was it possible that she had been jealous of her husband's affection for and pride in his "Lindy"? It would explain many unpleasant situations in the past. Love certainly did queer things to its victims.

Love for her elder daughter was making a mother unfair to her younger. She had extracted a promise that the visit to the Coltons would be given up. So that washed up that situation.

What would she do with the one she was in? Work for a man whom she liked but didn't trust? Suppose his sense of honor didn't come up to what she thought it should? Skid was right. It would be difficult to find a business conducted on purely altruistic lines. She meant to be just.

Even in this short time she felt that she had outgrown the harshness of her youthful judgments. One couldn't live in a mighty, tumultuous city like this and retain a small-town viewpoint, but heaven help her to keep her belief in the virtues which her father had considered the unshakable foundation for a life: decency, integrity, reliability and a deep spiritual faith.

"Yes, Mr. Sanders?" she answered a buzz on the interoffice phone.

"What have you done about the Steele estate? Have you seen the old lady again?"

"No."

"I told you to push the matter ahead, didn't I?"

He was in one of his nasty little tempers. She had a right to a temper too. Her mother's call had left her primed for a nice, snappy fight.

"You did and I told you that I did not care to handle the matter."

"Because you think you're treading on Greg Merton's toes, I presume. Now get this and no nonsense about it. Take the convertible, see Madam Steele this afternoon and ask for her lowest price for the Castle estate. Don't come back without it. Understand?"

"I understand."

"I don't like your voice and I don't like the chip you've had on your shoulder this last week, Miss Bourne. Do what I say or you're through here one week from today. Is that plain?"

"Very plain, Mr. Sanders."

"Come in here before you go."

She heard him snap off the connection. That settled the question as to whether she would keep on here. She wouldn't. Neither would she go to The Castle to query Madam Steele.

Madame Steele! Memory clicked. She pulled open her private drawer in the desk and found the letter. Read it eagerly.

"Don't answer at once," she had written. "Take a week to think it over, then if possible come and see me. A personal interview is more satisfactory than correspondence."

Linda frowned unseeingly at the spot where the mooring of the Empire State Building tower stabbed the clear blue of the sky. Was this an answer to her problem? Keith Sanders had told her to go to The Castle this afternoon, which order seemed a chance, if not divinely designed, at least to have been offered by Lady Luck. Was this opportunity calling? She would go and find out.

She crushed on her green turban, slipped a beaver jacket over her green-velveteen dress. Keith Sanders had told her to come to his office before she left. Had she better tell him of her decision? It was the honorable thing to do. Why not get it over?

As she opened the door, he was at his private phone. She knew by his voice that he was fiercely angry.

"Get it or lay off! Understand? Or I'll—" He looked up and saw Linda—"put someone else on the job." He clapped his hand over the mouthpiece. "Don't you see I'm busy, Miss Bourne?"

"Sorry." She closed the door. She couldn't tell him she was leaving if she wanted to. To which salesman was he handing his walking papers if he didn't "Get it"? Had he discovered that a rival firm was barging in on one of *his* deals? It would do him good to have a dose of his own medicine. Why was she spending a moment thinking of Keith Sanders' real-estate business? She had vitally important problems of her own to consider.

In the outer office she stopped to speak to Miss Dowse.

"If I'm not here at four please phone Miss Brewster at our apartment that I won't be back in time to go with her for the week end. I've been trying to reach Mrs. Colton but the line has been busy. Ask Ruth to make my apologies to our hostess, to say that I will write. That's all."

Opportunity calling! Opportunity calling Linda

Bourne! The words skipped on and on in her mind like a blown-off hat being scurried along by a gay young breeze as she walked rapidly to the garage.

XIV

"MISS BOURNE," announced Buff, the butler, at the door of the spacious book-lined library at The Castle.

The room was softly lighted. Dancing flames threw grotesque shapes on walls and hangings, blurred the corners into undefined shadows. A great Satsuma bowl of small yellow chrysanthemums was reflected in the polish of the grand piano.

As Linda approached the woman in the carved-backed chair near the fire, Cash and Carry, the Great Danes, rose, like the gentlemen they were, and regarded her tolerantly.

"So you've come," Madam Steele said and waited. The corners of her lips had the ironic twist Linda remembered; her black-satin dress, with fine white frills at neck and wrists, shimmered in the firelight. The jewels on her patrician hands shot out millions of iridescent sparks.

"Yes. It is just a week since I received your letter. You wrote me neither to write nor come to see you before."

"Sit down. Help yourself to tea. I remember you like it. After that we will talk."

Autocrat, Linda thought, as she tilted the massive Georgian silver water kettle to dilute the brew, which looked srong enough to curl her eye lashes up tight. So is Keith Sanders, she reminded herself, and lifted the cover from crisp cinnamon toast. Madam Steele tapped the newspaper she had been reading.

"What quality is it in some persons which keeps them hanging on in a desperate situation until they somehow, in some miraculous way, get out of it?" she demanded, "What is that something which won't let them give up, that nine times out of ten pulls them through? Here's the report of a man in the last ship disaster, who, though seriously wounded, clung to a spar for eight hours."

"And was rescued? That's a story to remember when in a jam, isn't it? In a desperate situation one is sure to lose by giving up, one can lose nothing by hanging on and may have the hundredth of a chance to win out," Linda observed thoughtfully.

"I believe I'm hungry," she admitted. "I had so much to think of I've just remembered I forgot to eat luncheon. May I feed them?" She nodded toward Cash and Carry who sat on their haunches watching each mouthful she took with wistful eyes and slightly dripping jaws.

"Yes. One piece for each. You like dogs?"

"I adore them. Can't pass one on the street without having to strangle an irresistible urge to drop on my knees and hug the dear, which, if you believe me, is more than I can say of most humans I pass." Either the tea or her decision to leave Keith Sanders' office was sending her spirit to a new high.

"The dogs will appreciate your affection and having someone young to play round with, that is, if you have decided to accept the position. Have you?" Madam Steele leaned a little forward in her chair.

"I will come a week from today. If that suits you."

"Why not stay now?"

"I must give fair notice to Mr. Sanders."

"I suppose you must. Doubtless you think it strange that I asked you to come on such short acquaintance but lately I have been taking stock of myself. I have been alone so much that I am garrulous when I get a chance to talk. If a person is agreeable to me I immediately suspect him of wanting something. I'm beginning to be age-conscious and that is nothing short of being stupid. I decided that I needed youth in the house. Then you walked into the garden and a voice within me said: 'And there it is! The best of it.'"

"I hope I will prove to be what you need."

"If you're not, I'll try again." Madam Steele was her practical, austere self again. "I have decided not to sell this place at present. I will write Mr. Sanders to that effect. It is my home. I can afford to run it. It grows more and more

costly but why should I economize for the benefit of my
heirs? They'll have enough to quarrel over as it is."

Linda wondered who the heirs might be. Had the son
who had died in the World War left children? It was a relief to know that Keith Sanders would not have the estate
to handle. If only the owner had made up her mind to this
before, she herself wouldn't have been suspected of being a
double-crosser by Greg Merton.

"I want you to encourage your family and young
friends to come here as they would come to your home,
Linda. Then you won't be lonely."

"Why should I be lonely? My duties as outlined in
your letter sound as if life here should be pretty interesting."

"Life! In God's name what is life? A merry-go-round
of excitement and adventure, luxurious homes and smart
clothes? Or is it building character and struggling forward
to one's ideal? Stumbling, extricating oneself from blind al-
leys of mistakes. Getting up and going on with gay courage.
Making the most of happiness, giving of one's help and
sympathy. That's real life." She rested her head against the
high back of her chair, her brooding eyes on the fire, her
sparkling hands clenched in her lap. The dogs laid their
chins on her knees.

Linda felt as if she had been swept off her feet by a
tidal wave of emotion and regret which had left her
breathless, gasping. Was she expected to respond to that
passionate outburst? As the silence persisted she said:

"You would have liked my father. You and he speak
the same language."

Madam Steele transferred her regard from the fire to
Linda.

"And I already like his daughter. Don't let my tirade
frighten you. I warned you I was garrulous when I met a
sympathetic human being but I rarely indulge in that sort
of thing. There is something about you—we'll let that pass.
Come. I will show you your rooms."

She rose. Linda was surprised at her height and slen-
derness and remembered that she had not seen her standing before. She had thought of her, when she had thought
of her at all, as a person who fancied herself an invalid.
She gave no indication of ill health as she walked easily,

gracefully as a fashion model to the door, the train of her black-satin frock making a soft swish as she moved. She appeared to be younger than she had seemed in the garden. In the hall she spoke to the butler.

"I don't need you, Buff, I will show Miss Bourne her rooms. She will be here for dinner one week from tonight and will remain permanently. She will be like a daughter in the house. Notify the staff."

"Yes, Madam."

Chrysanthemums, shading from bronze through yellows to white had taken the place of gladioli in the hall, Linda noticed as she mounted the broad stairway. She felt as if she were standing outside herself, as one stands in a dream, watching a stately woman and a girl in a green-velveteen frock going up step by slow step. What freak of Chance had landed her in this position? It seemed years ago that she had sat on the porch steps and Ruth had advised:

"*Do* something about it. Get out. Go somewhere. Follow a rainbow. New problems, harder ones perhaps, but new." She had done it. All that Ruth had suggested had come true, especially the new problems. What next?

Madam Steele opened one of the many ivory-and-gilt doors in the upper hall. Linda had a swift vision of herself trying to find the room in which she belonged in the dark, before she entered a charming boudoir done in green chintz and French furniture. Beyond an open door was a bedroom and beyond that was a dressing-room glitter of mirrors and chromium. Somewhere within the house a clock sonorously told the hour. One. Two. Three. Four. Five.

"They've left the apartment. My week end has gone up in smoke." Irrelevantly the words flashed through Linda's mind. Madam Steele's voice, which seemed to come from a great distance, asked:

"To get down to practical matters. What is your present salary?"

Linda told her.

"You will require more of a wardrobe here. I will pay you three times that. Come supplied with half a dozen dinner frocks and at least three for formal occasions. I will write a cheque for your first month's salary."

"Thank you, Madam Steele, but I don't want it until it has been earned. I have a nest egg upon which I can draw."

Buff, all deference and attention now that she was to be a member of the household, preceded her down the steps to the convertible. She stopped halfway to ask casually:

"The man waiting beside my car isn't the same one who brought it round the last time I came, is he, Buff?"

"*No,* Miss. That one heard that one of our men in the garage was sick and asked for a chance to fill in. He was here only a few days. I didn't like him, Miss. We don't have that class on the estate."

"I caught only a glimpse of him, but that glimpse was enough. I didn't like him either."

As she stepped into the car she wondered what connection the cadaverous-faced person could have with Sanders. Perhaps he was a family black sheep whom Keith had to help occasionally. Why think about it? Black, gray or white sheep, the man meant nothing in her life.

As she drove toward the city her thoughts were busy with the woman she had agreed to serve. Why had she so quickly decided to accept the position? The answer to that last was easy. Keith Sanders had given her the choice between barging in on business which belonged rightly to Gregory Merton or leaving his office. She had committed herself to the second course only to find that there would be no business to handle now that Madam Steele had decided not to sell the estate. Even so, she wasn't sorry she had made the change. She would acquire an absolutely new viewpoint. She would be out of Hester's way. Greg was at odds with his aunt so there was little chance he would come to The Castle. She would miss Ruth, but Ruth didn't need her financially.

The apartment when she walked into it felt lifeless, deserted. Libby had gone to the Brewster house to collect some articles Ruth wanted. She snapped on every light in the living room before she went to her own.

"The King of France and forty thousand men marched up the hill and then marched down again," she chanted as she looked at her week-end case which she had left partially packed that morning.

As she was replacing accessories in the dresser the bell rang. She opened the entrance door.

"I've been waiting across the street till I saw lights here. I've come to drive you to the Coltons'," informed Greg Merton.

Linda clutched the knob and began to close the door.

"But I'm not going to the Coltons'. I have sent my regrets." As he placed his foot in the narrow opening she accused: "Something tells me you were once a house-to-house salesman. You have the technique."

"Maybe you're right. I generally get what I go after." He stepped past her into the living room. "If you've given up going to Janet's because of our misunderstanding—"

"*Our!*"

"All right, have it your own way, *my* misunderstanding of you. Forget it, will you? Perhaps you didn't repeat Janet's news at the Inn. Perhaps you didn't intentionally put Sanders wise to the fact that the Steele estate was to be on the market, perhaps you just casually repeated what you heard."

"Delete those 'perhaps,' Mr. Merton. I did *not* mention the prospective Steele sale to Mr. Sanders. Having settled that to my satisfaction, I wish you would leave. I have work to do. I'm hungry. I haven't had my dinner and—"

"Janet phoned me to come here for you, that no matter how late you were she would wait dinner for us. And just in case it makes any difference, if you don't go, I shan't. So, trot along and finish packing your bag."

"I haven't said I was going."

"But I have. Why should you disappoint Janet because you dislike her brother? They'll wait dinner for us. On your way. Finish packing. Make it snappy. Scram."

"Oh, King live forever!" From the threshold she flung the mocking gibe over her shoulder.

In her room Linda regarded the partially packed week-end case. Greg Merton thought the reason she had sidestepped his sister's invitation was wholly because she disliked him. Even if she did, she wouldn't have given up the visit because of him; it was because her mother had made it a test of her affection for her sister. She had tried to accommodate, and here she was up against his ultimatum that unless she went, he wouldn't. He meant it. It would certainly put a crimp in Hester's love affair. if he didn't appear at all. She would go.

When ten minutes later she entered the living room, he suggested:

"You're not faring forth to your execution, you know. This is a party. Can't you smile for the gentleman, lady?"

She made a disdainful little face as he opened the door.

"You're not a gentleman. You're a dictator."

The motor-thronged streets were filling with before-the-theater diners. The music of horns, gleeful and windy, drifted from restaurants; imposing uniformed men opened and closed automobile doors; lights, blazing the surpassing excellence of merchandise from toothpaste to footgear, glowed on and above buildings and dimmed the shine of the stars within their radius.

Out of the city. A country highway. Greg Merton drove steadily, smoothly without speaking. Now that he had persuaded her to come—ordered, was the word—was he sorry that he hadn't a more entertaining companion? He was the first to break the silence.

"Saw you at the Brazilian Restaurant the other evening. More business to talk over with your boss?"

"I didn't see *you*."

"Which crisp answer tells me I was speaking out of turn when I asked the question. You're right, but I don't mind telling you that I was there on business, Skid's."

He told her of their decision to make friends with Alix Crane and her Brazilian in the hope of finding out how the night-club singer had come into possession of Mrs. Grant's emerald-and-diamond bracelet, of her statement that the gorgeous thing she was wearing was a costume piece.

"You should have seen Skid's face when she said she had bought it 'off' a friend."

"Did he believe her?"

"He knew it was his mother's barcelet; he thinks she may be on the level, suspects that things were getting warm for the 'friend,' who decided to get rid of it and pass the buck to the Crane woman. That means we've got to find that friend. Skid said I was to tell you our plan. It's on the hush-hush, remember. I can't believe that Alix Crane is mixed up with a criminal gang, can you?"

"No. She doesn't have to be. Apparently she is attractive enough to get what she wants without that. How about the fascinating Señor Pedro Lorillo?"

"We're looking up his background. Do you think him fascinating? He isn't the type I would have picked to send you off the deep end."

"Your mistake. He's my current rave. He brings out the *femme fatale* in me."

She settled deeper into the inviting depths of the leather seat. Any remark after that flippancy would be anticlimax. She had been on the move since seven this morning. Eleven epoch-making hours. Except for the tea, she hadn't eaten. Was hunger, combined with the smooth pace of the car, making her sleepy? Perhaps it was the air, which was unbelievably warm and fragrant for the season. Were there two moons? She forced her eyes wide. Only one. Good heavens, she mustn't go to sleep here.

"I hope—we—won't keep dinner—wait—ing . . ." What was she saying? She would die if she couldn't close her eyes for a minute. She had felt like this in church once, had suffered agonies trying to keep her heavy lids propped up. Why try to do it here? She would close them for a minute . . .

"Wake up, sweet thing. We've arrived."

Had she heard those words on had she dreamed them? She looked up directly into Greg Merton's face. Something rough under her cheek told her that her head was against his shoulder.

"Sorry to disturb you, but this is where we get off," he announced gruffly.

XV

AT NOON the next day the water in the swimming pool rippled in the light breeze. The sun stippled the surface with gold coins. Shrubs flamed with crimson, scarlet and

ocher against a dark background of spruce. The old chimneys and gables of the Coltons stone-and-oak house standing among lawns and a few great elms on a rise of ground
were outlined against a brilliant sapphire sky. The air was
sweet with a fallish fragrance of English box. It was warm,
unbelievably warm for the time of year. The world seemed
one hundred per cent silence. Only a faint, far motor horn
broke the drowsy calm. The guests, in swim suits, lay on
the emerald velvet grass or lounged in deep wicker chairs
with mid-summer indolence. Skid Grant flung himself
down beside Linda.

"Do I see your skin turning to gold, gal, or is it the
spiffy white suit which gives it that appearance?"

"I'm tanning, all right. I never burn. Hester is about
to dive. She's good. Watch."

His eyes followed hers to where her sister, in a scarlet
suit which fitted the perfect lines of her body like the skin
of a goldfish, posed on the higher of the two springboards.

"That's a pretty tricky dive," Grant suggested uneasily.

"She can make it." Linda glanced at Greg Merton,
who at the shallow end of the pool was teaching Billy Colton to swim. Why wasn't he watching Hester? The child
pointed and Greg turned.

"Look, look, Greggy." The boy's eyes were like azure
stars; his pearly teeth shone between vivid, parted lips.
"She's going to yump. Ooo! O-o-o!" he squealed as the
water closed over Hester's head. "I wan' to do dat, Greggy."

"Learn to swim first and then yon can, kiddo." His
uncle swung him to the grass. "Sit there and dry while I
dive. Everybody up," he called and raced to the springboard with the others in hot pursuit.

For ten minutes they dived, so close after one another
that they seemed like flying fishes. Janet green as a mer-
maid, Ruth and Linda in white, Hester with scarlet scales,
the men in navy or brown trunks and Skid in blinding
stripes.

Linda smiled at her host as he pulled himself from the
pool to the grass beside her. She liked his face, liked his
high forehead which suggested intellect plus, wondered if his
fine mouth would have had that discontented droop, if the
brain behind his brilliant hazel eyes would have made its

mark in the world, if he had had to use it to its limit to earn a living.

"Nice here, isn't it?" he asked.

"Nice is too colorless a work for your home. It's perfect. I'm so glad to meet you. Ever since I met your wife I've been wondering what her husband would be like. Now I know."

His laugh was boyish.

"Would it be intruding in the secret places of your mind were I to ask the verdict?"

Head on one side she pretended critical appraisal.

"Personality plus. Life of the party—when you like the party. Generous mouth. But I wonder if you're good enough for your lovely wife?"

"I'm not; who would be? Don't look so embarrassed. You've only said aloud what everyone thinks. Janet prophesied I would like you and—if it will make you feel happier—Janet is always right."

He sprang to his feet. His face was puckish with mischief.

"I may not be much as a husband but I'm a knockout as a host. I've invited your boss for the week end. Thought he was entitled to see his smart and beautiful secretary at play."

He laughed and dove. Linda's cheeks burned with annoyance. Keith Sanders coming here. Darn! Would she have to tell him that she had secured another position? Why worry? He had given her notice, hadn't he? Notice! That was too tame a word. He had fired her.

"A penny for your thoughts." Janet Colton sank down beside her. Before Linda could answer the gay challenge Billy snuggled his head against his mother's wet knee. She bent and kissed him swiftly.

"You ought to be napping, young Mr. Colton."

"Not yet, Muvver," he pleaded. "It's so nice here."

"It is nice; heavenly, I call it." She turned to Linda. "I let him escape from his nurse as often as possible, both for her sake and his. He's a strenuous lad." Her fingers gently smoothed the gold curls. "I'm thankful Greg shanghaied you yesterday. I wanted your sister and your friend to come but I especially wanted you."

"I knew I would be late getting back to the city and

feared the delay would inconvenience you. I hate to drag a serpent into this paradise but I hope you'll believe me when I tell you that I did *not* repeat your conversation with your brother at the Inn to Mr. Sanders. It's my word against his, I realize. I don't know why he lied about it, but he did."

"I believe you. The man has charm, my husband is fascinated by him; he has invited him for this week end. I hope you won't mind too much; you can't like him after that lie. He's due in time for lunch. I detest him. I think he's a bad influence." There was a betraying tension about her mouth. As Linda was silent she added:

"I shouldn't have said that. After all, he's your boss. Where are you going, Billy Boy?"

"Jus', jus' movin'," the child replied and began to roll over and over on the velvet turf.

"Don't move far. Nurse will be looking for you. Almost your luncheon time."

His mother turned back to Linda, who sat hugging her knees as she looked across the pool at Ruth and Hester. Bill Colton was sprawled at her sister's feet. She was laughing as she looked down at him, though she sat so near Greg Merton that her bare, wet arm touched his. Skid Grant was talking to Ruth. Janet's eyes followed hers.

"Your sister is one of the prettiest girls I've ever seen, but I can tell from her mouth that she lacks the sense of humor which pulls you through any situation, never lets you down. Am I right?"

"About my sense of humor, yes; about it's never letting me down—that's another thing again." On a sudden impulse she added:

"I'm getting through at Keith Sanders' next week. I —I have taken taken a position as social secretary, companion, what have you, with—with Madam Steele."

"With Aunt Jane! Oh, my dear. Why did you do it without asking me? Have you told Greg?"

"No. Why should I? Why bring up that unpleasant subject again just as we'd tacitly, if not verbally, signed an appeasement pact? Any special reason why I shouldn't work for Madam Steele?" Linda was instantly ashamed of her aggressive voice.

"Forgive me. I didn't mean that as it sounded. I do

appreciate your interest. I've been thinking of little else but making a change for the last week and the mental strain has begun to wear down my manners. Ever have a question start merry-go-rounding in your mind?"

"Have I? You're asking me! As for the reason why you shouldn't go to Madam Steele's to live, ask Greg. There's the dressing gong for lunch. I must scram. Don't hurry. Plenty of time. Billy! Billy! He must have gone to the house," she said as no answer came to her call.

Linda's eyes followed her as she walked lightly along the margin of the pool, balancing a little with her arms as she went, her slender, graceful figure, in its brief green suit, reflected in the blue mirror of water. She stopped to speak to the others. Her husband put his arm about her shoulders and they went on together.

Linda's thoughts returned to her own problems. Why had Janet Colton been so shocked to hear that her Aunt Jane had engaged a new secretary? What argument could Gregory Merton offer against her working for Madam Steele, if she asked him—which she would not do? She had decided to take the position. She would stick to that decision no matter what he said.

What was that queer little sound in the air? A bird? Laughter? She looked up. Her heart stopped. On the very edge of the highest diving platform balanced Billy Colton. He was laughing. The breeze lifted his gold curls. He stuck up his arms, laid his hands together:

"See me go!" he shouted.

If she made a sound he might be frightened. Why, oh why hadn't the others heard him? What to do? She couldn't mount to the springboard in time to stop him. She slid into the pool. If she could only catch him as he came down. She must. He might break his neck if he hit the water flat.

"Watch me yump," he called again.

A splash behind her. A frantic "Good God!" She was pushed aside. Greg Merton held out his arms as he trod water.

"Come on, Billy Boy, I'll catch you."

With a laugh, absolutely fearless, the child jumped. Greg caught him, the impact carried them both under. Linda waited only long enough to see two heads, one dark, the other golden, one face tensely white, the other laughing, rosy, come to the surface before she pulled herself from the pool and dashed toward the house.

She was dizzy; there was a yawning cavern where her stomach should be. She'd lived years for the instant she had seen the boy on the springboard till she heard Greg Merton behind her.

She stopped as she entered the cool, dark hall and clutched the top of a chair. Something inside her was churning. Could she get upstairs before she was sick? She dimly saw a figure outlined against the light from the open front door. The man's shoulders were familiar. Someone she knew. He would help. She tried to call.

He had gone. The hall was alive with red-and-green fuzzy-wuzzies. She drove her teeth into her lips and forced herself to the stairs. She must get to her room.

"I've been looking for you," said a voice behind her.

She saw Greg Merton through a purple haze. Tried to laugh.

"I—I—I've never done it before. I—I—think I'm going to—"

She struggled up from the dark. Someone was rubbing her arms. Someone held a glass to her lips.

"Drink this and don't try to talk. You're on the chaise longue in your room, if that answers the question you're trying to ask." The voice was gruff but she recognized it.

"Not that. It's Billy? Billy? Is he all right, Greg?"

"Sure, he's all right. The rascal. You saved him. I saw you slide into the pool and then—"

"No. No. I couldn't have held—" She shuddered.

"Take it easy." He sopped more water on her already dripping head. "The kid's all right."

She pushed away his hand and swung her feet to the floor.

"So am I. *Please* go. I'm all right, really I am. My R.Q.—recovery quotient to you—is one hundred per cent efficient. I'll dress and—"

"What happened to Lindy?" Janet Colton demanded breathlessly from the doorway. "Oscar said she was carried upstairs."

"Oh that husky son of yours decided he'd dive from the springboard, the highest one at that."

"Greg! The springboard?" Janet's eyes were wide with horror.

"But your brother caught him before he struck the water so he's perfectly all right, Mrs. Colton," Linda assured eagerly.

Janet sat down suddenly.

"I thought the burglary had turned my knees to gelatin but this—"

"Burglary! What burglary?" Linda and Greg demanded in unison.

"The jewel case on my dresser was forced open and a bracelet and my pearls are missing. Never mind that. Where is Billy Boy. Are you sure he's all right, Greg?"

XVI

THE ROOM was mellow, dignified, restful. Wood paneling blended with the leather of the bookbindings and the exposed ceiling beams. The heavy velvet hangings drawn across the long windows were the same shade of blue as the coat of the ruddy-faced admiral in the portrait set in above the mantel. Lamp bases were choice porcelains; light glowed through opaline shades. An old globe on a stand. Red roses in a tall silver vase on the grand piano. Deep, inviting chairs with arm tables. All this and no sense of crowding.

The red-faced man, with baggy jowls and sparse brown hair, in the black suit with fine white stripes, seated at the flat desk, had been presented to the company assembled as Jim Shaw, detective. A gray-haired man in sombre black, who had been introduced as "My print expert, Cox," guarded the door.

Bill Colton, Keith Sanders and Skid Grant in white dinner jackets and black trousers stood before the mantel like a line of defense. Greg Merton sat astride the bench at the piano; Hester in a shimmering orchid frock rested an elbow on its polished rosewood. Janet, in filmy white, leaned eagerly forward from the divan at a right angle to the fire-

place; Linda in a blacknet, the billowing skirt patched with
pink and blue like the suit of a Harlequin, perched on the
arm of it. The glow from a softly shaded lamp above the
chair in which Ruth Brewster sat threw a lovely light on
her violet crepe frock and the mass of rose-color wool in
her lap. The detective trotted one tan-leather-shod foot and
scowled at his notebook.

"You discovered the theft this noon, Mrs. Colton, and
yet Mr. Merton didn't notify me until an hour ago. How
come?"

"After the first shock of finding the jewel case open, I
thought I might discover that I had put that particular
bracelet and my pearl necklace somewhere else. Sometimes
I do that. I wanted to be sure they were not in the house
before my brother called you. I have looked in every possible place and haven't found them.

"You trust the servants?"

"Absolutely. They have been in my employ since I
came to this house a bride five years ago. I know they
wouldn't steal."

"I've questioned them. I believe you're right." His
greenish ferret eyes touched Ruth, Linda, Hester; passed
over Bill Colton, squinted at Keith Sanders, rested on Skid
Grant.

"Haven't known these guests of yours as long as you
have the servants, have you?" he asked with sarcastic emphasis on the word guests.

His tone brought Merton to his feet in protest. Bill
Colton took a step forward.

"Look here, Shaw, I don't like your intimation. Our
guests are our friends, no matter how long we have known
them. Sanders, here beside me, has week-ended with us
many times during the last year."

"You're laughing but your eyes are cold as blue ice,"
Linda thought as Keith Sanders tossed a cigarette into the
fireplace and answered his host.

"You might clarify the situation by telling him, Bill,
that I wasn't in the house at the time of the theft. I was expected for lunch. Couldn't make it. Arrived only in time to
dress for dinner. Oscar and the man who brought in my
bags will verify that."

Shaw trotted his foot. Consulted his notes. Nodded agreement.

"That tallies. You're out of the picture, Mr. Sanders. So are you, Mr. Merton; I've worked for you in real-estate cases for years. You wouldn't steal your sister's jewels." He fixed accusing eyes on Skid Grant. "I happened to be at a night club a short time ago when your friend with the spectacles and the young lady in the black dress with patchwork were put out."

"We weren't put out!" Linda denied furiously. "We —we went ourselves."

"We won't quibble over how you went. You called the young man 'Tom,' there. He gives his name here as Skidmore Grant. Sounds fishy to me."

"But Jim—" The detective held up his hand to silence Greg Merton's protest.

"Search my bags, Mr. Shaw," Skid Grant invited cordially. "I haven't been off the place since I arrived and as, apparently, you are convinced of the honesty of the servants I couldn't very well pass the loot to them. I suggest you leave Miss Bourne out of that incident at the night club. It isn't a girl's fault if her escort gets tanked and gives an assumed name, is it?"

"Oh, Madam! Madam! May I speak to you?"

A white-faced maid, whose bang of coarse hair was as black as her silk frock, dashed into the room. Janet sprang to her feet.

"What is it, Celia?"

The maid held out the hand which had been behind her back. From the shaky fingers dangled a string of lustrous pearls.

"My necklace! Where did you find it?"

"Nurse found it, Madam. She was taking soiled towels from the hamper in the powder room and she found the pearls in the bottom. She like to faint from surprise."

"The powder room! Where's that?" Shaw demanded.

"Near the entrance door."

"Entrance door!" Shaw held out an immaculate white handkerchief. "Put them in this, Mrs. Colton. Cox, set up your outfit in the dining room. We'll get all these fingerprints." He wheeled on the visibly terrified maid.

"Find the bracelet?" He had a gorilla trick of baring his prominent teeth as he listened.

"No, sir. No, sir. Nurse shook out all the towels thinking it might be there too, but there wasn't nothing else."

"All right. Tell her to turn out every hamper in the house. Miss Bourne, we'll take you first. As you weren't here, Mr. Sanders, we won't need your prints; you can come in and see how it's done, if you like."

"Thanks, I've seen the operation a number of times; in fact I have my own prints in the office. Don't look so frightened, girls. It's painless."

Keith Sanders might think this a joke but Linda didn't. In spite of his sudden shift to suavity, she felt that the detective regarded her with suspicious eyes as she pressed one finger after another on a smooth, blackened surface.

"That's all, Miss Bourne. You may go. Stay and help me, Mr. Merton," Shaw ordered curtly as Greg started to follow Linda.

As she left the room she wondered what Greg Merton thought of her now. He believed that she had sneaked information about his business to her boss; he had seen her drag Skid from a night club and now she'd been fingerprinted because, no matter what he said, that poisonous detective suspected that she had inside knowledge of the theft.

"Well, I see you survived," Keith Sanders observed as she entered the library. He was seated at the piano running his fingers over the keys. She regarded him with a tinge of wonder. Was this laughing, friendly man the employer who had roughly given her the choice between carrying out his orders or losing her job? Had that been only yesterday? It seemed years ago.

"What's the matter, Lindy? Don't you like me any more?"

Once on a time the tenderness of his voice might have quickened her heartbeat. Not now. She shook off the hand he placed over hers.

"Crazy about you."

"I don't like your flippant tone." He rose, linked his arm in hers and drew her to the divan. "Sit here. I want to talk to you."

"I prefer to stand. Helps preserve my size-sixteen figure."

"Just as you say. Look here, you're not sore because of what I said in the office yesterday, are you?"

"You mean about me getting fired next Friday? Of course not. It's all in the day's work. I leave on Friday and step into a new situation."

"What do you *mean?*"

"What I say. I have another position."

"You can't walk out on me like that. I've grown to rely on you. You're the best secretary I've ever had. I didn't mean what I said. I was upset about something outside business."

"That's just too bad but the effect was the same as if you had meant it."

"I admit I went cockeyed but when you've been in business longer you'll realize that that sort of a blowup is to be expected occasionally. You're pretty young, you know." He put his arm lightly about her shoulders and regarded her with the satisfied, tolerant smile which she had seen first at the Grant dinner.

"Don't speak to me as if I were a child."

"But such a lovely child. You've forgiven me, haven't you?" His arm tightened. "You always do forgive me, don't you? I was getting a little jealous of my business rival till I heard you tell your mother in the office that you couldn't love Gregory Merton if he were the only man in the world."

"I beg pardon," interrupted a voice. "Am I butting in on a—business conference?"

Had Greg Merton heard Keith Sanders repeat the silly defiance she had flung at her mother? If he had, so what? The question set Linda's pulses quickstepping. If he really believed he was intruding why didn't he back gracefully out instead of coming forward into the room? She tried to free herself from the arm about her shoulders but it tightened.

"How clever of you to spot a business conference, Greg. You are right. I was just telling Mr. Sanders that I am leaving his office next week to accept another position."

"Then what's the idea of holding Miss Bourne when she wants to go?" Merton's eyes rested suggestively on the arm about Linda's shoulders.

"Did you engage her?" Sanders demanded truculently and thrust his hands hard into the pockets of his jacket. Merton ignored the question.

"Where are you going, Linda?" he asked.

"Not that it's anyone's business but mine and the person who engaged me, I am to be a sort of secretary-companion to Madam Steele."

"Like fun you are! You—"

"You clever kid! You *darned* clever kid," Sanders interrupted Greg's shocked protest. "So that's the way you intend to put across the sale? I am to have a representative on the spot. You'll get your cut-in on the commission just the same as if you were punching the time clock at the office."

"Long distance for you, Mr. Sanders." The butler cut short Keith Sanders' exuberance.

"All right, Oscar. We'll talk this business matter over tomorrow, Miss New England. You're good; but even so, I may have some suggestions that will help."

Back to the room, he stopped in the doorway to speak to the butler. Linda had a flashing mental vision of herself dizzily clutching a chair in the dusky hall, of a man's figure outlined against the light. She knew now why it had seemed familiar. It had been Keith Sanders! But it couldn't have been. He hadn't arrived. Was she still dazed?

"Why are you brushing your hand across your eyes? Faint again?" Greg Merton inquired anxiously.

"*No.* I—I just remembered that I thought I saw Keith going out the front door when I came in from the swimming pool. As he didn't arrive till dinnertime my brain must have been addled by the sun or the shock of Billy Boy's crazy jump."

"You thought you saw Sanders," Greg Merton repeated sharply. With noticeable effort he lightened his voice. "Like him so much that you see him everywhere, I take it. Skip him. He's out. Did you *mean* it when you said you had accepted a position with Madam Steele? You can't do it. You mustn't go there."

"Why? Because you think I'll influence her to engage Keith Sanders to take care of *all* her real-estate business?"

"Hang the business. It isn't safe."

"Not safe! Don't be foolish. What do you mean by 'safe'?"

"If you need to have a simple English word explained, I mean that she insists upon keeping her jewels, which are fabulous, in the house and boasts of it, boasts that she is an excellent shot. She's one of those maddening women who knows it all. Can't be told anything. She exasperates her legal adviser, Judge Reynolds, to the verge of a nervous breakdown. Someday, someone is going to grab that loot and there will be one grand shootin' party with perhaps a smattering of blood or even a scatter of dead bodies."

Linda remembered her mother's anxiety to clear the matrimonial field for Hester; Sanders' voice as he exulted: "So that's the way you intend to put across the sale!" Better to let Greg Merton think that her reason for going to Madam Steele was to further Keith's interests. Then he would dislike her even more and her mother and Hester would be happy.

"Sounds exciting to me. Perhaps she'll arm me, too. I've always wanted to learn to shoot. This is a chance in a lifetime; I'm going."

"You're crazy!"

"It's fun to be crazy."

"Sure, why not? I'm speaking out of turn. I can see that you're in Aunt Jane's class, one of those maddening females who can't be told. Sanders was right; you are going as his Johnny on the spot, aren't you?" His eyes burned in his white face.

"That seems to be *his* idea."

"Then that's all I can do about it. But some dark night when you're waked up by a flashlight in your eyes and a masked face bending over you, don't say I didn't warn you."

"Who's warning who, or should I say 'whom'?" Skidmore Grant inquired from the threshold.

"Lindy has accepted a position as secretary with Madam Steele and I've warned her—"

"Practically ordered."

"Not to go." Greg Merton finished the sentence which had been indignantly interrupted by Linda.

"Why shouldn't she go? She wants to change her job.

Anything would be better than working for that big stiff she's with now, sez I."

Greg told of the owner's recklessness in hoarding cash and jewels in The Castle.

"It's not a safe place for a girl."

"Brother, haven't you learned yet that you can't stop an American from running to a fire? I'll bet it's as safe as this house where a person can enter and walk off with a diamond bracelet, drop a string of pearls in a hamper almost at the front door while the family is practically in the back yard, isn't it?"

"Thanks, Skiddy, for your moral support. Do you think someone came in from outside?" Linda asked hopefully. After all, Janet hadn't known Hester and herself long, and with Shaw filling the air with suspicion of her guests as a bomb spreads poison gas, it wouldn't be surprising if she began to doubt their honesty.

"I do. That boneheaded detective begins to think it was."

"Shaw's keen. He's the one I recommended to you, Skid. I still believe he could help us. Talk with him before he goes, to satisfy me, will you? He went a bit cockeyed tonight, I admit, but he's a good egg and a surefire sleuth. I wonder why the light-fingered gent or lady left that string of pearls?"

"It's a bracelet year, apparently. Greg told you, didn't he, that we're getting a trifle 'warm' about Mother's bracelet, Lindy?" Skid Grant inquired in a low voice as Merton turned to speak to his sister as she entered the room.

"Yes, and warned me that it was a hush-hush story."

"That goes too for the spectacle I made of myself at the night club. I'd like to see a movie of you and me sneaking out."

"Perhaps our detective friend, Jim Shaw, can accommodate you. He seems to be fully informed as to the act we put on even to your change of name. In spite of that I believe in him. I have a feeling that he is deliberately trailing a few red herrings across his trail. Is that mustache you're cultivating a disguise?"

"It's a beaut, what?" Grant tenderly stroked the stiff red sprouts on his upper lip.

"That's a matchless understatement. It's one of a thousand, fortunately."

"You're ribbing me but I can take it. Lindy, do you think you'd better put through the deal with Madam Steele? Greg's a bright boy. He's pretty sure to know what he's talking about."

"Objection overruled—That's a hang-over from Dad's court days. Think of the years she has lived at The Castle without its being burglarized. I like her. I will see a side of life I've never seen before. She will pay me enough to provide clothes suitable to a stratum of society which will be an education. In short I'm in luck. . . . Here's our ace sleuth with his suspects behind him. What has he up his sleeve now?"

Apparently Jim Shaw had nothing up his sleeve. He declared he was convinced that no one in the house knew the whereabouts of the missing bracelet, that he would follow clues which led outside.

"I'll shove, folks." His eyes traveled from Hester's flushed face to Ruth's beside her, leaped from man to man, lingered on Lindy, came back to Janet Colton.

"Just one thing more. What's the value of that bracelet, Mrs. Colton?"

Janet spoke to her husband who was standing between Skid Grant and Keith Sanders.

"Bill, Mr. Shaw wants to know the value of the bracelet which was stolen. It was the one you brought home to me two weeks ago."

"Oh, that! It cost *me* four grand. What the cost . . ." His voice was drowned in a crash as a Ming lamp toppled and fell, breaking into a dozen pieces.

"Sorry, Mrs. Colton. Did I do that?" Keith Sanders' face was a brilliant red. "I must have stepped back suddenly. I didn't know I was anywhere near the table." He knelt to pick up the pieces. Greg Merton bent to help him.

"I'm waiting to hear the value of that bracelet," the detective reminded acidly. "And tipping over that table isn't going to let you off from telling, Mr. Colton."

XVII

ALMOST three months had slipped away since she had come to The Castle, Linda reflected, as from the window of her boudoir she watched snow drifting and blowing in white sheets. The branches of a tree reached and writhed against the sky like an enraged octopus grabbing for its prey. The river was turgid gun-metal gray. October had gone and taken with it the last vestige of color from the garden, had left behind patches of black on the lawns. November had presented a parade of horses, their sleekness and beauty equaled only by the regally-furred-and-frocked women who flocked to admire them, heard John Barbirolli reviving Debussy's *Berceuse Héroïque* at the Philharmonic on Armistice Day—a mournful commentary on wars and their consequences; had loaded shopwindows with footballs, crimson and blue, and the miniature turkeys and pumpkin-orange of Thanksgiving. December had filled the shops with redbowed holly wreaths, glistening trees, multicolored lights and shining balls. Christmas was but two weeks ahead.

In all that time she had met Greg Merton only casually at Ruth's. He had been frigidly courteous. If he had come to The Castle it must have been when she was in the city for an evening of gaiety. Madam Steele had been wonderful, had invited young people to meet her, had entertained Ruth and Hester, Skid Grant and Keith Sanders for week ends.

Keith Sanders. She couldn't quite make him out. Her late boss had slipped easily from the role of employer to that of devoted escort, as devoted as she would permit. He had accepted the withdrawal of The Castle estate from the market with a resigned "These women!" shrug. Madam Steele apparently liked him. At first, she had looked at him with her sharp "Is it a touch?" expression when he had been at his smoothest and most suave.

After he persuaded her to turn the billiard room,

which was back of the stairs and had doors opening into both drawing room and library, into a movie theater, it was evident that she no longer suspected he had an ax to grind. He had arranged for an operator to be on hand week ends and holidays to project films. Madam Steele loved costume pieces and pictures which fictionally depicted epoch-making events in the United States. The more Indians and shooting the better. Money certainly made life's walk easy when it came to entertainment.

"With which not too original reflection I will go back to work," Linda derided herself and sat down at the table near the window. On it lay a loose-leaf album, a box of cellophane covers, hinges, perforation gauge, watermark detector, color chart, an adjustable magnifying glass, envelopes of stamps and a catalogue. She saw them through a mist. This was the first time since her father had gone that she had touched his stamp collection. Ruth had been right when she had said that working over these things he had loved would bring him very near.

"Mind if I come in?" Madam Steele inquired from the threshold. "It's such a gloomy day I can't stay put anywhere."

"I'd love to have you. Know anything about stamps? Come and look at this Postmaster's Provisional. Something tells me it's a reprint, but I wouldn't swear to it."

As Madam Steele took her chair at the table Linda picked up the stamp with the tongs and placed it under the magnifying glass.

"Reprint or not, it is an interesting item. . . . This array of implements has all the marks of a professional collector. How does it happen?" Madam Steele inquired.

Linda told her.

"I thought I had lost interest, but the moment I touched that book the thrill came back. The weather helps. This is just the sort of day when the world is hushed under the spell of falling snow that my father and I loved to work."

"Where did you get stamps; buy them?"

"Not often. We'd swap and occasionally a neighbor who was cleaning out an attic would send us a box of old envelopes. Dad and I would be thrilled speechless."

"I can believe it. The memory has set your eyes

glowing. I wouldn't be surprised if there were stamps you would like in a chest of old letters in one of the rooms upstairs. You may have all you find. Come with me and I'll give you the key to the door of the stairway which leads to the third floor. I had it shut off to save heating it, it is so rarely used now." She stopped before the green-lacquer-and-gold dressing table.

"What an exquisite Chinese box. I like the strings of different colored beads trailing from it."

"One of my sea-captain grandfathers brought that jewel case home from the Orient. It now holds my collection of costume jewelry, 'junk,' my father called it. Junk or not, it sparkles and I love sparkle.'"

"So do I. Someday I will show you my jewels. Meanwhile you'd better start stamp-hunting. Come with me; I'll give you the key."

Madam Steele never before had mentioned her jewels, Linda remembered as she followed her. Each time Ruth and Hester had come to The Castle for a week end they had confided that they were crazy to see them; Keith Sanders had been tepidly interested, Skid eager to compare them with his mother's. But no reference had been made to to them by their owner. That little remark about saving heat had been funny when one thought of the fortune in precious stones which was cached somewhere in this house, but apparently even the very rich had their pet economies.

Two hours later, Linda was still sitting on the floor near one of the rear windows of the room at the head of the stairs. Her cheeks burned with excitement though her hands were stiff from cold. She was thrilled to the marrow of her bones. Envelopes were piled in her lap. She had found rare stamps to fill several spaces in her books and in the chest remained packages of letters tied with strings. She would open just this one before she went down.

She squealed with excitement, rubbed her hand across her eyes, looked at the envelope again. It was! She wasn't mistaken! It was a 1901 Pan-American-Exposition issue. Carmine and black with an inverted railroad train in the center. The priceless two-cent error!

"Are you there, Miss?" The parlormaid, Annie, spoke from the head of the stairs. "The Madam told me to tell you tea was served."

"Good heavens, is it teatime? Come over here, Annie, and help tie up some of these envelopes, will you?"

Sure, Miss. Ain't you excited, though, about a lot of old letters?" She looked out of the window as she knelt beside Linda. "Gee, ain't this high! I'm glad we maids don't have to sleep here. We'd never get out if there was a fire."

"Yes you would. See the iron fire escape just outside the window? This house must have been built many years ago but even then safety was considered. You look white. Aren't you well, or is it this light?"

"I—I feel a kind of headache coming on. I'll be all right after I have my tea, Miss. We'd better hurry and get out of this freezin' room."

"What luck?" Madam Steele inquired as Linda entered the library. "No need to ask. Your cheeks are red. Your eyes shine like stars. You must have found something in those old boxes."

"Old boxes! Treasure chests! Look! What do you see?"

She held out the envelope with the Pan-American-Exposition issue. Madam Steele regarded it through her *lorgnon.*

"I see a red-and-black stamp. Nothing to raise my blood pressure. I presume it means something?"

"Means something! It's worth *hundreds* of dollars!"

"You're in luck, my dear."

"*You're* in luck. It's yours. I know where I can sell it for you. It's a sensational find!"

"I told you you could have any stamp you found and I meant it. Will you sell it?"

"Mine! Really! *Sell* it!" Linda gulped back a gasp of excitement. "Never! It will go into our book. If he were here, my father and I would be doing an Indian war dance. Are you sure you want me to have it? You could buy jewels with the money for your collection."

"It's yours. I'm glad you found it. Keep the key to the door of the third-floor stairway. You may find other treasures."

"Thank you a million times."

She had been here almost three months. The thought recurred to Linda as in a copper-gold lamé frock she entered the library before dinner. She stopped on the thresh-

old. Greg Merton was standing in front of the fire. Madam
Steele, in shimmering gray satin almost as white as her
hair, was talking earnestly, using her beautiful hands, sparkling with rings, for emphasis. Had she known he was coming? It looked like it. He was dressed for dinner.

"This is a surprise. Did you snow down, Greg?"

"No. Still sticking to the good old roadster. Aunt Jane
sent me an S O S. Haven't found out yet what it's all
about."

"I'll explain when we have our coffee, Gregory."
Madam Steele rose as Buff announced dinner.

In the dining room the butler drew out her chair. Gregory Merton performed the same office for Linda before he
took his seat, at the end of the shining mahogany table,
with its exquisite lace, massive silver and crystal, opposite
his aunt.

The conversation which ran to family matters, questions by Madam Steele, answers by her nephew, while the
butler, assisted by Annie in a maroon silk frock, deftly
served a delicious meal, afforded Linda's thoughts ample
time and opportunity to roam. Since she had come to The
Castle there had been days when she felt as if she were living in a dream, but never one which seemed so unreal as
this afternoon when she had crouched near the third-floor
window and found that sensational stamp. It was hers!
Hers and her father's.

She glanced furtively at Greg Merton. Dislike him as
she did, she'd have to admit that he was sensationally
goodlooking, that he had an endearing quality of warm
sympathy as he listened to his aunt. If her no-appeal asser-
tions were irritating he gave no hint of it. Did he still believe that Linda Bourne had come to The Castle in the interest of Keith Sanders?

She hadn't, but she felt sometimes that Keith was
smugly sure that under cover of the social-secretaryship she
was working for him. Was that why he invited her out so
often,—more often than she would go,—why he was so
charming to Madam Steele? Was he scheming to acquire
the management of her many real-estate investments? He
could be great fun, but she didn't trust him. Then why accept his invitations? Answer. First, because it was exciting
to go out with him; the second, and more compelling, rea-

son was that she had a curious conviction that he had some scheme in which he intended to use her. She was determined to find out and block him.

"Come back to the present and talk to us, Linda. Greg must be fed-up with family news by this time." Madam Steele's crisp suggestion brought Linda's reflections to a crashing climax.

"I'm sorry, terribly sorry, that I was woolgathering—there's-a question for 'Information Please.' How did the expression originate?"

"You and Greg can work out the answer in the library over the coffee." She rose. As Linda started to leave the room Annie touched her arm.

"Please, Miss Bourne, may I speak to you a moment?" The girl's voice was urgent, her face white.

"Of course. Don't wait for me, Greg." As he followed his aunt to the hall she asked: "What is it, Annie?"

"I've got to talk to someone, Miss Linda. I've *got* to. You were so kind of friendly this afternoon upstairs I thought you might be willing to listen. May I come to your room?"

"Of course. Ask Maggie to let you bring my breakfast tray tomorrow."

"Thank you, Miss. Thank you. I'll do that very thing."

Buff had served the coffee, had hovered devotedly about Greg Merton with the tray of cigars and cigarettes and had departed to his kingdom belowstairs. Madam Steele held out her fragile cup.

"Fill it once more."

"Are you sure you want it? You wouldn't have dared ask for it while Buff was here," Linda reminded and poured the coffee.

"He's a meddling old party. That reminds me, my dear—hold on to the key to the third-floor stairway. If he were to find it in the door, he would think someone had carelessly left it there and as a matter of discipline would add it to his bunch. He was almost senile with delight when I told you would be here tonight, Gregory. He sighed with relief, exclaimed: 'It will be a great help to have another man in the house, Madam.' "

"What did he mean by 'help,' Duchess?"

"Ask him. He likes to think that The Castle couldn't go on without him. I gave up having a houseman years ago because no one whom I engaged would endure his bossing. He heard the doctor tell me to go light on coffee, so he appointed himself my keeper. There is no reason now why I shouldn't drink it. I'm sleeping well."

"Not too well. I heard a sound in the hall last night and when I peeked out you were coming up the stairs looking like a modern Lady Macbeth with an electric flash instead of a candle. I expected to hear you mutter, 'There's blood upon these . . .' Oh, my dear! What have I said? You're white." Linda dropped to her knees beside Madam Steele.

"What's the matter, Duchess?" Greg Merton laid his arm across his aunt's shoulders.

"Sit down, Linda. Gregory, stop fussing over me and see if there's anyone in the hall. Then look behind the hangings."

"Not so much as a shadow," he reported as he returned from making the circuit. "What's happened? I never saw you nervous before."

"Come closer while I tell you. Last night I shot a man."

XVIII

THE ROOM was very still. Tragedy had stepped out of the shadows. Horror laid its icy finger on Linda's heart. Greg Merton stared incredulously at the woman in shimmering gray, sitting erect and composed in the carved-backed chair. She had made the startling statement in the voice with which she might have said: "Last night I danced with a man."

"I'll be darned! You—you sh—*shot* someone!"

"If I didn't stutter and stammer telling it, I don't know why you should repeating it, Gregory. I presume men who have been caught breaking and entering have been shot before."

"My mistake, Duchess. Shooting a person may be a

daily stunt in your life, but it just doesn't fit into my sched-
ule. Are you armed when you prowl? If so, you may bet
your bottom dollar you won't catch me leaving my room at
midnight."

"Of course I'm armed. Suppose I met a burglar? I
couldn't very well say 'Excuse me while I run to my room
for my revolver,' could I?"

In a low voice, with an occasional furtive glance over
her shoulder, Madam Steele explained that she had been
unable to sleep, that when the clock struck twelve she had
gone to the library to get a book, had switched on the light,
had seen a window hanging move.

"Come out or I'll shoot," she had commanded.

The hanging moved again. She shot. Hurried across
the room. The long French window was ajar. She flashed
her electric light on the floor, on the terrace. There were a
few drops of blood on the snow.

"That's why I turned white when you quoted Lady
Macbeth, Linda. I don't like blood. I got my man, Gregory. I've always told you I was the equal of any burglar who
walked."

"Sneaks, is a better word. You got him! Do you mean
he's a prisoner here?"

"No, worse luck. I stepped out on the terrace and—"

" 'Stepped out'! You're crazy. You might have been
shot yourself."

"I didn't think of that. I thought only that he might
have fallen, that I would have him brought into the house
and cared for. After all, I didn't intend to kill him. Snow
was falling. His tracks were already covered. We will cautiously inquire if a wounded man has applied at the hospital or to a doctor in the neighborhood for help. We'll get
him and find out who sent him. It isn't conceivable that a
lone man would try to steal my jewels. That's why I sent
for you, Gregory. I haven't forgiven you yet for saying I
thought myself smarter than my business advisers, but I'm
willing to admit that in some matters you have intelligence."

"That's a break. You mean you'll let me handle this
without interfering? If so, I'll get in touch with the police at
once."

"The police! Certainly *not*. Having carried on without them for years, I won't appeal to them now. *I* shot the man—you needn't remind me that I lost him; now you and Linda can find him for me."

"I! But there might be a dozen wounded men in the country! How would I know I had the right one?" Linda had a breath-snatching vision of herself speeding about inquiring for a man who had been shot.

"Your secretary will keep out of this or I wash my hands of the mess now. Take your choice, Duchess." Gregory Merton's voice rang with a hands-up quality which sent little shivers merry-pranking along Linda's veins. It had its effect on Madam Steele.

"Have your own way, Gregory," she acceded grudgingly, "I've tried battering at your will power before."

"One liability removed. You understand that you are *not* to muscle in on this mess under any circumstances, Lindy?"

"I would like to help."

"Skip it. If you help, I don't."

"All *right*. I'm out. The dictators are not all in Europe." She made an impudent little face at him.

"Now that that point is settled we'll get back to the business at hand. Know where you hit the guy, Duchess? Arm? Leg? Head?"

"Think. Use your brain. If I'd shot him in the head he would have dropped where he was. If in the leg, he couldn't have gone far. It must have been his shoulder or arm. There's your clue. You'd better start to hunt in the morning."

"Morning! I'm due at my office at nine-thirty for an important conference. Greg, the boy detective, will buckle on his trusty revolver and start tonight."

"You're laughing about a serious matter, young man. You haven't a permit to carry a gun; you'd better apply for it tomorrow. I believe you think I had a nightmare. Don't you realize that if I hadn't shot that man we might all have been murdered in our beds?"

"That's a cheery thought." Linda suppressed a shiver. "Though when you come to think of it, why would a person enter my room? Anyone with any sense at all—and it must take a heap of brains to be a burglar—would know that a girl who works for a living would have nothing worth stealing."

"She might have a valuable engagement ring," Greg Merton suggested before he held a lighter to a cigarette.

"She might. I hadn't thought of that," Linda countered noncommittally.

A red-headed, freckle-faced, black-silk-frocked maid hesitated on the threshold.

"May I take the coffee tray now, Madam?"

"Yes." Her mistress frowned as she approached. "Why are you doing this, Maggie? It is Annie's work."

"I know, Madam, but she has a bad attack of migraine, could hardly hold her head up while she was serving dinner, she couldn't. She'll be all right in the mornin'," she prophesied and left the room with the large silver tray.

"You'd better look in on Annie before you go up, Linda. See if she really is ill. She may have wanted to step out early. Such things happen. See her and report to me."

"I will, Madam Steele." Apparently the headache of which Annie had complained in the afternoon had developed into migraine.

"I'll go out now and take a look around. Which curtain did your deadly shot penetrate?" Greg Merton inquired.

"Hmp! Still making a joke of it, aren't you? Examine the right-hand hanging at the end window." Madam Steele leaned forward to follow him with her eyes as he crossed the room. He felt of the blue-damask hanging. His long, low whistle was expressive.

"I am limp with apology, Duchess. I did think you'd had a nightmare. I've found the bullet hole. Which fact convinces me that we'd better start the man hunt, pronto. Business will keep me in New York this week. I'll be back Saturday but I'll send up a man, Jim Shaw, who works for me, to carry on while I'm away."

What would the gorillalike Jim Shaw think when he found her ensconced in The Castle, Linda wondered. She was sure he had suspected her when Janet Colton's bracelet was stolen.

"Gregory Merton, I won't have a detective or the police on this place. Either you help me or I won't have anyone."

"Suit yourself, Duchess. I will do what I can tonight. I'll be gone in the morning before you're up. If I discover a clue I will leave a note for you. Good night, Aunt Jane."

Curious that he hadn't said good night to her, too, Linda thought. She might have been a chair or table for all the notice he took of her. Madam Steele's eyes followed him until he had left the room. She settled back in her chair.

"Earlier this evening you spoke of Christmas, Linda," she reminded, as casually as if, a few moments ago, she hadn't admitted that she had shot a man. "I have a plan for it. I want Gregory, Janet and her family, your friend Miss Brewster, your mother and sister, that amusing Skidmore Grant and of course Mr. Sanders, to come the day before and spend the holiday with us. Judge Reynolds will be here as usual."

"But, Madam Steele! Your nephew and niece of course, but why my family?"

"You'll want to go to them, won't you?"

"Why—why, yes. I hadn't thought of anything different."

"I need you here. Help me make this a joyous Christmas. There will be presents for everybody and a tree. I can't do it without you. Will your family and friends object to coming?"

"I can't answer for them but, whether they come or not, I will stay here till every last thing is ready and planned for your celebration."

"But I want them and you. Why shouldn't we have a merry Christmas in this house? I provide one for the townspeople. I need terribly to forget on that day that the life of my son and the lives of countless young men were a wasted sacrifice. Twenty-one years and Europe is again aflame. . . . Sorry, I didn't mean to refer to that tragedy. I will write the invitations tomorrow. Look around at the window fastenings, will you? Buff is getting careless. I should have asked Gregory to do it. That young man is obstinate as a mule—but I'm glad he's here. I feel as if I had something secure to grip." She waited on the threshold until Linda joined her and reported:

"Fastened tight as a drum."

"You're a sweet child. You make me feel that you like what you young moderns call your 'job.' "

"Like it! I love it."

"Thank you, my dear. Go now and inquire for Annie. If she's asleep don't disturb her. Sleep is the best remedy she can have."

"If I don't report to you, you'll know she's all right, Madam Steele. If you hear anything disturbing tonight, don't prowl—phone my room. I always leave my boudoir door unlocked so that you can come in if you want to. I'm not much of a shot, but I can scream. Good night."

Linda was thinking of that affectionate "my dear," as she knocked gently at the maid's door in the servants' cottage which was connected with the main house by a covered passage. Madam Steele had never before spoken to her in that tone.

No answer. She knocked again. Listened. Was Annie asleep? She turned the knob. The light from the corridor shone on the bed. No one in it or on it. The spread was undisturbed. No hat or coat in the closet.

She gently closed the door and tiptoed back into the great hall, ran lightly up the stairs. She thought of the maid's white face. Had she gone out in connection with the matter she wanted to talk about in the morning? A hand caught her arm.

"Is Annie in her room?" Greg Merton whispered.

She shook her head. "Shall I tell Madam Steele?" she whispered in return.

"No. What she doesn't know won't worry her. *Just* a minute. Nice of you to tell Sanders that you couldn't love me. Why not wait till I *ask* you to?"

Linda's lips flew open. Before she could answer the savage question, he threw open the door of her room.

"Go to bed and stay there. Understand? *Stay* there. Just in case you've forgotten, get this: You're to keep out of this mix-up, or there'll be trouble."

XIX

LINDA was standing at the window in a pale-blue lounge coat when Annie entered with the breakfast tray. She hadn't slept much. When she had dozed it was to chase a blackmasked burglar up one hall stairway and down the other, then skid across the flagged floor only to charge the stairs again to the accompaniment of Greg Merton's savage voice saying over and over, "Why not wait till I *ask* you to?" She felt as if she had spent the night on a merry-go-around that never stopped.

"Good morning, Miss Linda." Annie set the tray on a small table and placed a chair. "I think I've brought what you usually have, Miss. Maggie fixed things. She's my sister. She's awful good to me."

"It looks perfect, thank you." Linda sipped the ice-cold orange juice and looked up at the maid. Her eyes were heavy. Her face was pale.

"How's the migraine this morning?"

"I didn't have it, Miss Linda."

"I know that. I went to your room. You ran out, didn't you?"

"Did—did the Madam know?" The question was a whisper. The maid's mouth trembled uncontrollably; tears flooded her eyes. "Will I lose my place?" There it was again—everyone in the world in terror of losing a job.

"I didn't tell her. Sit down. Stop twisting your hands. What's on your mind?"

"It's Cline, Miss Linda." Her voice caught in a sob.

"Who is Cline?"

"He's a mechanic in a garage in the village. Sometimes the head chauffeur calls him in to repair the Madam's cars; though I will say she gets new ones so often there isn't much to do to them." Her voice held a resentful note.

"What is this Cline to you that you should cry about him?"

"He's my boy friend, my steady."

"Is that all, Annie?"

"That's all, honest-to-God, Miss Linda. We're going to get married as soon as he's saved money enough to take me to Canada. His brother has a garage there and will give him work. He thinks 'twill be sometime after Christmas we'll go." The light of anticipation faded. Her lips trembled again; her eyes suffused. "I guess we won't go now, though. He's had an accident."

"Accident!" The word slashed through Linda's preoccupation. She had been wondering if "Cline" really intended to marry the girl—that garage in Canada somehow did not ring true.

"What kind of an accident?" Could it have been Cline at whom Madam Steele had shot?

"He hurt his shoulder, Miss, terrible bad, I guess. He can't move his arm. He said something flew off and hit him when he was working on an auto. He wouldn't even let me look at it."

"When did he get hurt? How did you know about it? Why did he come out here if he was hurt at the village garage?"

"It must have happened night before last. Something hit my window. I was woke out of a sound sleep. I looked out. Cline was standing near a shrub beckoning to me. Honest-to-God, Miss, I've never met him at night before. I wouldn't want to and if I did, I'd be scared for fear I'd meet the Madam—she walks round the house at night, she does, like a banshee. He came to find me. Said he didn't know no one else who'd help him."

"You went out?"

"Yes, Miss. What else could I do? He was braced against a spruce tree white as a ghost. He didn't speak till we were out of hearin' of the house. He looked something awful. Sweat running down his pale face and him biting his lips as if holdin' back a scream. He leaned so heavy on me I almost dragged him to one of those benches on the garden path."

"Did you see the wound?"

"Oh, 'twasn't a wound, it was a bruise. He wouldn't let me look at it. Said if he could get to some place where he could lie flat, he'd be fine. I was at my wits' end to know where to take him and then all of a sudden I thought of that game house up in the woods. 'Tisn't used in winter, hardly ever. You've seen it, haven't you, Miss?"

Linda nodded. She remembered that she had thought the grotesque building looked like something which had been designed for the World of Tomorrow, had been rejected and cast outside the sacred gates.

"I stole back to the big house and got the key—it hangs in the back hall—fair holdin' my breath for fear I'd be caught. I thought I'd never get him there. I did though. I told him to lie quiet and in the morning I'd bring a doctor. He made me swear I wouldn't. Said he'd get on all right by himself, that if his boss knew he'd been so clumsy with tools, he'd fire him and it would be nix on gettin' married. Then he passed out. I dragged cushions from the window seat. Got him onto them. Covered him with my coat. After he come to again I left him. I went again last evening. He's awful sick, but he won't let me bring anyone to see him, says that would end everything between us. I don't know what to do. That's why I asked if I could talk to you, you were so kind of friendly yesterday afternoon. I was crazy to tell you then but I didn't dare."

Undoubtedly Cline was the man at whom Madam Steele had shot. She would make sure, though, before she reported to Greg. Had Annie read her thoughts? The maid was colorless.

"I've told you this in confidence, Miss Linda," she reminded passionately. "If you tell anyone about it or where Cline is you'll make terrible trouble for me. Promise you won't. Promise!" The girl's voice cracked on a hysterical sob.

"Be quiet, Annie. I shan't tell anyone till I have seen your boy friend. I've had three years' Red Cross training. I'll go to the game house with you after dark. Persuade Cline to let me look at his shoulder. If the skin isn't cut or bone broken, it won't do any harm for him to stay where he is until the worst of the pain is over. I'll take along something to ease that and you can apply it."

"Will you really, Miss Linda?" The maid's mouth quivered in a smile. "I'll bet Cline will let you look at his shoulder. He's asked a lot of questions about you. I've told him about your boy friends who come here and your swell looks and clothes. What time had we better go to the game house, Miss?"

Linda considered. Usually Madam Steele went to her room promptly at ten. Her dour maid was in attendance after that. Greg Merton's business would prevent his return to The Castle until the week end at least, thank heaven. By that time Cline would be on his way if the injury to his arm or shoulder was a bruise and not a bullet wound. What would she do if it were the last? Why cross that bridge until she came to it?

"I ought not to stay here any longer, Miss," Annie prodded. "What time will you meet me?"

"After dinner I play rummy with Madam Steele. At ten she goes to her room. I'll meet you in the shadow of the great pine near the game house as the church bells chime eleven. If for any reason you can't be there, get word to me. Understand?"

"Yes, Miss. Thank you a lot." With her hand on the doorknob she turned. "Will you cross-your-throat-an'-hope-to-die that you won't tell anyone about Cline, Miss?"

If Cline were, as she suspected, the man who had entered The Castle at midnight he had been there dishonestly and should be punished, Linda reflected. In that case, she must expose him; the safety of the entire household would be at stake—it was human lives she wanted to protect, not jewels.

"I can't promise that, Annie. Suppose, when I see him, I discover he is so ill that he'll die if a doctor doesn't attend him? You and I would be practically murderers if we didn't call medical help. A sick person isn't capable of deciding what is to be done for him. Can't you believe that I want to do what is right?" Would that go down on the Judgment Day book as a gray lie or a white lie?

"Gee, you scare me, Miss, with the word 'murderers.' I guess I'll have to trust you. Someday your fella may get into troub—get hurt and you'll know how I feel. I'll be at the big pine at eleven, Miss."

Annie had betrayed herself when she had broken the word "trouble" in half and substituted "hurt," Linda decided. Did the girl suspect that her "fella" had not told her the truth or did she know what a sordid story was back of his injury? What was she letting herself in for? She had an instant's clear perception of possible consequences which closed her throat tight and shut off her breath. Greg Merton had said that if she muscled in on the mess, he was out of it. But she didn't know that the man in the game house was the man he was hunting for, did she?

If only she and Greg were better friends. How could they be when he believed she had double-crossed him? Her heart smarted unbearably when she thought of his distrust of her. His fierce "Why not wait till I *ask* you to?" still echoed through her memory. Sounded as if he were on the verge of a nervous breakdown fearing that she might think he wanted her love. He needn't worry. She had decided that Sanders was using her to take Madam Steele's business away from her nephew. She would do her best to stop him, not because she liked said nephew, but because she detested underground methods of getting business.

She never had known such an interminable day, she thought after dinner, as Buff set the coffee tray on the small table in the library. Guests at luncheon, tea at a neighbor's with Madam Steele, while all the time beneath the talk of war and the fight in Congress on Neutrality had run the anxious self-query, "What shall I do if I find Cline is the man who was shot?"

The butler fussed over the tray. His face was a shade more pasty than usual, his humorless mouth more grim.

"It's a great pity Mr. Greg couldn't stay with us this week, Madam," he complained. "He told me when I served his breakfast that he wouldn't be back till Sunday. We need him."

"What do you mean, 'need him,' Buff?"

He coughed behind his hand in the best movie-butler tradition.

"I followed you when you came into the library the other midnight, Madam. I heard the shot."

"You couldn't have heard it. There was a silencer on the revolver."

"Being so near, I heard the sound, but I kept out of sight. I knew you would be angry if I appeared. I watched till you went upstairs. I always hear you when you prowl at night, Madam. I've been with you thirty years. I feel a great responsibility about your safety. If the coffee is as you like it, I'll go now." He paused to add, "Your secret is safe with me."

Madam Steele's startled eyes followed him and came back to Linda.

"Well, of all the melodrama! 'Your secret is safe with me.' Gives me the creeps. Makes me feel as if I had hidden a body. Meddling old party. Fancy his following me about the house when I prowl. It's spooky. A lot of protection he'd be. Get out the cards, Linda. It will take about four games tonight to calm my nerves. That's a figure of speech —I haven't any."

Four games! They would make her late to meet Annie at eleven. Then what?

"Did Greg report any progress?" Linda inquired as she dealt the new, shiny cards. "He said last night that he would leave a note for you."

"He left the note. He had discovered nothing. I believe that in spite of the bullet hole in the hanging, he still thinks I had a nightmare. You can't build that way, child. Keep your mind on the game. Anyone would think you had a gunshot wound on your conscience."

"Perhaps I have," Linda told herself. Aloud she said, "You'll have to admit that a burglar in the house might have a machine-gun effect on the imagination. Your deal."

"Here's your bad penny back again, Duchess," a voice announced jovially. "I've arranged my business to take the rest of the week off. How's that for efficiency?"

Greg Merton! Linda stared at him incredulously. Greg Merton feeling terribly pleased with himself. Grand chance she had now of meeting Annie by the big pine as the church bells chimed eleven.

XX

WOULD Madam Stelle never call it a day, Linda wondered feverishly? Why of all nights should she select this one to stay downstairs beyond her usual hour, which was ten? Every tick of the clock made the rendezvous with Annie more difficult. As if Greg Merton's sudden appearance hadn't complicated it enough.

He stood back of the fire, smiling, smoking, while the minutes were racing, racing, *racing* toward eleven o'clock.

"By the way, Duchess, how's the maid who had the sudden attack of migraine?" he inquired. His eyes above the light he was holding to a cigarette flashed from his aunt to Linda. The look sent her heart zooming to her throat. Was it because of a guilty conscience that she had sensed suspicion in that glance? He had warned her not to "muscle in." Why worry? She wasn't sure that Annie's "Cline" was the man he had been asked to look for, was she?

"She served at dinner tonight. She had piled on rouge. I presume she thought I wouldn't notice. She knows I won't keep a maid who can't do her work. Good night, Gregory. I'm going to my room."

"Isn't it part of your secretary's duty to entertain your guests, Duchess? Tell her to stay here and talk to me."

Linda held her breath waiting for the answer. Suppose Madam Steele said "Stay"—she never would get away to Annie.

"Hump! If you aren't interesting enough to keep her, why should I interfere? She's a free agent after I go to my room. Good night, again, Gregory."

When with Madam Steele she reached the top of the curved stairs, Linda looked down.

"Good night, Mr. Merton." Her voice was low, amused and cloyingly sweet.

He didn't answer. Just stood in the hall looking up, hands thrust into the pockets of his blue-serge coat. Had he noticed her eagerness to leave the library? He had an uncanny way of sensing what was in the wind.

In her room she hastily pulled on warm socks, fastened overshoes, wound a green-and-white-striped scarf about her head, zipped her ski suit and thrust an electric torch into the pocket of her trousers. She glanced at the clock. Only ten minutes in which to reach the big pine. She ran to the window.

The snow had stopped. Gorgeous moon. Full. Luminous. A lump of bluish silver hammered flat against indigo velvet. Its light had put out the lesser stars but red Mars and Jupiter retained their brilliancy. A blue moon. Wasn't

it supposed to be a good omen? Not this time. Better for
her errand had the sky been overcast.

She picked up the bag which held her first-aid kit. She
had considered taking the revolver which Madam Steele
insisted she should keep in the drawer of the bedside table,
and decided against it. She hated the thing, never had loaded it. If there were a possibility that she would need a gun
she wouldn't go to the game house. That settled that.

She opened her door. Listened. Tick-tock! Tick-
tock! Only the tall clock in the hall, the sharp crack of a
burning log in the fireplace broke the silence. She stole
down the stairs. Suppose Greg Merton appeared at the library door? What would she say? He was in the room—
she could hear voices. Lucky he was talking with someone.
He couldn't possibly hear her. She made her cautious way
across the flagged floor to the hall. The walls seemed
weirdly sibilant. Were they whispering that this was old
stuff, that they had seen a girl stealing out many, many
times before?

She gently closed the side door behind her. She was
out of the house and Mr. Gregory Merton was in the library. Hooray! If she were seen now, it would be pre-
sumed that she was a maid sneaking out for a rendezvous.

Even in a good cause it was a strange and lonely feeling to turn one's back on warmth and security, she discovered, as she plodded on. Once out of sight of the house she
hurried. No path to guide her, not even Annie's footprints.
This expedition would have been thrilling if she could have
told Greg about it, if they had set out together. Why had he
watched her so closely in the library after dinner? Had he—.

She stepped into a hole. A thousand stars rocketed.
The fall shattered her introspection. "Serves you right," she
accused herself and struggled up. "Keep your mind on your
feet instead of on a man named Merton, Brainless."

She wasted a few precious minutes hunting for her
bag. Found it open. Groped for the scattered contents. Replaced them. Clutched the handle tight. Proceeded cautiously. Bells. How they shortened time with their fifteen-
minute chimes. She counted the solemn strokes. Eleven.
She was late.

Snow whitened stumps, boulders and holes with lavish
impartiality. The walk which, in the fall, had been a pleas-

ant stroll over pine needles and fallen leaves had become a
way as full of pitfalls as an old-time tin Lizzie with dents.
The sudden, clear snap of frost had the startling effect of a
popgun. The evergreens rustled with whispers.

The tall pine! At last! She stopped a moment to draw
a deep breath of the sparkling air. How still the world was.
Almost as light as day. Time was ticking on like a metro-
nome. The temperature was dropping fast; her scarf was
coated with frost where her breath had frozen. She stood in
the shadow of the great pine. Annie had not arrived. Had
she been unable to steal out? It must be five minutes after
eleven.

The grotesque shape of the game house crouched a
short distance away. Back and forth she paced, wondering
what she would do if she found that the man's wound was
a gun-shot, wondering if he had entered The Castle to steal
the jewels. That last didn't seem plausible. Madam Steele
had been right. What could a man accomplish alone? Perhaps he hadn't been alone. Perhaps he was only the tip-off
man. Perhaps—the chimes again. Had she been under this
tree ten minutes? She had been a little late. Distraught with
anxiety Annie might have gone ahead. That was a thought.
She'd follow and be quick about it.

Scrunch! Scrunch! Did her feet have to make such a
racket? She might as well have brought a brass band to an-
nounce her arrival. Unless his sweetheart had prepared him
for her coming, "Cline," if guilty, would make a desperate
effort to escape. Then what?

Was that a fire behind the game house just to make
things harder? Fire! No. It was the aurora putting on a
theatrical show. Waving green streamers of light, stabbing
with scarlet spears, washing the dark sky with shimmering
violet and rose. Still as a snow maiden she watched it glow
and fade. In the gorgeousness of that heavenly spectacle
this affair of Annie's seemed of small importance.

She shook off the spell of beauty and went on, her
heart thumping like an Indian war drum. The maid's affair
might seem negligible to her but it might mean danger to
Madam Steele.

Close to a window of the game house she stood motionless as an inactive bank account. The curtain was tightly drawn. Not a splinter of light visible. She listened.

Voices? No. Only the swish of snow-laden branches above her head.

Why linger here as if she were afraid to be seen? She had come on an errand of mercy. Why should she gumshoe round as if she were a G-man or a racket-buster on the trail of his quarry?

She scrunched to the entrance door. Touched it. It swung open slowly, in uncanny invitation. She swallowed her heart which was now beating an alarm in her throat.

"Annie! Annie!" Her voice trailed into a hoarse whisper.

Scuttling? Mice? Rats? Steady. Suppose it were? What harm could they do? All her life she had heard the expression "buckled on courage." As a child she had taken it literally, had pictured courage as a sort of material harness. Well, here it went, over her head. Would it work a magic spell? Make her invulnerable to fear?

She flashed the light of her torch along the wall. The game house was wired for electricity. Nothing so outdated as an oil lamp or candles would be relied on for a building on Madam Steele's estate. She pressed a button. The large room blazed with light. With a bang which shattered the stillness the door shut behind her.

Step by lagging step, she reached the middle of the floor. Pivoted like a dummy model in a fashion-shop window. Tennis racquets, croquet mallets, a shabby green cardigan, an eyeshade in an open closet. No one here— Her heart froze. Something long. Something limp. Something stretched on cushions! Something covered with an automobile rug! What was that on the floor of the bay window?

Her breath stopped. Her feet took root. She clenched her teeth. She couldn't quit. She wouldn't. She must move. She must speak. She owed it to her employer to find out what this gruesome thing was.

She tiptoed toward it. Silly! Why tiptoe? She had made noise enough entering to rouse the dead. She shivered. That last word hadn't helped. The tip of a boot stuck out from under the rug.

"What are you doing here?" The voice she had geared to a clarion call emerged a whisper. Shaken as it was, its effect was instantaneous. The rug was thrown back. A man sat up.

"For the love of Mike!"

"Skid! S—Skid! I don't believe it! I'm seeing things! I just don't believe it."

She dropped to the floor and went off into gales of laughter, laughter punctuated by sobs. Grant gripped her shoulder, shook her.

"Snap out of it, Linda, or you'll have hysterics."

"Your eyes are so—so funny! They l—look like mar—marbles. B—Big b—brown glassies. I—I—I—never had hys—hysterics in my l—life."

"Well, you're darn near having them now. Your nerves are shot. What are you doing here? Loosen up, gal, and—" A discordant screech split the air, dwindled into a prolonged hiss—s—s.

"Gosh! So are mine! What in thunder was that? My hair's standing on end! A signal, I'll bet. Listen!" He caught her arm. "Hear that scrunch? Someone's coming." He dashed for the light switch. Blackout.

"Lindy! Come here!"

She followed his whisper. Chimes again. Time was marching on. It must be eleven-thirty.

He seized her shoulder. Drew her into the closet. Closed the door. Scrunch! Scrunch! Someone was stepping cautiously on the porch.

"Leave it open a crack so we can see," Linda whispered.

"No. Don't move."

A knob turning. They stood rigid. Whoever had come had flicked on the light. Silence. Spooky, terrifying silence.

"Why doesn't he move?" Linda whispered close against Grant's ear.

Her movement tumbled the racquets to the floor. The crash brought action. Running footsteps.

"Hands up," growled a voice. The door was yanked open.

XXI

THAT morning Gregory Merton had thoughtfully paced the floor of his office, hands in his pockets. His hunt last night after his aunt and Linda had gone upstairs had amounted to nothing. Snow had covered all tracks. In the early morning he had called on the nearest physician and the two adjacent hospitals. No one with a bullet wound had been treated. He had hated to come away without even a hint as to the midnight marauder but he had to keep his date in the city.

He had disposed of that matter satisfactorily, had arranged with his head salesman to take over for the rest of the week and, if inquiries were made as to his whereabouts, to say that he was making a quick trip to the Coast. Better not have it known that he was at The Castle. Staying there wasn't disappearing into the wilderness. He could be reached by telephone and could be back at the office in an hour. He was uneasy about his aunt and he might as well face it, about Lindy's safety. It had taken only the possibility of danger to her to make him acknowledge that his distrust of her was a big bluff, that he was madly in love with her.

He stopped his pacing and visualized her proud head, her sturdy chin; her clear, glowing brown eyes as they had flashed last night when he had told her to wait till he asked her to love him. What demon had possessed him to crack at her like that? Since Alix Crane at the Brazilian Pavilion had declared that Keith Sanders had Linda fascinated his heart had been raw; it had needed only the man's repetition of her declaration that she couldn't love Greg Merton to—

"Hey! In a trance? What's happened? Got a line on your sister's bracelet yet?" The sepulchral voice came from the ruddy face protruding round the partially open door and shattered the apology he was formulating in his mind.

"Come in, Skid." As Grant perched on the corner of the desk, Greg added, "I wish I had a clairvoyant power to

130

locate missing articles. I'd find a man, darn quick. I wouldn't waste it on a bracelet."

"What man?"

Merton told him. Added that he had arranged his business to spend the remainder of the week at The Castle; concluded:

"I'm uneasy about Linda. I told her to keep out of the mess but something tells me that she'll get into it up to her neck if I'm not there to stop her."

"You've guessed it. If you think you can stop her doing what she thinks she should do you're an optimist."

"I don't see any 'should' about it. She wasn't hired to hunt criminals."

"She'll consider whatever Madam Steele asks her to do as part of her job. I don't care what she does so long as it keeps her from stepping out with that guy Sanders."

"Is she with him often?" Would Skid notice the strain in his voice?

"I hear she is. She comes to the city at least two nights a week for fun. Evidently she considers him four-star entertainment. I haven't been able to date her since Thanksgiving. When Linda loves, her man will own all the earth and a good-sized chunk of heaven. I know now I won't be the lucky guy. Signing-off on Lindy. Hasn't Jim Shaw traced your sister's bracelet yet, Greg?"

"Not so much as a sparkle of it. Our idea that its disappearance was linked up with the theft of your mother's jewels wasn't so hot."

"I'm not so sure of that. I see light! A blinding light! Madam Steele has jewels. That house of hers is a small diamond mine, isn't it? I'll bet a hat the man she took a shot at was one of the same gang."

"There may be something in what you say." Greg caught the contagion of his excitement. "No. Nothing doing, it doesn't sound reasonable. One man wouldn't tackle the job alone—"

"Unless he had inside help."

"Inside help? You've said it! Annie with the attack of migraine!" He told of the maid's alleged illness, that when Linda went to her room she was gone.

"Perhaps she had skipped out to meet the wounded hero."

"Looks like it. I'm going back to The Castle tonight. I'll arrive too late for dinner; then Annie, who assists the butler in the dining room, won't know I'm in the house. Come along with me. That's an idea. Aunt Jane likes you —considers you 'brilliant'—she must enjoy your ribbing of her guests. We can work on different angles of the case and compare notes."

"Sounds darn exciting but I'm on another job. I've been getting fratty with the suave Señor Pedro Lorillo. If he isn't a bad boy I'll eat my hat. Gosh, when he looks at me with those white eyes of his, so help me, my spine curls up like a gelatin film in heat."

"Ghoulish, I calls 'em. I have a hunch that the Brazilian business at the Fair was a front. Now that the World of Tomorrow has shut up shop, why is he still hanging round New York?"

"He isn't. Gone back to Brazil, Alix reports. She left town at the same time to fill a night-club engagement."

"Still sure that bracelet she sported is your mother's?"

"Sure as shootin'. The diamonds in that figure 8 flashed me a wicked wink, that night at the Brazilian Pavilion. I'll swear they knew what I was thinking. I believe the girl was honest when she said she'd bought it 'off' a friend. But later, she wouldn't give me a hint as to the friend's name. I didn't dare urge it. If Lorillo knew where it came from—I'm sure he did—he wasn't taking any chances of my getting wise. He watched me as a dog watches a nice juicy chop just out of reach. At times I wondered if he was on to the fact that my name isn't Sterling. Now they've both lighted out and the girl's taken the bracelet with her."

"I wish you'd give Jim Shaw a look-in on the case, Skid."

"He's in. You sold him to me. He knew who I was, knew all about me that night at your sister's. He was putting on an act for reasons he won't give at present. I decided that the Lorillo-Crane axis was getting too hot for me to handle alone. I've turned the girl angle over to him while I concentrate on the Señor. I'm making plans to fly to Brazil. If you pick up the trail of Madam Steele's burglar here in the city before I leave I'll bet a grand our paths will cross. When you're after an international ring look for links in the most unexpected places. Happy landings!"

As that evening Greg Merton watched Linda mounting the stairs he thought of the conviction in Grant's voice. She had been startled at his unexpected appearance in the library, had betrayed an eagerness to escape to her room. Guilty conscience? Was she mixing into the business of running down the missing man? There had been a mischievous challenge in her "Good night, Mr. Merton."

Back in the library he sank into his aunt's favorite chair, lighted a cigarette and stared at the glowing logs above the bed of red and gray ashes. The suspicion that Annie was implicated in the presence of the unknown man in the library had assumed immense importance. Had she hidden him somewhere? In between business appointments, during the afternoon, he had planned a campaign. The maid, if she were going to the wounded man, wouldn't leave the house until she was sure everyone was asleep, which, in this establishment where early hours were the rule, would be between eleven and twelve. He would be where he could watch the door of the servants' cottage at that time.

"Oh Mr. Greg, Mr. Greg!" The butler sent his hushed voice ahead of him as he hurried forward. The man's excitement brought Merton to his feet.

"What is it, Buff? What has happened?"

"It's one of the men from our garage, sir. He said to tell you that a man with a bullet wound in his shoulder has been reported to be at a cottage just outside the village. It may be our burglar, sir."

"A man from The Castle garage? How long has he been employed here?"

"I O.K.ed him for the job last September, Mr. Greg."

"Where is he? Bring him in. I want his story first hand."

"He went away. He acted kind of frightened. Perhaps he was afraid of reprisals in case it was discovered he had squealed."

"You seem to have all the gangster terms at the end of your tongue, Buff."

The butler coughed behind his hand.

"I'm like many of the great men of the country, Mr. Greg—I prefer detective stories for my reading and I go to the movies."

"That does educate—in a way. Did this man tell you how to reach that cottage?"

"Yes, Mr. Greg. And to be sure we'd make no mistakes, I wrote it down." He offered a slip of white paper.

Before he glanced at it Greg looked sharply at the butler. What was behind that pasty face, with its faded eyes and drooping mouth? Could he by any chance be the "inside help" which Grant suspected? It was an absurd suspicion. Buff had been at The Castle thirty years and in all that time not so much as a silver fork had disappeared. It was nothing short of cockeyed to suspect the man. Yet—he couldn't rid himself of the feeling that there was something fishy about that address.

"When it comes to an international ring, look for links in the most unexpected places," Skid had warned. There could be no more unexpected link than Buff. He would watch him.

"Know where this cottage is?"

"Yes, Mr. Greg. It's a poor neighborhood, but quite respectable."

"How far away?"

"Not more than five miles. It won't take us long to get there."

" 'Us'? Where do you get that 'us,' Buff?"

"Of course I'm going with you, Mr. Greg. There may be danger. If he's the man the Madam hit, he won't allow himself to be taken without a fight. I'm a good shot, sir."

"That shooting might work two ways. Listen, Buff, you're not going with me. I'm going alone."

"But Mr. Greg. I've seen you grow up, you were a little boy when I came here. I couldn't let anything happen to you." His chin quivered. If this was acting, some Hollywood talent scout was missing a sure bet.

"Nothing will happen to me. Stay on the job here. If Madam Steele or Miss Bourne—or—or—any of the maids should inquire for me, I've gone to bed, get it?"

"Why should the maids inquire for you, sir?" The butler drew himself up several inches. "Why should they inquire for the master of the house at this time of night, Mr. Greg?" He was impressive in his indignation.

"While we're on the subject, Buff, get this straight— I'm not 'the master of the house.' I don't know why I dragged in the maids—just to cover everyone I presume. But you get what I mean: No one is to know that I'm not in the house. Say I've gone to bed with a raging headache, toothache, anything so long as they don't know I'm out. Understand?"

"Yes, sir. Will you want your roadster?"

"Yes, I left it in the drive."

"I'm sorry, Mr. Greg, but when the man from the garage was leaving he suggested that he put it up and I told him to take it."

"But you knew I would want the roadster to follow up that address." Had his car been sent to the garage to delay him? Was Buff in on this?

"I—I—didn't connect the two then, sir. I'm sorry. Very sorry for the mistake. I'll phone at once to have it brought round."

"No. I prefer to go for it. Is that clock striking *eleven,* so soon? I'd better get going."

"I'll bring your coat and hat, Mr. Greg."

"I have a cap and a heavy coat in my room. I'll wear those."

He was out of the library and up the stairs before the butler could protest. At his door he listened. Buff crossed the flagged floor of the hall. A door closed. He ran down. Jerked his coat from the closet. Pulled a soft cap from the pocket and drew it low on his head. Noiselessly unlocked the massive door. Squeezed through a narrow opening.

On the terrace he drew a long breath of the cold air. Moonlight made the world almost as bright as day. He had the address Buff had given him in his pocket, but he would try smoking out Annie before he went to the garage for his roadster. He still believed that was his best bet. The wounded man in the cottage five miles away smelt of red herring.

He kept in the shadow. Moved cautiously between the shrubs which banked the terrace. From the security of the purple shadow of a spruce he glanced up at the servants' cottage. Not a splinter of light. He could see footprints which trailed away from the door. Someone had gone out since the snow stopped. That couldn't have been very long ago. It had been snowing when he left the city. Not until he reached the gates of The Castle had the moon come from behind the clouds.

He went on, keeping to the trail already made. Small footprints. A woman's. He was right in his suspicion of Annie. He stopped. Someone had fallen into a hole and had thrashed around getting out of it. What was that? Looked like a piece of cloth. He picked up a roll. A strip of bandage. The maid had gone along this trail to the wounded man. He was hidden in the game house, of course. Why hadn't he thought of that before? Because it was too easy?

He plodded on in the footprints until he reached a huge pine. Someone had paced back and forth here. Waiting? Waiting for whom? For Annie? He could see the outline of the hideous bit of architecture Aunt Jane fondly called the game house against the pyrotechnics of the aurora. He stopped for a second to watch the color shift. Went on to the entrance steps. The place was lighted.

The steps cracked under his feet. Behind him a discordant scream rose to an incredibly high note, dropped, quavered into a long hiss—s—s. Splinters of ice prickled through his veins, tingled at the roots of his hair.

"I must have the jitters, if an owl hoot can set my teeth chattering," he told himself. "Evidently scared the party inside too. The light's gone out. Who's there? It's up to me to find out." He squared his shoulders:

"Get going, fella. Make it snappy or they may get you first."

XXII

HE CAUTIOUSLY opened the door. Listened. Had someone moved? It might be a mouse scuttling across the floor. He switched on the light. A window cushion on the floor. An automobile rug in a heap beside it. A bag. Had Annie been about to treat the wounded man when she heard footsteps? Where had the two gone? Not out the entrance door. They would have run into him. A clatter! The closet! He drew a revolver.

"Hands up!" He growled to disguise his voice. Yanked open the door. Skid Grant faced him. Skid, with his arm tight about Linda Bourne.

There was a split second of stunned silence. Then Grant's shout of laughter, the memory of his ridiculous, melodramatic approach, the sight of Linda encircled by that arm, sent a surge of fury through Greg's veins.

"What's so darn funny, Skid? It wouldn't have been a joke if my gun had gone off, would it? What are you doing here, Lindy? Didn't I tell you to keep out of this mess?"

"Just when did I consent to take orders from you?" she demanded as she stepped from the closet.

"Cut it! *Cut* it! Stop fighting, you two," Skid Grant commanded. "Gosh, I never saw anything so funny as your face, Greg, when you opened that door." The attempt to check another guffaw choked him. He coughed and strangled. "Quiet cuss when you're sleuthing, aren't you, Skidmore? You have a police siren beaten at its own game for noise. What are you doing here?"

"Shadowing Señor Pedro Lorillo."

"Lorillo! Here? In The Castle grounds? You said he'd gone to Brazil."

"That's what I thought. Listen, my child, and you shall hear of the evening ride—this is where I desert the classic. I went to the garage in town to get my roadster when in sneaks the smooth Brazilian. Could hardly believe my eyes. I slipped out of sight but not of hearing.

" 'I want to hire a two-seater,' says he to the boss. 'I'm going into the country. Put in plenty of rugs. It's likely to be cold before morning.' All this minus his Spanish accent.

" 'Country,' thinks Mrs. Grant's little boy, and then somehow the word linked up with what you told me had happened at The Castle. Why had he given out that he had gone to Brazil when he hadn't? It was a crazy hunch but I followed it—and Lorillo's car. Lost it—the car, not the hunch—as we entered the village which we pass through before we reach The Castle. Sure that he was making a strategic detour, I came on. Parked on a dark side of the road outside the gates and stole into the grounds. Remembered the game house and came here. No footprints or tire tracks to provide a clue. If a person or persons had left the place it must have been before the snow stopped. I skulked around the outside. There were slits of light beneath the shades. Made a lot of noise tramping up the steps and into this big room."

"What did you find?"

"The seat and the rug on the floor as you see them now. Heard footsteps approaching on horseback—"

"Skip it. Tell this straight."

"All right, all right. Something tells me you don't appreciate the light touch, my boy. Where was I?"

"Seat and rug on the floor and footsteps approaching on horseback," Linda prompted. She swallowed a nervous giggle as Greg glared at her.

"I doused the light pronto and crept under the rug. Sez I to myself, 'X marks the spot where the body was found. Someone's coming for it. This is my chance to find out who.'"

"Who was it?" Greg demanded.

"'Lovely Lindy,' herself. Now may I tell my story?"

Quickly she told why she had promised to meet Annie at the tall pine and of what had followed.

"Why didn't you tell me all this before you went upstairs?" Greg Merton's face was colorless. "Didn't you know that you were being dragged into a criminal net?"

"I had a suspicion that all was not sweetness and light but I gave Annie the benefit of the doubt until I was sure. What do we do now?"

"Go back to the house, quick. Skid, we'll put you up for the night."

"Thanks. I'll pick up Lorillo's trail in the morning. I am more than ever convinced he's mixed up in this. Never did believe he hailed from Brazil—'where the orchids come from.' If it was his scout whom Madam Steele winged you'll all be able to sleep easy for some time to come. They won't try it again until they think this episode has been forgotten. Let's push off."

It was a silent trio which tramped back through the snow. Linda was wondering what had happened to Annie and her Cline. Greg was seething with impatience to get her safely into the house before he told Skid of the injured man in the cottage.

"Come into the kitchen and I'll make hot chocolate," Linda whispered as they entered the hall at The Castle.

Greg shook his head. Put a finger to his lips to ensure silence. Placed his hands on her shoulders. Steered her gently but steadily toward the stairs. For an instant she resisted, then ran up and disappeared into the upper hall.

"That's that. She's safe." The words were more a long-drawn breath of relief than a sound. "We'll drop our coats here, Skid. I've got something to tell you before we go out again. Gumshoe into the library."

They stopped halfway across the room. Madam Steele sat erect in her usual chair. She must have replenished the fire for scarlet flames leaped and licked up the great chimney, threw grotesque, dancing shadows over the amethyst satin of her tightly belted housecoat. She impatiently tapped ringless fingers on the chair arm and frowned at the two astonished men.

"What's going on?" Her keen eyes raked first the face of her nephew and then that of the man beside him. "Do you think I'm an imbecile that I don't know that there's been a lot of running in and out of the house tonight? What's it all about?"

Greg faced her from before the fire. As if to render moral support in this crisis, Grant stood beside him.

"It's about that would-be burglar you took a shot at, Duchess." Greg told the story, from Annie's talk with Linda to the climax in the game house, leaving out only the part Buff had played in it. That was too important a link to be made known at present.

"Hmp! Why didn't you go directly to the wounded man in the cottage? Who gave you the information, Gregory?"

"I can't tell you. I didn't go because I had a hunch that the information was a ruse to keep me from the game house."

"And what are you doing here, Skidmore Grant?"

"I was in this neighborhood, Madam Steele. Ran into Greg and he insisted that I should spend the night here. If I am intruding—"

"Of course you're not intruding. Don't be silly. What are you going to do next, Gregory? Isn't it thrilling?" Her dark eyes snapped with excitement. Her voice was eager.

"Break a record getting to that cottage. Skid has a plan. He has the immortal Sherlock beaten at his own game as a detective. Upstairs you go, Duchess." He caught her hand and drew her to her feet. "We ought to get started."

"I'll wait here till you come back."

"Nix." He slipped his arm under hers and led her, still protesting, toward the hall. "I don't stir from this house again till you are in your room."

"Very well. Very well." She stopped at the foot of the stairs. "I'll go if you will promise to report to me when you come back."

"I promise—if there is anything to report, Duchess."

"Here's hoping I'll be as peppy as she is when I'm old," Grant confided in a low tone as she mounted the stairs.

"A woman with a spirit like hers isn't old. She hasn't a wrinkle in her face, perhaps you've noticed." A door closed. "Come on. We'll take your roadster, Skid. Mine's at the garage. Why advertise the fact that I'm going out at this time of night?"

As the car sped toward the village in a world of moonlit magic, Greg told of his suspicion of Buff, to the accompaniment of the scrunch of tires on snow.

"What do you make of my hunch, Skid?"

"He's been with her thirty years? You're screwy."

"Perhaps, but if you had seen and heard him you might not be so sure. If we find the wounded guy at the cottage I'll believe the old boy is on the level."

"If—" Grant repeated skeptically. He stopped the roadster in a purple pool of shadow. "Look at the directions again. We're at a crossroads."

There were no lights in the story-and-a-half cottage when they reached it. It stood quite by itself in the midst of fields. The snow in the path to the front door was untrodden.

"It's empty!" Grant whispered. "I believe you are right about Buff."

The uncurtained windows of the house stared at them with blind eyes. They walked cautiously to the back which looked as if plated with silver where the moonlight struck the glass panes. A light snow didn't quite conceal tire tracks, which led through an opening where part of a fence had been removed, then stretched across a field. They were mere dark shadows but they told a story.

"The getaway must have been made while it was still snowing, between ten and eleven," Greg whispered. "But the snow on the porch has been trodden flat. Let's go in."

The unlatched door opened at a touch. Greg flashed the light from his electric torch about the small kitchen. No furniture. No sign of occupation except—Grant's eyes followed his pointing finger. Drop by slow drop, water dripped from the old-fashioned pump.

They tiptoed through two rooms where the wallpaper hung in moldy strips, creaked up the stairs. No trace of anything living, not even a mouse. The drip, drip, drip of water sounded like a ghostly rap, rap, rap, through the silent house. On the porch again they looked at the almost undistinguishable tire tracks.

"This is where we stop for the present, or are you game to follow those tracks in the roadster, Skid?" Greg's voice sounded in his own ears like a shout, the air was so clear.

"Sure, I'm game. We'll keep at this mystery till we bust it wide open. Come on."

He drove across a bumpy field. Came to a road well worn by traffic.

"Where do we go from here?"

"Hold everything!" Greg jumped out, flashed his torch on the snow. "They entered from the direction of The Castle. Did their best to obliterate their trail. Missed one betraying curve. The tracks going in the other direction are lost in the highway. No use following them. Our best bet is to find out where the car came from."

"That makes sense to me. I still have a hunch that I'll find Señor Pedro Lorillo mixed in this somewhere."

They sped along the highway. It was darker now. The moon slid down behind tall pines. Before its light vanished they saw a broad ribbon of white turning left into a heavy growth of trees.

"Look, Skid! A road! I bet we've got something there."

On his knees Greg felt for ruts. He was right. A car had passed this way. He waved to Grant. Beckoned. Swung to the running board as the roadster turned in between the trees. The road was so narrow that the car brushed pine branches which by way of retaliation spatted soft snow in their faces.

"Dark as Hades," Grant whispered. A discordant shriek like a soul in torment rose, dwindled, died away. "There's that fiendish yell again. What is it?"

"Screech owl. The thing set my hair on end when I heard it before. It makes the sinister setting of this mystery-busting job just one hundred per cent perfect."

They had run five miles when Greg exclaimed:

"I'll be darned! Do you see what I see, Skid?"

"If you're seeing something that looks like a prehistoric monster crouched to spring, I am. It's the game house."

"They must have picked up the guy Cline here before the snow stopped. This clears the butler of complicity. I'm pro-Buff, now. The tip the garage man gave him was straight goods."

"But why in thunder should he give it to him? Why should the garage man squeal, Greg?"

"We'll get at that when we get at Annie. Better park the roadster here and foot it to the house."

As they silently opened the front door and slid into the hall, Linda, in Imperial Chinese-yellow lounge coat and vermilion-satin trousers, streaked down the stairs like a flame.

"She's gone!" she whispered.

"Who's gone?" Greg demanded.

She caught his arm and Grant's. Drew the two men close.

"Annie. Bag and baggage."

XXIII

LINDA entered Ruth's living room to find it in the state of colored paper, brilliant ribbons and glittering tinsel which immediately precedes Christmas. There were packages already tied and labeled for the post, others swathed in gay wrappings; there were books and handkerchiefs, bags and scarfs on a table awaiting their turn. Ruth Brewster stopped snipping at a sheet of red paper.

"Lindy! As I'm alive. I'd given up expecting you. Thought you had hurried back to The Castle because of the snow. Ring for Libby. I told her not to bring the tea tray till I had reached the place where if I tied another ribbon I would have a nervous breakdown. I'm there."

Linda rang the bell and crossed to the window. The skyline beyond the Park was like a bespangled panorama where lighted holes pierced towers and pinnacles, where geometrical silhouettes gave shape and substance to what otherwise might seem a mythical, snowy fairyland.

"Each time I return to it, this city seems more wonderful, Ruth. If it hadn't been for your suggestion, 'There is only one common-sense move when you don't like your life. *Do* something about it,' I might still be working for Sim Cove and hating it. I did something and I'm everlastingly grateful to you for the push. I'd love to tie some of the packages."

She pulled a chair to the laden table and cut a sheet of silver paper to fit a book. Ruth paused in the act of looping red-satin ribbon into a flamboyant bow.

"It's a ticklish thing to give advice. Sometimes I wish you were still in the town and the house in which your grandfather was born."

"Wish I hadn't come to New York? You *can't* mean it. My mental horizon has had a coast-to-coast extension. At home I was smugly aware that we were First Family; here I'm nobody unless I make good. In Keith Sanders' office I came up against hard, modern, complex problems. They shredded my heart to ribbons but the experience has made me more helpful, I hope."

"You've always been helpful, Lindy."

"Helpful, perhaps, but pretty cocky. Not very understanding. And as for living with Madam Steele, that has been a liberal education in culture and the arts. Distinguished guests. People who are *doing* things. The newest books. Magazines galore. The latest records, from swing to classics. Her house is full of beautiful things. Not too full. No clutter. She's modern. Every little while she has a lot of treasures put away to be replaced by others. But with all her wealth—sometimes I'm terribly sorry for her."

"I suspect you're wasting your sympathy. She impresses me as being a woman who is a law unto herself."

"She is, but because of her immense wealth she is suspicious of everyone. If a person is nice to her, her eyes narrow, harden, as if she were preparing to repulse a touch of money. I don't wonder. Some days her mail is made up of begging letters. That's another thing I've learned: Too much money is a disillusioning thing."

"I wasn't referring to your viewpoint or your character. They have developed, all right. I don't like your friendship—I hope it is only that—with Keith Sanders."

"Why not? He's gay, charming, makes a spectacular income for so young a man and when we walk into a night club or the theater he has a headline personality. I'm not in the least in love with him, if that's what you mean. Speaking of love, I presume Greg Merton is still devoted to Hester?" She perked the loops of a green-satin bow and regarded it critically.

"They drop in here occasionally together, but I can't see symptoms of intense devotion on his part."

"Mother will see that devotion develops." Linda was ashamed of the betraying bitterness of her voice. She looked at Ruth quickly, hoping she had not noticed it. Apparently she hadn't. She appeared absorbed in the relative values of silver or gold ribbon for a package wrapped in star-sprinkled blue paper.

"Keith is coming here to drive me home." Linda reverted to the subject of her late employer. "You're unfair to him. He can be very thoughtful. He suggested the cinema outfit at The Castle, has taken the care of installing it." No need to tell Ruth that she believed it was done to make himself solid with the owner of vast real-estate holdings—the mean suspicion might be merely her hectic imagination working overtime. "Madam Steele has ordered two pictures for the holiday. He's coming for Christmas. I hope it won't spoil your day."

"Of course it won't. Because I don't want you to marry him doesn't mean that I'm allergic to him. Has that playwriting germ he had picked up before he went to the Grants' ever developed into a serious attack?"

"Haven't heard of it since. Perhaps he tried, perhaps he discovered that it isn't the 'cinch' he thought it."

"That and portrait painting! You don't have to tell *me* they're no cinch. Libby Hull is a problem. I want her to go home for the holiday. She won't. Says that there's no one there for whom she gives a tinker's darn."

"Abracadabra! Vanish your problem. Madam Steele met her here. Thinks she's a 'colorful' character. Told me this morning to invite her. She would have her meals with Buff and the maids. Will she do it?"

"Never. But it's only fair to extend the invitation. Here she is. Watch for fireworks." Liberty Hull was smiling as she entered with the tray; her black eyes snapped like jet beads reflecting the light.

"Thought I heard your voice, Lindy. Glad to see you. Mrs. Bourne phoned she and Hester would be here for tea, Ruth, so I brought extra cups."

"Goodness! Look at this room! Quick, Lindy, help clear away these ribbons and papers." Ruth opened a blond-mahogany chest. "Drop them in here. Libby, pile the packages on the end of the piano."

"That's pretty near magic," she approved as she set an enameled box from Norway back on the cleared table. "Libby, wait a minute."

"Can't. I've left the marmalade rolls toasting and the puffed-cheese crackers in the oven."

"They can wait. Madam Steele has invited you to The Castle for the holiday." Ruth swallowed twice before she explained, "As—as a sort of maid for me."

Liberty Hull's mouth tipped up at one corner.

"That means that I'll eat with the servants, I suppose. Well, my great grandfather had the intelligence to serve as Speaker of our State Legislature for eight years and I guess he handed down enough common sense to me so I'll take the chance to see life above- and below-stairs in one of them big houses, what, with one thing and another, you see pictured in the magazines. Thank Madam Steele kindly, Lindy, and tell her I'll be pleased to come." She paused on the threshold.

"Who knows but what I'll make such a good impression that I'll get a job as housekeeper. You won't be needing me, Ruth, when you and Skid Grant get married." With which exit line she vanished into the hall.

Linda stared at the crimson face of her friend.

"Ruth! Ruthetta Brewster. What did she mean? Are you and Skid, are you—?"

"Engaged? No. Now that you are in love with Keith Sanders—Skid thinks you are—" she corrected in response to Linda's protesting gesture—"he has turned to me. I'm shameless enough to admit that I've loved him since we were children. When I was convinced you didn't want him, I—I *did* something about it. New setting. New hair-do. New clothes. New interests. He began to notice me. A little make-up is a wondrous thing," she paraphrased. "I am no longer 'good-old Ruthetta' but a girl he likes to take out."

"You schemer! You female Menace! You, you *dear*." Linda's voice was breathless with excitement. "Skid Grant hasn't a chance of escape. How can he help, how could any man help loving you?"

Ruth's cheeks were warm with color. She laughed unsteadily.

"It's surprising how many to date have been immune to my lure. Seriously, Lindy, what I have told you is in strict confidence. No one is to know how brazen I am. Most especially your mother. She might ask me to step aside and give Hester a chance. I thought so," she added cryptically as a pink stain crept to Linda's hair. "She said 'Hands off' to you about Greg Merton, didn't she?"

"Ruth! How did you—"

"Libby, someday I'm going to kidnap you and put you in charge of my apartment. You're the best housekeeper in the country," announced a resonant voice in the hall.

"The old applesauce," Ruth commented in a whisper. "You'd think Liberty Hull had lived long enough not to be taken in by it but she laps it up." Almost in the same breath she greeted the man who entered. "So glad you've come, Keith."

"Thanks, Ruth. You're looking out of sight, Lindy. Country life is agreeing with you." He deposited a flower box on the table.

"Roses for my tea hostess and a gardenia for Libby." He turned to the woman who had entered with a tray of toasted marmalade rolls and puffy cream-cheese crackers. "It's your movie night, isn't it, Miss Hull?"

Her dark eyes in her long, narrow, bony face glittered with tears, her high-bridged nose twisted ludicrously.

"Why, why, Mr. Sanders, ain't you thoughtful? I never had a flower given to me before in all my life—by—by a man, I mean. What with one thing and another, I never had a beau you might call 'special.' "

"You have a flower now, Libby." Ruth handed her the box. "Put the roses in a vase for me and the gardenia in the icebox till you wear it."

"It was sweet of you to think of Libby, Keith," Linda approved as the woman left the room. "But watch your step—breach-of-promise cases have been started on less. She'll adore you." She flung a now-what-do-you-think-of-him glance at Ruth.

"I'd much rather you would adore me, but I've discovered that I can't buy you with flowers."

That was as definite as he ever had been in expressing his feeling for her, she thought.

"Or anything else. Hullo, Mother. Hester, that fur jacket and black gown of yours are as up-to-the-minute as milk wool," she approved, as Mrs. Bourne and her elder daughter entered. "Greg! Skid! Did you come with them?"

She tried to view the occupants of the modernistic room impartially. Her mother in a brown costume and a matching toque, sitting erect on the edge of a divan, could easily be mistaken for the sister of Hester whose slim figure was engulfed in a deep chair and whose eyes and lips were smiling at Keith Sanders as he stood looking down at her. Ruth was pouring tea. Skid, near the piano, was swaying to the rhythm of the dance music Greg was playing softly.

Ever since the moment twelve nights ago when she had stopped him and Skid in the hall to whisper the news that Annie and her belongings were missing, she had been waiting and hoping for a word from one of them as to what they had discovered about the man whom Madam Steele had shot. She had even given up two evening engagements thinking that Greg would appear at The Castle to tell her what clue he was following, if any. Didn't he know, didn't he care that she was anxious for the solution of the mystery? Seated at the piano now, he appeared engrossed in the soft barcarolle from the "Tales of Hoffman" flowing from the tips of his fingers.

"Oh, night of love." Jewels of sound. What did he know of love?

As if he felt her question he looked up. His eyes met hers and suddenly the room was blotted out. She saw him smiling at her with a question in his eyes. Somewhere outside an automobile horn was sounding. Inside there was low laughter, voices, tinkle of silver on china, a rippling accompaniment of music, but she heard only the pound of her heart and an astonished inner voice declaring over and over:

"I love him! I *love* him!"

The soft melody was like a irresistible tide sweeping her on. She couldn't stop those words going round and round in her mind, "I love him." The music ended with a crash of chords.

"My signature tune," he said and rose. Immediately Hester was beside him. Linda drew a deep breath as if she had emerged after a long time under water. She resisted an impulse to draw her hand across her dazed eyes.

"Keith, if we intend to reach The Castle in time for dinner we should start at once," she reminded.

"I'm ready. I'm always ready to go with you, Lindy." His look brought the color to her face. She wished now that she were not driving back with him. She had steadfastly refused his kisses, refused to permit an encircling arm. "Miss *Puritan* New England," he called her now with an edge of sarcasm in his voice. It was getting more and more difficult to hold him off.

"Good night, Mother." She fastened her short beaver jacket. "See you all tomorrow. Be sure and arrive in time for tea."

"Hester and I are depending on Greg to get us there, so give him directions," Mrs. Bourne instructed complacently.

"Sorry to revoke," Gregory Merton apologized quickly. "Can't make The Castle till later. I've got to entertain a customer at dinner, Mrs. Bourne. I've arranged with Skid to take you and Hester in his large car with Ruth."

"Greg!" Angry color rushed to Hester's face. "You can't mean that you're turning us over to *Skiddy*."

"That's the general idea."

"I won't go. I won't go at *all*."

"Hester!" reproved her mother half-heartedly. "Of course you'll go."

"Cut the kid stuff, Hester. I'm not crazy to take you, believe it or not. I had other plans. I'm doing this to oblige Greg," Skid Grant explained impatiently.

"I won't go unless I go with him, that's flat."

Linda glanced at Ruth. There was a faint suggestion of a satisfied smile upon her lips. Had she had anything to do with this sudden change of plan? Under cover of showing him the array of gaily decorated packages on the piano, she had talked earnestly to Greg for a moment before she served tea.

"I ask you, what's the matter with me?" Skid Grant's injured question broke the strained silence. "When I have a balky horse I hold a carrot in front of it and it gets going. Guess you'll have to play carrot, Greg, if we want this gal to join our Christmas party."

"Sorry, it can't be done, Mrs. Bourne."

She rose and laid her hand on his arm.

"I'm sure it can't, Gregory." She patted his arm maternally. "I know that you wouldn't break an engagement with Hester unless you were forced to."

The emphasis on the word Hester sent little chills feathering through Linda's veins. Sounded as if he had committed himself, as if he were practically engaged to her sister.

"I hope you'll not let Hester's obstinacy cheat you out of a grand holiday, Mother," she said, as evenly as she could with her emotions still in a tumult over the discovery of her real feeling toward Gregory Merton. Whom was he taking to dinner tomorrow?

"Oh, I shall go." For once Mrs. Bourne opposed her adored daughter. "What time shall I be ready, Skid?"

"Come on, Hester," Keith Sanders interrupted before Grant could answer. "Of course I haven't Merton's what-have-you, but why not let me pinch hit for him? I'm going alone. Drive up with me, will you?"

The smile which dispelled the sulkiness of her face was like the sun shining through thunderheads.

"I'd love it," she said sweetly. "You're a dear to think of suggesting it."

"Now that a peace pact has been signed and sealed suppose we start, Keith." Linda wondered if the edge in her voice would be construed by the others to mean jealousy. "See you all tomorrow."

Gregory Merton crossed the room and held out his hand. "*Au revoir,* Lovely Lindy."

She wanted to be caught in his arms, to feel his mouth crushing hers. In her mind she was crying out to him, "Greg! Greg! Come with me now! I love you!" and aloud she was saying gaily:

"Happy evening—tomorrow, Mr. Merton."

XXIV

ON CHRISTMAS EVE a sliver of gilt moon coasted down the purple-velvet sky and disappeared. The river which had been a shining silver ribbon darkened to polished gun metal and reflected the trembling stars. Port and starboard lights on passing boats sparkled like broken rubies and emeralds on its rippling surface. Tall rows of elms and solitary massive oaks moved skeleton arms in a cold wind. Linda wished she could see the great house from the outside. Every window was candlelighted and holly-wreathed.

She pulled the heavy blue-damask hangings in place and looked at the colorful group by the fire at the end of the long library. For some inexplicable reason she had a sudden, frightened sense that she didn't want time to go on, that she must seize it and hold it back.

Why? Why should she feel apprehensive about persons who had apparently banished their problems and perplexities and were definitely in holiday mood? Even her mother in shimmering silver lamé, usually as inarticulate as a dummy model, was laughing as she looked up at Judge Reynolds, buggy of chin and ox-eyed, who appeared amorous rather than judicial as he leaned on the back of her chair. Janet Colton's gold frock, Hester's turquoise-blue glinting with silver paillettes, Ruth's orchid velvet and Madam Steele's amethyst satin added rich variety to the kaleidoscope of color which shifted with dramatic effect against the black-and-white of the four men.

Four. The Judge, Keith Sanders, Bill Colton and Skid. Where was Greg? Who was the customer he was entertaining at dinner? Was it a girl?

"Come away from the window, Lindy. You look like a chilly white ghost against the dark background. Gives me a creepy fear that you may vanish into thin air." Keith Sanders' voice banished the heaviness of her spirit.

"Does a ghost have gold stars on its frock or whatever the white thing is it wears?"

"It might have collected a few drifting through space. Where were you when Hester and I arrived this afternoon? I expected you would be on the terrace waving a spray of mistletoe to encourage an affectionate greeting."

"You have such original ideas, Mr. Sanders—Personal Service is missing a sure bet by not engaging you. To return to practical matters, sorry I wasn't on hand to welcome you—with or without mistletoe—I was finishing tying up packages for Madam Steele when Buff told me you had arrived. She showed me her jewels this afternoon. My goo-goo eyes haven't yet returned to their normal size. The diamonds, rubies, emeralds and what-have-you, arranged in flat trays are as unbelievably sumptuous as the exhibits in the house of Jewels at the Fair. Remember, when I showed you my sketch of the second floor of this house, that I described two red-lacquer cabinets against the walls of the solarium? They hold the treasure."

"I do. I remember, also, that when I inquired for what they were used you replied snootily, 'I didn't consider it my—your business.' "

"It wasn't, Keith, and something tells me I shouldn't have told you now that they hold the jewels. What's so funny about that?"

"I laughed at your superactive conscience, Miss New England. Don't you realize that the contents of those lacquer cabinets is no more a secret than is the location of the gold the U.S. has cached in Kentucky? Some towns have their Stone Face, their Continental Tavern, or their Biggest Manufacturing Plant in the State to boast about; this has

Madam Steele's jewels. I heard of them the first time I stopped at the village garage. It's the ninth wonder of the world that they haven't been stolen long before this."

"Thanks a million for relieving my mind. I would hate to betray a confidence." She thought of Greg Merton's belief that she had repeated his sister's news about the sale of The Castle. Why think of it? That hadn't been a confidence. It had been a conversation and she *hadn't* repeated it. "Now that my conscience has been polished till it shines, let's join the others," she suggested lightly.

"Mewry Chwirstmas," a high childish voice shouted.

Startled, the group by the fire turned to watch the sturdy little figure in a one-piece nightie approaching. His short yellow curls were tousled; his eyes were like rounds of sapphire sky at its clearest; his cheeks were as rosy as the cheeks of a Delicious apple; his teeth between parted lips were as softly white as his mother's pearls. Under one arm he clutched a timeworn Teddy bear. From the other hand trailed a rope of green leaves. He laughed gleefully.

"I guess I su'pwized you, I guess."

"You guessed right, young Mr. Colton." Janet caught him in her arms. Snuggled her nose into his neck till he squirmed and giggled. "Now, we'll surprise you. Bill, carry him back to bed, will you?"

"Just a minute, William. Let him come to me," Madam Steele held out her hand. "Come here, Billy Boy."

He leaned against her knee and smiled enchantingly up into the stern face.

"Where are dose big dogs, Aunt Jane."

"Shut up in the kennel. Cash and Carry go to bed early. They're sleepyheads. Are you happy tonight?"

The child's dark brows drew together in a puzzled frown.

"What's happy?"

"Oh, liking to be where you are and—and the people you're with and—"

"I know. I *know*." He wriggled with eagerness. "It's what nurse an' Libby were talking about. Nurse said she 'posed dat Miss Lindy would make Mr. Sanders happy tonight and Libby said dat 'twas time she made somebody happy, she'd kep' twee fellas danglin', long enough. What's danglin'?"

His imitation of the voices of the nurse and Libby Hull, which had been perfect, set Linda's face on fire, started a ripple of laughter. Bill Colton seized his son.

"That's enough from you, young man. I can see your finish. You'll be one of those chaps who do 'imitations' at night clubs. Say good night."

With an arm about his father's neck, with the bear clutched under the other, the rope of green trailing from his hand, young Bill looked appealingly at Janet.

"Comin' to tuck me in, Muvver?" he cajoled.

"Of course I am, ducky," she said with a break in her voice.

Madam Steele's eyes followed them, came back after they left the room.

"I always think of the Holy Family when I see Mother, Father and Child together." She cleared her throat. "Ring for Buff to set out the card tables, Linda."

Keith Sanders joned Linda as she crossed the room:

"Who are the three 'fellas' you're keeping dangling, Lindy? I thought I was the only one with whom you stepped out now."

The autocratic demand, his assumption that she had given up all other men friends for him, set off a little flare of anger which she camouflaged with a laugh.

"Really, Keith, you're not the only man in my life. Buff, the card tables, please." She was glad that the entrance of the butler prevented Keith's reply. Buff waited till Sanders had stalked away before he confided in a voice more suited to a conspirator than a butler:

"Mr. Greg phoned that no one was to wait up for him, Miss. Said he wouldn't get here till midnight. Will you tell the Madam, please? She might be prowling when he comes in and shoot at him. You know her little ways, Miss."

"Yes. I know her little ways, Buff, I'll tell her."

She returned to the group by the fire. Madam Steele was talking while she impatiently tapped a book on the small table beside her chair.

"I liked the story very much indeed. The author has written to entertain, not to educate. That's what I want when I pick up a novel in the middle of a sleepless night."

Mrs. Bourne turned the pages and nodded approval.

"It looks entertaining. I'm like Alice in Wonderland. I like plenty of conversation. Is it a love story?"

"Yes. I like them. They are based on an invincible truth. The world may be convulsed with war and hate; the earth may tremble from the onward march of army tanks and heavy guns; our economic caldron may boil violently; empires may rise and fall, yet there is always love. Love between husband and wife, between parent and child, between friends, between boy and girl, love for the Church. There's been such a lot said about the modern angle for the writing of the so-called love interest that I've been doing a little research. I can't see that the expression of a lover's eyes, or the caressing inflection of his voice, is an iota more casual than when I was young. The way of depicting it in print may have changed, but the way of a man with a maid hasn't."

"Lady, you've said it," Skid Grant agreed. "The modern method can't give the old-fashioned one any serious competition. So help me, though, now that you have gone in for research and have the human heart under your microscope, I'll have to watch my eyes, Duchess."

Linda caught his swift glance at Ruth, saw her color rise in response. Skid and Ruth would be a perfect combination; she would bring out the best in him and he would add gaiety to her life, which had been rather colorless.

"One can see a lot of the game of Life from the sidelines, Skidmore. William, we've been waiting for you," Madam Steele announced as Colton and his wife entered the room. "I want you to play with me."

"Where's your white-haired boy, Greg, Aunt Jane? You scorn me as a rummy partner when he's around."

"Don't be foolish, William. Where is Gregory? Isn't it time for him, Linda?"

Linda delivered the message.

Buff told me to warn you not to prowl tonight with your trusty gun."

"Does she prowl? With a gun?"

"One might think from your startled voice that you

did some midnight prowling yourself, Sanders." Skid Grant's voice was edged with suggestion.

"Not while I'm in this house. When I'm once in my room tonight I'll not leave it. I wouldn't dare. With the two dozen doors in the upper hall identical, I'd be afraid I would stumble into the wrong room."

"You're right, Mr. Sanders. I've often thought they should be numbered," Madam Steele agreed with surprising affability, "but numbers smack so of an hotel. I couldn't do it."

"The planets in their stations list'ning stood"—how often she had heard her father quote that lovely bit from "Paradise Lost," Linda thought, as from her bed at midnight she watched the sector of star-powdered sky she could see through the open window.

Listening to what? Certainly not to the perplexities and heart throbs of an atom like herself. Throbs was too tame a word to describe her feelings when she thought of Greg Merton. "There is always love," Madam Steele had said. Did it always bring this unbearable heartache with it? She had said, also, that the way of a man with a maid had not changed. She remembered Keith's voice when he had said, "I'd much rather you would adore me." She had sensed a lack in it, had attributed the feeling to her old-fashioned ideas of what love should be. After all, perhaps it wasn't love he felt for her. She remembered Greg's gruff voice as he had declared that afternoon at the Inn:

"I wanted you, all right. But not for a secretary."

After that, all had gone smash between them. Did he still believe she was here to influence Madam Steele in Keith's favor? Where was he now? The bells. The carillon Madam Steele had presented to the village church as a War Memorial was chiming on this Christmas eve:

"It came upon a midnight clear."

She listened with tear-wet eyes until the final rich chord died away. How still the world seemed after it. Not a sound outside or in. What was that? The boudoir door opening. It couldn't be—

If only her heart wouldn't pound so deafeningly. If

she couldn't hear she could see, see a faint light in the oth
er room. Was it Madam Steele's burglar back again?

Holding her breath in fear of making a sound, she
swung her feet to the floor and waited. If someone were
looking for jewelry he would have the setback of his life
when he saw her collection of rhinestones. The light went
out. Silence. Was the intruder waiting to be sure he had not
been heard?

Straining her ears, clamping her lips between her teeth
to steady them, inch by cautious inch she opened the draw
er of the bedside table, drew out a revolver. In bare feet
she stole to the threshold. She could see a dark shape mov
ing toward the door. The sight drained her of fear. She
touched an electric switch. Light flooded the room. The fig
ure, back to her, stiffened.

"Did you knock? It's still being done, you know," she
suggested jauntily. The man wheeled.

"Keith! Keith!" she whispered incredulously.

XXV

THE SUDDEN brilliance revealed the startled whiteness
of the man's face; set agleam the silver ribbon around Lin
da's hair, the rosy polish of the nails on her bare feet; light
ed the blue of her satin pajamas, picked out the steel of the
revolver she had dropped to the floor.

"Keith!" she whispered. *"Keith!"*

The color swept back to his face. He set his shoulders
with a swagger, chuckled, whispered:

"Good lord, Linda, you frightened me out of a year's
growth. I thought I was in my own room, discovered my
mistake and was pussyfooting out when you flashed that
light. I told them downstairs I bet I'd mistake the door
didn't I? And here I am."

"Is it your custom to enter a room, when you're a
guest, with an electric torch?"

"Never go without one, anywhere." He laid his hand

on her shoulder. "You're a knockout in that rig and you were lovely enough before to set a man crazy."

She shook off his hand. His lips were smiling but his eyes were rapier keen.

"Cut out the compliments, Keith. Leave the room at —" Her voice caught in her throat as through the open window in the bedroom drifted the scrunch of feet on snow. Greg! Greg arriving! Suppose he met Keith coming out of her room? "At once!" The final word was a whisper. "Get out! Quick!"

"And if I don't get out?" He smiled with the superb assurance which always maddened her.

"Then I will." She opened the door. Someone was crossing the flagged floor downstairs, someone stepping lightly. Greg! She drew back quickly and closed it.

"Wait!" she whispered. "Don't go yet."

"But now I want to go." His smile was sardonic. He put his hand over hers on the knob, slipped out and closed the door behind him. Ear close against the keyhole Linda heard him say in a low tone:

"Confound it! I've done it, Merton."

"Done *what?*"

"Blundered into the wrong room. I don't know whose. Fortunately I didn't wake the occupant."

"If I find in the morning you've been lying, Sanders, I'll break every bone in your body. Get going. I'll wait here to be sure you make no mistake in the room this time."

"You're screwy, Merton. Had too much to drink, what? Oh, I'm going."

"Make it quick!"

Linda hadn't known that whispered words could be so savage. Greg knew it was her room into which Keith had "blundered." Would he hear if she moved? Could he see the light?

She tiptoed to the revolver, swept it up. Switched out the light. Crept into bed and shut her eyes. Held her breath. Listened. Heard only the snap of frosty twigs, the hiss of a meteor as it shot across the heavens. What was Greg thinking? That Keith had been here at her invitation? He couldn't, he wouldn't believe that, he—

A tap at the boudoir door. Who would knock at this time of night? No one. Her imagination had seized the bit in its teeth. Not surprising that the last few minutes had set it galloping. The sound again. Could it be Greg? He had said he would stand at the door till Keith found his own room. Did he expect her to answer? She wouldn't. She was asleep. If questions were asked in the morning she would be wide-eyed with surprise, she had slept like a top all night. Why not, had she missed some excitement? That was her story. She wouldn't be questioned by anyone but Greg. He was the only person—

"Linda. *Linda!*" The low call came from the boudoir. He was there. Thank heaven, the revolver was tucked under her pillow. No danger of its going off. She never had loaded it. She was too afraid of the darn thing.

"Lindy." The voice came from the threshold. She lay motionless. Breathed softly. One uncovered foot was freezing in the cold air blowing in from the window, but she didn't dare move it. Someone looked down at her. She heard a hard-drawn breath. An insane urge to laugh possessed her. Good heavens, had her lips twitched?

The down puff was pulled over her bare foot.

"Good night my—" the husky voice broke abruptly.

From under her lashes she saw a figure on the threshold of the boudoir. Blackout. A door closed. Exit Mr. Gregory Merton.

She sat up. Snapped on the bedside light. Lived over the instant when Keith Sanders had faced her in the next room. Of course he had entered by mistake. There was no other believable explanation. That he had come because she was there was inconceivable. He wasn't that kind. She wouldn't have put it past fat Sim Cove—her inner self had shrunk away from him whenever he came near—but she never had had that feeling about Keith Sanders, never until he laid his hand on her shoulder a few minutes ago—then her heart had gone dead with fright. What reason could he have had for entering her room if he hadn't mistaken the door?

The question popped up at intervals during a day packed with hilarity, outdoor sports—a day all green and white and turquoise outside, all glitter and tinsel, all spruce-scented and poinsettia-crimson inside.

It came again as she ran up the broad stairs to shed her snowy ski suit before dinner. How could a man as keen

as Keith Sanders make a mistake in the door? She entered
her lighted room. Who was the woman by the desk? It
wasn't—It was—

"Libby! *What* have you done to yourself?" Surprise
doubled her knees. She sank into a chair. "You've—had a
haircut and a *permanent*," she accused, as she took in the
import of the plastered waves and flat pepper-and-salt
curls. "You've spoiled yourself."

"What do you mean 'spoiled,' Lindy Bourne?" Miss
Hull complacently regarded her changed appearance in the
mirror. "That's a great way to talk when, what with one
thing and another, I spent hours waiting in a hairdressing
place that was open last evening!" She patted the stiff
curls. "I guess it will look a little more natural when it
wears soft, but I paid twenty dollars for it and I didn't dare
risk combing it out."

"Twenty dollars! Spendthrift. They cheated you."

"Well, if I've been cheated I ain't going to let it spoil
my good time. Ruthetta's dressed. She sent me to help you.
I guess you earn your pay, Lindy. You 'bout run this big
house, don't you? Here, let me pull them wet boots off."

Linda relaxed in the deep chair. Beneath her brusque-
ness, Libby was a dear. She was tired. She hadn't slept last
night and the day had been strenuous, with a tree for
young Mr. Colton after breakfast, one for the servants after
luncheon and the "Snow White" picture for the child and
the maids in the afternoon. The film operator was staying
over to show "Union Pacific," which was to follow the
grown-up tree after dinner.

"The housekeeper and I run it under Madam Steele's
direction. She has her hand on every switch in this house.
Start my bath, will you, like a dear?"

"Sure."

Liberty Hull returned from the dressing room armed
with brushes. "Sit down, Lindy. I'll brush your hair. You
look kinder tuckered out."

"Tuckered!" Linda sank into a chair before the mirror in the bedroom. "I'm all in. Glad you've having such a
grand holiday, Libby. What have you been doing?" Not
that she really cared, but conversation kept her from repeating mentally Greg's cool "Good morning, Linda," at
breakfast, kept her from seeing him skiing with Hester,

skating with Hester, dancing to radio music with Hester, kept her from remembering her mother's complacent smile as she looked on.

"Did I pull?"

She shook her head in answer to Libby's concerned eyes in the mirror. Had she winced at memories?

"What with one thing and another I've been doing a little of everything," Miss Hull answered her question complacently. "Made the hard sauce for the plum puddings. Would you believe it, Mr. Buff whispered to me that Madam Steele said the cook's always made her think of the sand pies she used to make as a child." She bridled with pride. "Mine was as smooth as whipped cream."

"I know your sauce, Libby. It's a dream. What else did you do?" The woman's voice was soothing. While it flowed on she couldn't think.

"I helped Mr. Greg and Mr. Buff hang the mistletoe and—"

"Where, Libby?"

"Sit down and face the mirror again. How can I brush your hair if you go to twistin'? I promised I wouldn't tell. But there's lots of it an' in the most unexpected places too. You watch out if you don't want to get kissed—by the wrong person."

"Perhaps I don't want to be kissed by anyone."

"Tell that to the Marines, Lindy Bourne. I *will* say, though, it's high time you made up your mind as to Mr. Right. There! Your hair shines like a burnished copper saucepan. What dress you goin' to wear?" Her voice came from the depths of the wardrobe.

"The gold-net skirt and the scarlet jacket. It looks Christmasy. Toss me the gold sandals." The crystal clock on the dressing case chimed. "Glory, I'll be late. Get out the rhinestone and pearl clips from the Chinese box in the other room will you, Libby, while I'm taking my tub?" She disappeared into the dressing room and plunged into a bubble bath.

"My, ain't you got a lot of pretty jewelry?" Libby pitched her voice to carry. "I guess these are them clips you want. Will you wear any bracelets? Sakes alive, haven't you got a lot of 'em. Why, come in, Mrs. Colton. Lindy's in the tub. Shall I tell her . . ."

Linda heard the murmur of Janet's voice. Then the door closing.

"Libby, what did Mrs. Colton want?" she called.

"She jest come in to ask if you had an extra Christmas tag she needed for a package. I gave her one on your desk. I must have looked like the Queen of Sheba with my hands just dripping rhinestone bracelets. They're awful pretty. I guess what with one thing an' another, Mrs. Colton ain't very well. I hear her husband's kind of a philanderer. Come to think of it, perhaps 'tain't that. I wouldn't be surprised if there was another baby comin' to town. Kinder looks that way. She was white as a ghost when she went out. You'd better hop out of the tub if you calculate to be ready for dinner, Lindy."

"I'm out. It was marvelous. I'm fresh as a daisy. On top of the world.

> " 'The inner side of every cloud is bright and shining,
>   Therefore I turn my clouds about
>   And always wear them inside out,
>   To show the lining.' "

She laughed as she finished chanting the verse.

"That was Dad's philosophy of life, Libby, though Doctor Oliver Wendell Holmes thought of it first. I've given my silver lining an extra rub and now it's bright side out."

"Your father was a fine man, Lindy. High-hearted like you. I remember once . . . Someone's knocking. I'll go see who 'tis."

"She's dressing. You can't see her now," Libby protested at the door of the boudoir.

"Who says I can't see her? You're sure putting on airs in this house, Miss Hull." Maggie's face was redder than usual, and that was red enough. Her nose wrinkled with disdain as she brushed by and saw Linda in the room beyond.

"Oh, there you are, Miss Bourne. Please may I speak to you private? It's something terrible important."

"Come in here. Close the door." Linda paused in the act of drawing on a gossamer stocking. "What is it, Maggie?" The maid looked to right and left and behind her.

"It's my sister. It's Annie, Miss," she whispered.

"*Annie!* Has she come back?" Maggie nodded. Her eyes popped like a Boston Bull's. "Does anyone know she's here?"

"Nobody but me, Miss. She's in my room. She's been hidin' in the woods since noon, waitin' fer it to get dark. Every one of us maids is going to a ball in the village as soon as we get through clearin' up dinner—we've been talkin' of it for weeks—so 'twill be safe enough for Annie to come out then."

"Did anyone—a man, come with her?"

"Do you mean that Cline fella? I always had the feelin' that he was a bad egg, but Annie was mushy about him. She sneaked him into this house one day when the Madam was away, she said he'd never seen the inside of a big house and would like to just once. She didn't count on his having a camera and takin' pictures. She was scared, I guess, made him promise he'd never let on he had 'em."

"When was that?"

"Now you're scared. It was a couple of months ago. Didn't amount to nothing. She came alone today. Says she's got to see you. It's a matter of life an' death. An' will you meet her somewhere private soon's you can after dinner?"

"*Private!*"

"Yes, Miss. She says 'twon't be safe for either of you if you're seen together." She wrung her hands. "I'm scared for her, an' for you, Miss."

Not safe. Had Annie brought news of Cline? How had he used those snapshots? She must talk with her. Where? She had it. She opened the drawer of the green-lacquer chiffonier.

"Come here, Maggie," she whispered. "Give Annie this key. Tell her I'll meet her in the room on the third floor where she helped me with the envelopes. Tell her to leave the key in the door to the stairway. I'll slip away while the picture is being shown in the billiard room. I won't be missed in the dark. I may be late but I'll get there."

"Don't fail her, Miss. I'd stay an' help, but she said that would be a giveaway. She acted kind of wildlike. Muttered something 'bout ten o'clock. Said somethin' terrible would happen if you didn't come 'fore then."

XXVI

THEY were all in the long drawing room, the room with the pale-green Louis XIV furniture, the white-and-gold and mirror-paneled walls, and the yellow-damask hangings. A massive spruce towered at one end. It shook out spicy scent and a melodic tinkle with every current of air, glittered with silver tinsel and shining balls, twinkled with a hundred lights in every tint and shade of the color spectrum. From the radio poured the music of woodwinds and shimmering, brilliant, singing strings in the rhythm of a Strauss waltz. Keith Sanders looked down at Linda as they danced. His arm about her tightened.

"Come out of your dream. You appear to be in a state of suspended animation, Lindy."

Just as if his midnight entrance into her room hadn't contributed to her preoccupation. That and planning to steal away without being missed to meet Annie in the storeroom were running her mind ragged.

"How can I help feeling that this lavish Christmas must be a dream?" she countered lightly. "It's as unbelievable as Cinderella and the Pumpkin Coach. Cast your eye on this gorgeous thing, then pinch me that I may be sure I'm really seeing it."

They stopped dancing near the tree. She held out her right hand. On the third finger sparkled the diamond setting of an emerald ring which extended from second to third joint. Sanders whistled under his breath.

"Our hostess certainly took the lock off her jewel box tonight. Gave each one of her women guests a sample, didn't she?"

"Yes. There's no reason why she shouldn't have given that pair of diamond daisy pins, with the yellow-diamond centers, to Janet—she's a relation—but to count Ruth, my family, and me in the jewel shower is unbelievable. It's like an Arabian Nights' tale. It was too much for us to accept but had we protested it would have spoiled her Christmas."

"Sounds kind of screwy to me."

"Screwy! Don't you recognize extraordinary thought-fulness when you see it, Keith? She said she wanted to see her treasures worn and enjoyed while she was alive. This is my dream ring. It is the first piece of real jewelry I ever owned."

"When you come to think of it why shouldn't she distribute them? She has plenty more. According to your say-so, a diamond mine in South Africa is a piker in comparison to what she has stored in those lacquer cabinets upstairs. Look here—" his voice had changed abruptly from amusement to concern—"you haven't told anyone I blundered into your room last night, have you?"

Linda's eyes went past him, followed Bill Colton and Hester, Greg and Ruth, Skid and Janet as they danced. Judge Reynolds and her mother were doing the polka which at long last had come into fashion again. How soon could she meet Annie?

"You haven't, have you?" he persisted.

Her attention came back to him. "Of course I haven't."

"You wouldn't try to fool me, would you?" His hand gripped her wrist, his eyes were hard as blue rock.

"*I* fool *you!* It just couldn't be done." She freed her hand. "Is it likely I would broadcast a mistake like that? Besides, I've had too many things of real importance to think of today. We're not being very polite to our hostess, Keith. She is sitting by herself, looking like a queen in white velvet and those gorgeous rubies, but living over the tragic past, I judge by the ironic line of her mouth, while the rest of us are having fun. Let's get the picture started. She'll adore this one. 'Union Pacific' is old but she asked for it because her grandfather was a railroad builder. I must speak to Buff about the snack she wants served after it. Every servant on the estate but he—he preferred to see the picture—has gone to a dance in the village."

"Wish you and I were going. It's one night in a million." He pushed back the yellow-damask hangings and un-locked the long French window near which they were standing. Opened it wide. "Look! Let's you and I beat it, go for a ride. I've got something special to say to you. I'll never get a chance in this mob."

For the length of a lightning flash Linda hesitated.

Why not? If she went, she wouldn't suffer the intolerable hurt of Greg's devotion to Hester, she wouldn't have to hear Annie's sob-story about her boy friend. "Quitter!" she flouted herself and drew a deep breath of the cold, clear air.

"It's perfect. The world glitters like a frosted Christmas card. Perfect as it is, I can't desert the party. I must go at once and order the snack. My word, as if we could eat again after that dinner."

"How long will it take?" He caught her hand as she started to leave him. She laughed and twisted free.

"I've never measured the distance between here and the butler's pantry in time, but I'll be in the front row for the picture. Hunt up the operator, please. Close the window and draw the hangings before you go. Madam Steele believes that uncovered lighted windows attract trouble."

"What you say goes. You *are* a movie fan, you're fairly jittery with excitement. Don't worry. I won't start the picture till you and Buff come in."

"The show will be on in a few minutes," Linda encouraged Madam Steele as she passed. On the threshold of the hall a hand with a green signet ring gripped her shoulder. So far she had successfully evaded lingering under the bunch of mistletoe hung above it. The color flew to her face as she looked up and met Greg Merton's determined eyes. Much as she wanted him to kiss her, she didn't want it this way. He shook his head, glanced up briefly.

"No. It isn't what you think it is. I've got to talk to you. Come to the library."

"Can't now. I must find Buff."

"Not yet. Come on before the others notice us. Make it snappy."

"Mr. Merton in the Dictator mood," she mocked, before she crossed the flagged hall with him. Would she ever get to Annie? Her breath caught as Maggie's words echoed through her mind.

"Don't fail her, Miss. She acted kind of wildlike. Muttered something about ten o'clock. Said something terrible would happen if you didn't come before then." The clock was striking nine-thirty now.

"What's the matter?" Greg Merton demanded as they

reached the fireplace end of the library. "You act as if you thought I was going to beat you?"

"Don't be absurd. What have you to say to me? Hurry! Keith has gone to get the picture started. I don't want to miss a footage of that and I must see Buff first." He hadn't touched her but she felt as if she were being held by steel chains.

"You'll get there, but before you go, you'll answer a question. Sanders came out of your room last night. He *said* he went in thinking it was his. Did you know he was there?"

His face was white. His eyes burned straight down into her pounding heart. What should she say? If she admitted that she had, he might think she had asked Keith to come. If only they were good friends, if only he didn't think she was a double-crosser, she could tell him the truth and they would laugh about it. He wouldn't believe her. A storm of emotion was gathering within her, rising, rising, until her heart and mind were in a tumult. She shook her head slowly, speechless.

"Look at me. You can't?" His voice was rough with anger. "All right, you did know he was there. It seems I'm speaking out of turn, again. That saves him from getting the licking of his life. If it was okay with you it's nothing to me. That's all."

He stalked down the long room. She held out her hand, opened her lips to cry out the truth to him, shut them hard. What difference did it really make to him except that he thought now he had one more proof that she was a detestable person? Would her heart ever stop aching after this?

The butler wasn't in the pantry. She discovered him at last in the drawing room, straightening the hangings at the window from which she and Keith had looked out. What an old fusser he was. He'd doubtless have a nervous breakdown if the damask didn't fall in straight folds. She delivered the message.

"That's all about the supper, Buff. Come quickly. Mr. Sanders is holding up the picture for us."

Their entrance into the billiard room was the signal for the lights to go out. Keith must have been watching for them. She sat on the edge of her chair while the cast of actors was being shown on the screen. Waited impatiently through the first two scenes. Now was her chance to get away without being seen. Ten o'clock, Annie had set the zero hour. Zero hour for what?"

Stealthily, soundlessly as a ghost, she reached the door that shut off the stairs to the third floor. The key was in the lock. Annie was waiting for her. A chill shivered through her veins. What would she hear? Why wouldn't it be safe for the maid or herself if they were seen together?

"Annie? Annie?" she whispered. She didn't dare switch on the electricity for fear the light would be seen outside.

"Here I am, Miss. Near the old chest by the window."

"What has happened? Tell me. Quick!" Even as she asked the question she knew with blinding suddenness that something dreadfully wrong threatened.

"Oh, Miss Linda, I had to come! A couple of guys took Cline away that night you were to meet me at the game house and me with them. He'd told me to bring my clothes, that I couldn't ever go back to the Madam. When I found what kind of company he was keepin' I was scared stiff. They took him into the hospital and I beat it and hid. I saw him on the quiet last night. If they find me here they'll . . ." The dusk caught up her hoarse whisper and sent it echoing from corner to eerie corner. Sobs shook her, deep smothered sobs, terrible to hear.

Linda gripped her emotions tight. No time to be frightened. No time to imagine. The faint sounds of yells, whistles and shots rose from below. The picture was getting into its stride. Luckily it was a long one.

"Annie," she urged close to the girl's ear. "Tell me what this means. Who will follow you?"

"Cline's pals and Cline's boss, if they find out he told, Miss. He's terrible sick in the hospital an' scared to die with this sin on him. It was planned weeks ago."

Linda strangled an urge to scream with impotence. The church bells were chiming the three quarters. Only fifteen minutes till ten o'clock. Danger was creeping toward them.

"Stop sniveling, Annie, or I'll go down and tell Madam Steele you're here. I'll shout, 'Come and get her!'"

"You wouldn't do that, Miss?" Annie's voice was horrified.

"I would and a lot more. Quick. Tell me or I'll go—"

"Don't! Don't! I'll tell . . ." She whispered her information, stopping between every few words to listen. Linda shut her teeth hard into her lips. She mustn't let the girl know she was terrified.

"At ten! It is almost ten now."

"Listen!" Annie's fingers bit into her arm. They crouched side by side, ears strained. Came the click of a key in a lock.

"Someone saw us come. We're locked in. We can't help now, Miss." The girl's shudder made Linda fighting mad.

"Oh, yes we can. I won't stay here and let a lot of crooks harm my relatives and friends." Brave words but it was action, not words needed now. At ten it would happen. The human brain was capable of holding three billion separate ideas and she couldn't rake up one that would help. What could she do? As clearly as if it had been radioed she heard Madam Steele's voice:

"What quality is it in some persons which keeps them hanging on in a desperate situation until somehow, in some miraculous way, they get out of it? What is that something which won't let them give up? That nine times out of ten pulls them through?"

Had she that intangible something? She had been handed the chance of her life to find out. Her blood which had been chilled rushed through her veins in a warm tide. She was angry enough to take chances, frightened enough to be shaky, determined enough to carry on.

"I'll crawl through the window to the fire escape and go down that way, Annie."

"You can't, Miss. It'll be icy. You'll slip."

"Stop crying and help. People don't slip when something *has* to be done."

"But, Miss, if you fall?"

"I *won't* fall. Stay here. I'll send someone to let you out if I make it. I must make it. Quick. Help push up the window. It's frozen! Darn! Push! *Push!* Only a few minutes to go before ten. There! It's up. Don't move. Someone may have heard the squeak."

They waited motionless. No sound broke the stillness.

"Now!" Linda whispered and caught up her gold skirts. She squeezed through the opening. Holding her breath to hear the hour chime. Praying that the minutes would lag. She slipped on the icy iron grating. Caught frantically at the rail. Looked down. The steps led only to the next floor. Some helpful person had removed the ladder to the ground.

"Oh, Miss! Oh, Miss. Take care! You'll fall!" Annie's whispered protest followed her like a refrain. Her skirt caught. She tore it free. Step by cautious step she backed down. Slipping. Clinging. A sound! Her heart drummed. She flattened herself against the steps. Clung desperately. She mustn't be seen. A window was gently raised. Madam Steele's bedroom! Annie's story was true.

"A dull thud. Had someone swung from the window? No. It was being softly closed. She held herself rigid. Every nerve in her body twanged, "Hurry! Hurry!" Quiet again. Down she went. Minutes were racing. No more steps. She'd have to drop. She peered at the snowy ground. Some drop. Lucky there was no terrace below. Her bones would be mush were she to land on that. Perhaps she could reach the conductor at her left and slide. The carillon! Chiming "Silent Night." Striking ten. Too late! Late or not she must go on.

Every home should have a fire-house pole, she thought with a hysterical chuckle as she caught the iron pipe of the conductor and swung her feet from the steps. She gripped it. Slid. Lost her hold. Plunged. Landed in a snowdrift. Her outflung hand struck something hard. A big, knobby white-canvas bundle. Madam Steele's jewels!

Her heart pounded as she plodded through snow to the terrace steps. Crept along close to the house. The bundle in her arms was heavy. Annie had whispered that the crooks would enter through the library, that the end window of the drawing room would be unlocked for their quick getaway. The very window at which she and Keith had stood looking out at the perfect night. Suppose she had been a quitter and gone with him as he suggested? Why let that thought stop her breath? She hadn't. She was here to do what she could.

She touched the window cautiously. It swung slowly

open. Someone had unlocked it from the outside since she
and Keith had been there. She had heard the click as he
turned the key. Outside? Maybe it had been unlocked from
the inside. Who would do it? Buff! Buff arranging the
hangings. Had it been he? Memory raced on. He had heard
Madam Steele's shot that night in the library, had not gone
to her assistance. Buff, *Buff,* was the helper inside!

The thought set her ashiver. She held her breath to
listen. "Union Pacific" should be at its noisiest by now. Engine whistles. Yells. Gunfire. Instead the house was deathly
quiet. A shot! Real. Not from a sound track. She was too
late. It was just one of those things that couldn't happen—
but it had.

XXVII

AS HE walked the length of the library Greg Merton resisted the urge to turn back and catch Linda in his arms, to
hold her close till she told him the truth about Sanders'
presence in her room last night. It had been easy enough to
say, "If it was O.K. with you, it's nothing to me." It was
something to him, something that hurt unbearably.

He had been a fool to pay so much attention to Hester through the afternoon and evening. He had been on top
of the world when Ruth had intimated in her living room
that Mrs. Bourne was responsible for Linda's coolness to
him, that she wanted him for her elder daughter. He had
come to The Castle determined that there should be no
doubt in anyone's mind whom he loved—and then he had
seen Sanders slip out of Linda's room.

"What's on your mind, Greg? You look as if you were
about to chew nails." Grant's low voice greeted him as he
stepped into the hall, Grant's arm slipped within his. "Got
to talk to you. Anyone in the library?"

"No."

"Come back there."

"What's all the mystery about?" Greg asked as he was
conveyed to one of the long windows. The hangings

dropped between them and the room—the hangings which had been pierced by Aunt Jane's shot, he remembered.

"Lorillo's in the neighborhood."

"On Christmas Day! Sure, Skid?"

"Saw him in the village when I went there after luncheon. Had a hunch he might be using that cottage we visited as a hangout. Remember I left the skiing party at dusk? Beat it to the cottage by the back road. Splinters of light at the windows. Something submarinian going on there and I'll bet the suave Señor is the master mind. We *know* Alix Crane sports one of Mother's bracelets. She *says* it's costume stuff, that she bought it 'off' a girl friend. I know she's lying. Jim Shaw agrees with me that the Brazilian gave it to her."

"That doesn't necessarily mean he stole it, Skid."

"No, but I'll bet he did. What's he doing in this neighborhood? It doesn't look good to me. Madam Steele has jewels to burn. She surprised a man in this room, didn't she?"

"She did. You've got something there. The servants are making a night of it in the village. Just to ease our minds, let's you and I go the rounds of the house after the others have gone to bed. You take the servants' cottage, check up on them when they come in. I'll patrol the front. We'd better get back to the billiard room before the lights are turned off for the picture. The reconnaissance may seem wheelly when we get through but it won't do any harm."

"It can't be more wheelly than parking a lot of fabulous jewels in an unprotected house like this one. If you ask me, you should have had a conservator appointed to take care of Madam Steele's property."

"Conservator! When she can outguess most of the men I know in a business deal? They are her jewels; if she's willing to run the risk of losing them, it's all right with me—so long as no one is hurt. If Lindy—"

"Love her, don't you?"

"Yes."

"So much that your voice is husky when you admit it. Fair enough, fella. I hope you get her. To return to our G-man stunt. Buff will be the only servant left on the place. You suspected him before."

"Yes. But I changed my mind. He's on the level. Come on, let's go to the billiard room before we're missed." They stepped from behind the hangings. "Janet! What's happened?" Greg demanded as his sister hurriedly entered the room. Her face was colorless. She caught her brother's sleeve with one hand. The other was clenched till the knuckles showed white.

"Greg! Greg! I've found my bracelet!" He put his arm about her shoulders.

"Take it easy, honey. Where did you find it?"

"She looked from him to Grant and back at him with anguished eyes.

"In Linda's room."

"*Linda's* room!" Gregory Merton stared at his sister. "*Linda's* room! My God!"

"What are you muttering, Greg? You look as if you'd been blinded by lightning. You can't believe that Lindy stole it." Grant glared at Janet. "You're crazy. Where was it in her room?"

Breathlessly she told of seeing the bracelet dangling from Libby Hull's hand when she had gone to Linda's boudoir to ask for a Christmas tag. Had doubted her eyes. Had stolen back when they were all dancing. Had found the bracelet in the Chinese box.

"*Sure* it's yours?" Greg Merton's voice was hoarse, his face livid.

In answer she opened her hand. Crushed in the palm lay the diamond bracelet he had seen her take from the case her husband had tossed into her lap. With a muttered execration Skid Grant snatched it. Held it under a lamp. His face was colorless.

"See that 8 in small diamonds beside the big yellow one, Greg? It's one of Mother's."

"Your mother's!" Janet Colton repeated. "You're losing your mind, Skid. How could I get *her* bracelet? It's mine. Don't you remember the afternoon Bill gave it to me, Greg? He had been away for two days—" Color rushed to her face, tears came to her eyes. "He dropped it into my lap and said he hoped I'd wear it, that it was designed for a lovely woman. You *must* remember. Skid's looking at me as if he thought I had stolen it."

"I remember," her brother attested gravely.

"I'm more interested to know how it got into Lindy's jewel box than in how you got it, Janet. You surely don't believe she stole it?"

"Unclench your hands, Skid. Neither Janet nor I think she stole it. We're not that crazy. It looks as if the person who snitched the bracelet from Janet must be in this house."

"You've said something, Greg." The angry flush faded from Grant's face. "Brought that nurse of Billy Boy's with you, didn't you, Janet?"

"Yes, Skid, but I know she's honest. I *know* it."

"She has a beau, hasn't she?"

"She has, Greg, but—"

"You told me the day the bracelet disappeared that she was in tears most of the time because he was a rounder, didn't you?"

"Yes, but—"

"Quit the third-degree business, Greg. Janet, put that bracelet into your pocket—"

"I haven't one." She slipped it under the square neck of her crimson moire frock between the diamond daisy clips. "This will do." Her eyes were enormous as she admitted: "I felt like a thief myself when I took this from Linda's jewel box, but I *had* to be sure. Suppose she misses it?"

"What do you mean, 'misses it'? She never has known it was there. Get that and don't forget it." Greg Merton's voice was savage with fury. "It's that nurse of yours. She's been fratty with Libby Hull since she came, hasn't she?"

"I didn't mean it that way, I honestly didn't, Greg. I love Lindy. I—"

"Forget it, Janey. Listen carefully. One by one we'll drift into the billiard room. After the picture, which is full of yelling, shooting and engine whistles, while we're having the 'snack' Buff brings in, I'll ask you if Billy Boy has slept through the racket. You grin and say—"

"I know. 'Don't you and Skid want to see him, Greg? He's a cherub when he's asleep.'"

"Perfect. Then we three will race upstairs and hand that nurse the surprise of her life. Now for the picture. Go first, Janey."

"I know Nurse didn't steal the bracelet," Janet reaffirmed from the threshold.

"We'll tackle said nurse before we make our rounds, Skid," Greg said in a low voice. "She may be in on the Lorillo scheme, he may be the 'rounder' she's in love with, if you and I haven't gone haywire and there is a scheme. We'll put her where she can't do her stuff."

"If she hid that bracelet in Linda's room, I'll get her if it's the last thing I do on earth."

"Take it easy, Skid. We'll make someone pay for that and pay to the limit. I have a hunch I know who it will be. Come on. We've got to sit through the picture."

As they entered the billiard room Madam Steele and her guests were seated facing a screen. On the gallery at the opposite end of the room a man was working over the projector. Linda hadn't come in. Was she still busy with Buff, Greg wondered uneasily. Hester slipped her hand under his arm. She pouted engagingly.

"I missed you. Hasn't this been a gorgeous Christmas? Look!" She held out her lovely hand, made to seem even whiter than it was by the pure blue of a diamond-set turquoise ring. "Nice, isn't it? Not as valuable as Linda's emerald, but then Linda always gets the breaks." She cleared her voice of petulance. "Don't think I'm complaining. It was wonderful of Madam Steele to give me anything."

"Better not flash your jewels. Someone looking in the window might try to snitch that ring off you someday. . . . That cheery crack adds to the holiday hilarity, doesn't it? Forget it. Here come Linda and Buff. There go the lights. The show is on."

His voice had been casual while his heart burned and smarted. How had Janet's bracelet come in Linda's jewel box? How had Mrs. Grant's come in his sister's? Was there any truth in the suspicion which had blazed like lightning through his mind a few moments ago in the library or had he gone screwball?

As he sat in the dark his thoughts were concerned wholly with ways and means of clearing up the mystery. His eyes were on the screen but they were blind to the conspiring, fighting, laboring, cheating, courageous and inspired human beings working out their celluloid destinies; his ears were deaf to the clank of iron wheels on steel rails, to the shrill engine whistles, thud of axes, shouts of soldiers, war whoops of Indians, to the constant volley of guns.

In the midst of his preoccupation he was suddenly aware that all sound had ceased. Lights were on. Had the film broken?

"Hands up! Make it snappy!"

The voice had come from behind him. He turned. His heart went cold. Two masked, raincoated men, stubby automatics drawn, threatened from the threshold of the doorway to the drawing room. A holdup! Timed at the height of the picture's din. His eyes flashed from them to the guests grouped about Madam Steele, who stood, white head erect like a queen, in their midst. All present but Linda and Buff! He had seen them come in. Where were they? *Buff!* Was he behind this? Had he enticed her out of the room? Was he holding her? Bill Colton's laugh broke the tense silence.

"What's this? A neighborhood joke, Aunt Jane? For a minute these guys had me fooled. I—"

"Shut up! Hands up! Everybody!" The snarl came from the taller of the masked men. "Keep 'em up! Get into the other room. Scram."

Disguised as it was there was a hint of familiarity in that voice. Where had he heard it? As they were being herded into the next room Greg's eyes met Grant's whose lips formed a word.

Lorillo! Lorillo in person! Who was his pal? Someone in this house had made their entrance easy. Their exit would be made hard, damned hard, if he got drilled doing it. If it weren't for the glittering tree he would be sure this was a nightmare. Not a chance. Those two toughs were real. Lucky Linda was out of the mess. Was she? Someone had set a pitcher of claret cup, glasses and small cakes on a table. Buff had been here. He had been at the picture. Had he stolen out to let these men in? Had Lindy seen him and followed? Had he seen her and—"Steady! Steady, or you won't have the nerve to think this through," he warned himself.

"Do your stuff! I've got 'em covered."

At the rough command the short man snatched the

diamond clips from Janet's frock. Greg lunged toward him. Her husband, ghastly with anger, dropped his hands and struck.

"Put 'em up," the tall man growled, "or else—" He fired a shot into the wall behind Colton. "Get the old woman's rubies!"

Greg's eyes flashed to Sanders at Madam Steele's right. Would he dare protect her? His face was a mask of fury, his eyes were daggers of hate as he glared at the man with the gun. Had his head moved in a slight negative shake? It had. Smoldering suspicion blazed to certainty. Sanders was tied up in this. Sanders had—

"What's this? A shootin' party?" inquired a gay voice, from the other end of the room.

It was Linda! Linda with a knobby white bundle clasped in her arms! Her bedraggled frock trailed streamers of gold net. Her hair was tossed. Her colorless face was smooched. Her brown eyes glowed. The holdup men wheeled. In that instant Bill Colton sprang. Sent the short one crashing down. Reynolds, Grant and Buff flung the tall one to the floor. Greg wrenched the automatic from his hand. Leveled it at Sanders.

"Sit down!" The words crackled with fury.

The man's eyes burned like live coals in his livid face. His stiff lips widened in a sickly grin.

"Gone screwy again, Merton? Forget it! Colton needs help."

"Sit down! Lindy, drop that thing you're holding. Quick! Pull the light wires off the tree! I'll tie him up. He's in on this."

"I'll help with that wire." Madam Steele had emerged from a coma of surprise at the holdup. "I've suspected he was up to some deviltry. He hasn't had me fooled for a minute, though I thought it was my business he was after." Her eagle eyes blazed. "So this is why you accepted my hospitality, Sanders. To pave the way for a gang of cutthroats."

"But, my *dear* lady—"

"Shut up! Or I'll—"

Sanders sprang. Caught Merton's throat in a stranglehold and choked off the sentence. Gripped his wrist and seized the gun. Through a red haze Greg saw a girl in a ragged frock running toward him.

"Keep back, Lin—" Something burst in his head. The room went black.

XXVIII

LINDA ignored the broken command, dashed forward on a surge of outraged fury. She grabbed Sanders' hand which held the automatic.

"Keith! Keith! You struck Greg! Are you crazy?"

"Let me go! Quick!" His voice was murderous, his eyes were savage. He tried to shake her off. She clung desperately. Dragged at his wrist. Subconsciously she was aware of Madam Steele pulling and jerking at the light wire on the tree, of Buff helping; of Bill Colton struggling with someone on the floor, of white-faced Janet standing over them with a heavy vase poised to drop; of Skid perched on the head, the Judge seated on the midriff of the prostrate form of a long, raincoated figure, of Ruth kneeling on one of his arms; of her mother and Hester huddled in a corner.

"Mother! Hester! Help Greg! Water!" she called over her shoulder. "Come somebody! He's getting away! He's getting away!" She clung to Sanders' arm as he dragged her from her feet toward the window.

"No he isn't." With incredible dexterity Madam Steele flung a loop of wire dangling with colored glass bulbs over his head and pinioned his arms. Round and round she went —as Buff freed more and more from the tree—winding, pulling with unbelievable strength while the blond man ineffectually struggled and fought.

"You needn't hold him any longer, Linda. I've got him. He can't walk; he'll have to hop. Take that revolver away from him," Madam Steele ordered.

"Let it alone!" Greg Merton snatched the gun from Sanders' useless hand. His eyes were dazed. Moisture dripped from his hair and chin, ran in red rivulets down his white shirt-front. Hester or her mother must have emerged from their coma and emptied the pitcher of claret cup over him, Linda decided, and fiercely choked back a rising tide of sobs and laughter.

"Buff! Buff!" Janet called frantically. "Upstairs! Quick! See if Billy Boy and Nurse are safe." She brandished the vase above the struggling man her husband was holding to the floor. "If you've harmed my child I'll beat your brains out with this . . ." she threatened fiercely.

Madam Steele gave a vicious pull to the wire around Sanders. "And they call this Christmas! 'Peace on earth to all men of good will,' " she quoted grimly.

"What's going on here?" From the open window a man followed his gruff query into the room.

"Another of the gang! Give me that!" Madam Steele snatched the automatic from Greg's hand. "I'll get him!"

"Take it easy, Madam. I don't belong to any gang." Jim Shaw's protest showed strain. He bared gorillalike teeth in a chalky face. "Take it easy, Madam."

"For the love of Pete!" Skid Grant shouted. "If you've got any men with you, call 'em in quick, Shaw!"

"Men! *More* men! Has the boy gone crazy? God knows we have all the men here we can handle, Gregory!"

"Shaw is an officer, Duchess. He'll help."

Sanders took advantage of their diverted attention to hop cautiously toward the open window. He stopped with a muttered curse. Two officers and a girl had stepped into the room, a girl in a leopardskin coat with a matching turban crushed down on her yellow hair. Her eyes shone hard and green as emeralds in her colorless face. Her scarlet lips twisted in a sneer.

"Alix! What . . ."

"What am I doing in the mansion of a socialite?" Miss Crane finished Sanders' hoarse question. "I've come to see you, darling. And what a sight! The irresistible Great Lover trussed up like a Christmas goose!" Her harsh laugh flooded the man's white face with turbid red.

"I've come to hear you swear, Keith Sanders, that I *didn't* know that the 'costume bracelet' you gave me was the real thing, that I *didn't* know it was part of the Grant loot, that you *did* make me promise not to tell who gave it to me, promise to say I bought it off a friend." Her voice lashed. She pulled a pistol from her pocket. "Come across with the truth, you heel, and come across *quick!*" Jim Shaw seized her wrist.

"None of that, Miss Crane. My men will take care of him."

"Shut up, Shaw." She jerked her hand free. "You've been shadowing me for days. Yesterday you had the nerve to accuse me of having knowingly received stolen goods. You brought me here tonight to face Sanders. And was I *glad* to come. Glad to put a crimp in his Christmas. When he gave me that bracelet I was a fool not to have known he was doing me dirt; one look at his cold-storage eyes ought to put even a dumb cluck wise. Well, I'm here. He'll talk if I have to shoot to make him. Speak your little piece, *darling,* or . . ." She stared incredulously at the battered men being roughly forced forward by two in uniform.

"*Pedro!* What are you doing here?" The question was a shocked whisper. Her amazed eyes rested for an instant on his handcuffed wrist. "My God! You! *You,* a gangster! I'm catching on; Now I know why you urged me to let you take my bracelet to have it copied in genuine stones for me. You knew it was the real thing. And—I—poor fool —thought you loved me." She drew a deep, shuddering breath. "Señor Pedro Lorillo from Brazil, where the or— orchids come from. It's a scream, a . . ." High, discordant laughter broke in a harsh sob. She buried her face in her shaking hands.

Shaw hurriedly picked up the pistol she had dropped. The onetime Brazilian's face was the color of dirty wax, the whites of his eyes rolled like the eyes of a racehorse on the homestretch. The crafty eyes in the dead-pan face of the man beside him met Linda's.

The room whirled. She drove her teeth into her lips till her brain cleared. It was the cadaverous man who had called at Keith's office, the man who had brought round her car the first time she had come to The Castle. He had been sent to prepare for this night!

Fragments of memory slipped into a pattern. Sanders' eagerness to handle the sale of Madam Steele's estate; his interest in the lacquer cabinets; his livid face when the Crane girl had brought the Brazilian to their table. . . . His savage "Get it or lay off!" at the phone had meant he was ordering Lorillo to get the emerald bracelet from her. . . .

Her dazed impression that she had seen him going out the door at noon that day at Janet's; his devotion to herself, a cover to become familiar with this house, when she had thought he was after business; his suggestion that a cinema outfit be installed; his opening of the drawing-room window tonight (his click of the key had been faked)—he, not poor old Buff, had paved the way for the thieves. . . . Cline and his snapshots; the holdup at the peak of the din of the picture . . .

Through the memories glinted the callous iciness of his blue eyes. Alix Crane was right, those eyes should have put even a dumb cluck wise. The scheme was as plain as if set in a blazing neon design, all but the reason for his midnight entrance into her room. Had he mistaken it for Madam Steele's? Had he been after the jewels then?

"Stop staring at those crooks and look at Libby." It was Greg Merton's low voice, his hand on her shoulder.

Liberty Hull stood in the hall doorway. Her cherished permanent resembled nothing so much as a floor-mop rampant; her gray mohair dress had been torn. Red spots burned in her cheeks. She held a man by the collar of his shirt. His eyes bulged with fright; his face was mottled.

"I caught this stealing away." She shook him by way of emphasis. "He's the picture operator. He had supper with us so I know. What'll I do with him? What with one thing an' another, I'm too busy to hold on to the rat much longer."

"I'm not. He's my meat." Jim Shaw turned the operator over to one of his men to be herded from the room with Sanders and the other two. He spoke to Alix Crane who nodded and followed. He lingered to confide to Gregory Merton:

"I'll say that Sanders is some organizer. Even had his own picture operator on the job. 'Tisn't any international gang as we thought, it's a close corporation, just the three we caught tonight with an occasional sucker to help, like the guy that got shot. They couldn't get rid of the Grant loot the usual way so Sanders planted some of it where he could get it again. Smart fella. Lucky I had a hunch to bring the Crane girl here to face Sanders or you folks would have found the goin' tough. I'm taking her along in my own car. She's straight. Had a crush on that slick Lorillo, I guess. I'll shove. See you tomorrow." He followed his men from the room.

"Libby! Libby, dear, are you hurt?" Ruth asked anxiously.

"No. Don't take on so, Ruthetta. Mad as a wet hen, that's all. Your boy's safe, Mrs. Colton, s'pose that's why you're grabbin' my arm and trying to speak."

"Thank God! Bill! Bill! Come!" Janet and her husband raced from the room. Liberty Hull rubbed a red welt on her wrist.

"That shorty, who was just dragged out, tied me and the nurse up and taped our mouths, while the tall fella pointed a revolver at us. We didn't have a chance to yell. You wouldn't have heard us anyway with all that shootin' an' shoutin' goin' on in the picture. They didn't so much as look at the boy in the other room. They had that much sense.

"What with one thing and another, this has been quite a holiday, Madam Steele. The lock of one of the big cabinets has been jimmied and every jewel's gone. They put the alarm out of business, too. Those fellas could have lifted the roof without anyone's hearin', with that bedlam downstairs. Now that I've broken the cheerful news, I'll go make some sandwiches. You'll feel better if you eat," she advised before she left the room.

"Gone! *Gone!*" Jane Steele sank into the nearest chair. "I thought all they were after were the diamonds we had on."

"You haven't lost the jewels. You haven't. I have them." Linda swooped up the knobby bundle she had dropped to the floor at Greg's command to pull off the tree wire.

"Don't look at me as if you thought I had stolen them. They're here, every last sparkle of them." She knelt beside Madam Steele and tugged at the fastening of the canvas bag she had laid in her lap.

"I'll open it." Greg Merton looked at the girl's wet, torn skirt which trailed over the floor in ribbons. "Lindy, Lindy, how did you get these? Are you hurt?"

"No. *No.* I hope they're all there," she exclaimed as the jewels in the wide-open bag flashed and sparkled in the light.

"You're here safe, my dear child. That is more important than the jewels." Madam Steele's voice was shaken. "How did you save them?"

They gathered round—her mother, Hester, the Judge, Ruth, Skid and Gregory Merton—as, still on her knees, Linda told of Annie's warning, of her own icy descent. Janet, with her husband's arm about her, joined the circle before she had finished.

"Where's the girl now?"

"On the third floor, probably, Madam Steele. She didn't dare get out of that window."

"But you dared. What you intended to do was reckless enough, what you did, sliding down that icy conductor, was suicidal," Greg protested huskily.

"Your mistake, I didn't slide all the way—I fell into a snowdrift, Mr. Merton."

"Whatever you did, you were a crazy kid, you sweet thing. Get up." He pulled her gently to her feet.

Linda steadied quivering lips. His tenderness was more devastating than his scorn had been. She felt tears rising like a flood and rallied all her pride to crowd them back.

"Lucky for us she was a 'crazy kid.' Gregory, take the jewels to my room. Unlock the door for Annie. I wonder why the burglars opened only one of the cabinets?"

"It takes time to disconnect the alarm and jimmy a great lock, Duchess. Darned fools. Why didn't they make their getaway with the jewels? Why tuck on that holdup, Greg?"

"I'll bet Sanders was asking himself that question, Skid, that the holdup was not part of his program. His pals got out of hand. He was ghastly from fury. If they hadn't been so greedy he wouldn't have been caught *this* time. . . . He might have bluffed it out even then if Alix Crane hadn't appeared."

"The law will put that trio where they won't try a return engagement during my lifetime; after that, you and Janet can do the worrying, Gregory," Madam Steele declared. "While you're upstairs change your clothes. You look as if you'd been sticking pigs. Also, hurry up the sandwiches. Our skirmish with the underworld and the vice squad has given me an appetite. You look as if you'd been

shot over Niagara Falls in a barrel, Linda. Change to a
house coat and come to the library. Then we'll hear the de-
tails of this night's melodrama. If only I could have taken a
shot at one of the thugs, it would have been a perfect ending to a perfect day."

"You bloodthirsty female!" Skid flouted affectionate-
ly. "Come on, Duchess." He held her under the mistletoe
and kissed her cheek.

They were gathered about the library fire when Linda
joined them wearing the yellow coat and vermilion satin
trousers. Greg in a green brocaded lounge robe and folded
white scarf was standing by the mantel; Bill Colton, on the
divan beside his wife, had his arm about her shoulders as if
he never would let her go. Her eyes were starry with happiness. Ruth, Hester and her mother were relaxed in deep
chairs. Judge Reynolds, Skid Grant and Greg stood back
to the mantel.

"We've been waiting for you, Linda," Madam Steele
greeted eagerly. "Greg and Skid are about to tell us what
started their suspicion of that smooth Sanders."

The contempt in her voice hurt Linda. She had liked
Keith. Since he had declared that he had heard of the sale
of Madam Steele's estate through her, she had distrusted
him, had suspected that he was scheming, but her attack of
first love had been a high-pressure affair the short time it
lasted—she couldn't quite forget that.

"I stopped to speak to Annie. When, in the dusk of
the third-floor room, she whispered that there would be a
holdup at ten, I almost lost my mind. There was so little
time. The minutes raced. The carillon chimed zero hour.
The holdup was on. I was sliding down that icy iron conductor! I lived years getting to the drawing-room window.
I was too late."

"In the nick of time, sez I. Your dramatic entrance
was a wallop. Instinctively the thugs turned. Gave us a
chance to gang up on them. Found out yet who locked that
stairway door, Lindy?"

"It was Buff, Skid. He told me that he slipped out on
the picture, thought he heard a sound, stopped in the upper
hall to listen and saw the key in the door. Thinking it might
be a temptation to the servants to explore, he turned it,
dropped it into his pocket and went to the pantry for a nap.

'Union Pacific' was too noisy for him. It is unbelievable that he wasn't seen or heard by the burglars. I'll never doubt after this that miracles happen."

She sank to the floor at Madam Steele's feet and clasped her hands about her knees. "All set for the next installment of this thrilling serial."

"Your chapter first, Skid," Greg prompted. Grant flung his cigarette into the fire.

"To give you a rough idea, I'll begin with the theft of Mother's jewels soon after Sanders visited us. I had no suspicion of him then. He had gone back to New York several days before they were stolen. Remember when I went blotto at the night club, Lindy, and you recognized the sequined gal who wore Mother's emerald bracelet as Alix Crane, the night-club singer who had come to Sanders' office?" She nodded. "Even then I didn't suspect him. Greg and I shadowed Lorillo—he was the tall guy tonight, Madam Steele—but couldn't discover that he was in any way linked up with Sanders. They sure were experts at covering their tracks. Next your bracelet was stolen, Janet. Remember, Lindy, that you told Greg you thought you saw Sanders going out of the door, as you came in dizzy from the swimming pool?"

"'But it wasn't he? He didn't arrive until dinnertime."

"He *said* he didn't but our hero—Merton by name— had a hunch that perhaps you hadn't been so dizzy as you thought, got busy and discovered that Sanders' car had been serviced at a garage at noon. Bill, do you remember that when you were about to tell the cost of the bracelet the Ming lamp crashed?"

"I do. I recall also that your sleuth, Jim Shaw, accused me of tipping that table. I didn't."

"He knew you didn't. He saw Sanders do it, but he didn't want him to know it. Where did you buy that bracelet, Bill?"

"From Sanders. He needed money to pay racing debts. Begged me to take the jewels he had bought for a woman who had double-crossed him. I knew I'd never get my money any other way so took it."

"Presumably he didn't tell you that the bracelet was one which had been stolen from my mother?"

"What?"

"Sit down, William. For goodness' sake, don't interrupt again!" commanded Madam Steele. She sat forward on the edge of her chair. "Where is it now?"

"Janet has it. She found it in Linda's jewel case."

"Your mother's bracelet!" Linda was on her feet. "In my—" Her voice broke. "In my jewel case! What do you *mean*, Skid Grant?"

"Easy does it, Lindy. Listen to Greg. Take over, fella."

Greg admitted that always he had had a feeling that Sanders was tricky. That when Linda said she had imagined she had seen him in the doorway after he had declared he hadn't arrived until later, he, himself, had smelled a rat and had begun to check up on the man's activities. When, just before the movie, Janet had produced the missing bracelet and told where she had found it, in a blinding flash of certainty her story linked up with Sanders' stepping out of Linda's room at midnight.

"Your room! At midnight! *Daughter!*" Mrs. Bourne protested in shocked surprise.

"Don't get me wrong!" Greg Merton's voice was savage. "She didn't know he was there. He had come to get rid of the bracelet which was getting too hot to hold. Nice fella. The Crane girl had his number when she said he would stab his dearest friend in the back if it would forward his own fortune. He snitched Janet's bracelet because he knew if she wore it Skid would recognize it, took the pearls as a blind and dropped them into the hamper."

"Merton, you and Grant have worked up quite a case. But have you found the man Madam Steele shot?"

"It was Annie's boy friend, Cline, Judge Reynolds. He was a mechanic at the village garage. Got pulled into the scheme by Lorillo. He was here that night to try to take a near look at the locks of the cabinets of which he'd taken snapshots. I've just talked with Annie. She came clean, told all she knew about the case. Except for letting Cline into the house, she isn't to blame. A job like the one they planned takes a lot of preparation. You hit the boy in the shoulder, Duchess. In conclusion, Sanders is the tip-off man of the gang. He never did the dirty work. That's why he was so savage to be in on the holdup. He was a wizard at real estate but it was a front. Gave him a chance to look over big houses."

"I can't believe it," Linda protested passionately.

"Believe it or not, you knew he drew large sums from his business which he said was for expenses, didn't you, knew he gambled on the races?"

"I didn't *know* it, Skid."

"All right, all right, if you want to stand up for him, it's nothing in my young life. For the love of Pete, where's that snack we were promised? I could eat raw dog." Grant snapped his teeth.

"Linda, hurry up Buff. Greg, go with her. Before you come back, see that she puts something on those skinned hands she's trying to hide. Don't go, Hester. They won't need your help." Madam Steele smiled complacently. "As I remarked yesterday, I have been doing a little research on the subject of the human heart."

In the hall Greg Merton caught Linda's arm.

"What's the rush?"

"They're hungry."

"Let 'em wait." He put his hands on her shoulders. "How about being friends with me?"

"Not if you still believe I told Keith Sanders that Madam Steele had decided to put The Castle on the market."

"I don't. All the time I knew in my heart that you didn't. You treated me like the dirt under your feet. I had to have some excuse for pretending that I didn't care. Funny how two usually sane persons can get the wires crossed, isn't it?

"I never felt the least tinge of love for Hester; I wouldn't marry her if she were the only woman in the world. Her mother is all wrong. Your startled eyes and color betray you." He slipped an arm about her. Was it the pounding of his heart she heard or her own?

"I have a Christmas present for you in my pocket. The Duchess hasn't cornered the market on rings. That afternoon at Ruth's something told me I had a chance. You know I love you, don't you, Lindy? You knew I loved you the moment I saw you, didn't you?"

"I did not." The denial was spirited. "How could I when you—you seemed to despise me?"

He kissed her. Kissed her fiercely, passionately, thoroughly. Held her close, his lips hard on hers; asked unsteadily:

"Know it now? If not—" He kissed her again gently. "Stop me if I'm wrong, you sweet thing."

She had known his arms would be like this. Strong, possessive, enclosing her in a world of tenderness and protection. Head tipped back against his shoulder her radiant eyes met his.

"Mr. Merton in an ardent mood," she flouted with unsteady gaiety. "I'm not stopping you—or am I?"

EMILIE LORING

Women of all ages are falling under the enchanting spell Emilie Loring weaves in her beautiful novels. Once you have finished one book by her, you will surely want to read them all.

☐	NO TIME FOR LOVE	2228	$1.25
☐	LOVE WITH HONOR	2237	$1.25
☐	BEYOND THE SOUND OF GUNS	2249	$1.25
☐	ACROSS THE YEARS	2278	$1.25
☐	FAIR TOMORROW	2287	$1.25
☐	WITH THIS RING	2294	$1.25
☐	WHAT THEN IS LOVE	2302	$1.25
☐	WE RIDE THE GALE	2320	$1.25
☐	UNCHARTED SEAS	2330	$1.25
☐	FORSAKING ALL OTHERS	2382	$1.25
☐	HOW CAN THE HEART FORGET	2390	$1.25
☐	TO LOVE AND TO HONOR	2391	$1.25
☐	TODAY IS YOURS	2394	$1.25
☐	THE SHINING YEARS	2410	$1.25
☐	HILLTOPS CLEAR	2496	$1.25

Buy them at your local bookstore or use this handy coupon for ordering: